Maxine has wanted to be a writer for as long as she can remember and wrote her first (very short) book for school when she was ten. As time went by, she continued to write, but 'normal' work often got in the way. She has written articles on a variety of subjects, as well as a local history book on Brighton. However, novels are her first love.

In August 2015, she won HarperCollins/Carina UK's 'Write Christmas' competition with her first romantic comedy, *Winter's Fairytale.*

Maxine lives on the south coast of England, and when not wrangling with words loves to read, sew and listen to podcasts. Being a fan of tea and cake, she can (should!) also be found doing something vaguely physical at the gym.

Twitter   @Scribbler_Maxi

Instagram   @scribbler_maxi

Facebook   www.Facebook.com/MaxineMorreyAuthor

Pinterest   ScribblerMaxi

Website   www.scribblermaxi.co.uk

Email   scribblermaxi@outlook.com

Readers love Maxine Morrey!

'I've fallen **head over heels** for Maxine's writing style'

'I'm a **big fan of Maxine's writing** and I love how she is able to write **lighthearted romantic comedies** that have **serious issues** at their centre'

'I **love** Maxine Morrey's books'

'Hand on heart, **I could read a Maxine Morrey novel every day** of the week without getting bored'

'I'm a **big fan of Morrey's books**'

'Maxine has this way of **captivating her readers** with **charismatic and memorable** characters'

This novel is entirely a work of fiction. The names, characters and incidents portrayed in it are the work of the author's imagination. Any resemblance to actual persons, living or dead, events or localities is entirely coincidental.

HQ
An imprint of HarperCollins*Publishers* Ltd
1 London Bridge Street
London SE1 9GF

This edition 2019

First published in Great Britain by
HQ, an imprint of HarperCollins*Publishers* Ltd 2019

Copyright © Maxine Morrey 2019

Maxine Morrey asserts the moral right to be
identified as the author of this work.
A catalogue record for this book is
available from the British Library.

ISBN: PB: 978-0-00-832297-7

Typeset by Palimpsest Book Production Ltd, Falkirk,
Stirlingshire

All rights reserved. No part of this publication may be reproduced, stored in a retrieval system, or transmitted, in any form or by any means, electronic, mechanical, photocopying, recording or otherwise, without the prior permission of the publishers.

This book is sold subject to the condition that it shall not, by way of trade or otherwise, be lent, re-sold, hired out or otherwise circulated without the publisher's prior consent in any form of binding or cover other than that in which it is published and without a similar condition including this condition being imposed on the subsequent purchaser.

No Place Like Home

MAXINE MORREY

ONE PLACE. MANY STORIES

To those readers who have ever messaged me to say how much they've enjoyed one of my books, you totally made my day. Thank you.

Chapter 1

Ellie's back went rigid as the door slammed. Quickly pulling the bedroom door closed, she turned as a bunch of keys were thrown down on the hall table.

'You're home early.'

'Problem with that?' Carl sneered in a voice thick with sarcasm and alcohol. Ellie swallowed and tried to push back the panic she felt rising within her.

'I just lost a bloody contract I've spent the last six months fighting for to some hot shot who just happens—' he made inverted commas in the air with his fingers '—to be the son of the boss' golf partner!' He poured himself a triple whisky and threw it back, grimacing as the liquid seared its way down.

'Shit!' Carl spun and slammed the glass against the far wall. Ellie jumped and he turned his eyes on her. The fear he saw there seemed to only infuriate him more.

'S'pose you think I had it coming?'

Ellie shook her head and backed away. His eyes had turned almost black with fury.

'No! Of course not. I know you worked hard on it!' Ignoring her protest, he grabbed her arm. Ellie winced.

'Don't think I'm good enough to get the contract? Think the little shit probably deserves it?'

'No!' she said, trying to pull away. 'You know I don't think that!'

'Don't bloody lie to me!'

The slap split her lip and sent her tumbling backwards into the drinks cabinet, smashing glasses and sending bottles crashing to the floor. Ellie stared at the mess in shock.

'You clumsy cow,' Carl ground out as he began to advance again.

Her head snapped up and she stared at him for a moment. His face was red and contorted in fury, with no sign of the anger abating. It had been the same last night when she'd begged him to stop. But he hadn't. That was why she was finally leaving – something she knew she should have done a long time ago. But he wasn't supposed to have been home for hours yet. Carl raised his fist. Scrambling to her feet, Ellie screamed, half running, half stumbling into the hall. Behind her, the fist connected with the doorframe.

'Shit! You little bitch!'

Her hand was on the latch of the front door. A gap to escape opened but Carl was too fast.

'I don't think so,' he sneered, slamming the door with such force that one of the stained-glass panels within it shattered. The momentary distraction enabled Ellie to push away but Carl caught her hair, balling it in his fist. Her hands went to his as she screamed again in pain and fear, begging him to stop.

The next punch sent her reeling into the hall table. She tried to steady herself unsuccessfully as the table tipped, its contents spilling onto the floor.

'Now look what you've done.' The voice, thick with alcohol and hatred, was close again as Ellie tried to get up. There was a crack as his handmade, Italian leather shoe connected with her ribs.

'Get up!' Carl screamed at her as she lay sobbing on the floor. She didn't move. Couldn't move. 'I said, get up!' he shouted, hauling her up viciously. Ellie saw the punch too late as his fist slammed into the side of her face and sent her back hard against the wall. She tried to find the strength to keep upright. Keep off the floor. But she couldn't. The pain of the attack, on top of last night was too much. As much as she wanted to fight, she had nothing left. Her legs gave way and she slid down into a ball as her focus blurred and the tears soaked her cheeks. All she wanted was to sleep. Through the fog she could hear voices. Someone was calling her name.

'And stop fucking crying!' Carl loomed in again.

*

Ellie tried to open her eyes. Someone was holding her hand. She looked up and made an effort to focus on the face looking down into hers.

'Hello,' the policeman said.

She tried to sit up but he put a hand gently against her shoulder.

'You just lie still, sweetheart. The ambulance will be here in a minute.'

'I don't need an ambulance,' Ellie croaked out, but she didn't move. The policeman smiled at her. He had a nice smile. Kind.

At the moment the smile was hiding the fact that he wanted to tell the young woman next to him that she didn't have to take this. Blokes like that bastard they'd just hauled away to the station didn't deserve to walk the earth. The neighbour who'd called them had been almost hysterical, swearing that the man was going to beat his girlfriend to death this time. She could see it all, she'd said, through a broken pane in the front door.

Luckily, they'd been close to the apartment block when the call came across. The caller's urgency had ensured they'd hurried their pace which was just as well. Forcing the door, they'd managed to pull the man off just in time. He'd been aiming a blow to the young woman's head that may well have ended the dispute once and for all.

The police sergeant glanced around at the disarray of what was obviously a lovely flat. Modern and spacious, it was in a nice area in London's Canary Wharf, with stunning views of the city from the large, floor to ceiling windows. Judging by its location, and the items in it, the occupants were doing pretty well for themselves. His eyes fell on a picture that had fallen from the hall table. The glass in the frame had smashed and as he picked it up, shards tinkled onto the polished wooden floor.

She was almost unrecognisable. The photograph showed a laughing, carefree woman with bright green eyes and long, red hair being whipped by the wind. He looked back down. The hair was much shorter now, though still fiery red, the fragile beauty masked beneath layers of bruising and blood.

'Wonder if this was what started it, Sarge.' The other policeman had been surveying the apartment as they waited for the ambulance. His partner craned his neck round to look through into the bedroom where the other officer was standing. Two suitcases were packed and the room had been cleared of any female touches.

'Seems like she wised up.'

Turning back to the semi-conscious figure on the floor, his colleague moved a strand of hair, sticky with blood, from across her eye. 'Yeah. Just not soon enough,' he replied sadly as a wailing siren began to close in.

*

Ellie blearily opened her eyes. Rather she opened one. The other remained swollen and shut.

'Zak?' she squeaked out. Her throat was sore and tasted funny. Like blood.

Across the room, a mop of floppy blonde hair in a chair started

6

out of a doze. Zak scooted the chair up to the bed and took her small hands in his.

'Ellie! How are you feeling?'

Ellie raised her one working eyebrow.

'Sorry! God! Stupid question.' There was a pause. 'Bloody hell, Ellie, you look dreadful.' At least he was honest.

'Thanks. I feel dreadful.'

'Sorry.'

'It's OK. I think we've known each other long enough to be insulting. Why change the habit of a lifetime?' She tried to smile in a way that involved the least amount of muscles as possible.

'The police are charging him with resisting arrest and assaulting a police officer for a start.'

Ellie nodded, as he continued. 'They said they'll be in touch with regards to any charges you want to press.' He paused. 'Ellie?'

She knew what was coming. Zak was her closest friend this side of the Atlantic, ever since she had joined his infant publishing group as a contract illustrator seven years ago – an endeavour which had since gone from strength to strength.

Initially Ellie had to admit that she'd thought Zak was the clichéd public-school-boy type who had been given a company to play with by a rich daddy. She soon realised that she'd been too hasty in her assessment of his character. The money to start the company had indeed come from his family but it was in the form of a business loan, to be paid back with interest, just as a standard bank loan would have been. Zak's father had built up his own very successful business from nothing and Zak intended to do the same. The only thing his father was prepared to offer for free was advice, and then only when it was requested. But Zak had worked hard and his business was doing well, and they were currently in the process of recruiting several more staff.

'No.'

'No what?'

'I'm not going back to him. That is what you were going to

7

ask, isn't it?' Ellie turned her bloodshot eye on him.

'Yes. It was.' Relief flooded Zak's face, as he tenderly found an un-bruised piece of Ellie's and kissed it, very gently squeezing her hands. Ellie looked back at his handsome face. Normally it was full of smiles and laughter, but now it was filled with concern. Concern for her. It was the catalyst she needed. A big tear plopped onto the starched sheets.

'I'm so sorry!' she sobbed, emotion breaking her voice. 'I should have listened to you. I should have left before. It's just that he would apologise and he seemed to mean it. He really did and then...' The sobs became more continuous, painfully wracking her broken ribs.

'I know darling, I know,' Zak soothed as he stroked her hair. 'I know.'

*

Three days later, Ellie was released from hospital. Zak collected her and they drove back to his apartment.

'I am quite capable of being on my own, you know,' she said, leaning against a countertop in the large kitchen of his Kensington apartment.

'I know that,' he replied, glancing back at her bruised face as he poured freshly brewed coffee into two bone china mugs. 'I just don't want you to be at the moment.' He handed her one, taking in her expression as he did so.

'Indulge me just for a bit,' he said. 'After all, isn't that what friends are for!' he asked before proceeding to sing an appropriate line or two in his best, not-very-good Dionne Warwick voice.

'Zak!'

'Please. Just for a while.'

Ellie sighed. 'OK. So long as you promise not to sing.' Taking her drink, she headed through to the living room and eased herself down on the squashy sofa. Zak followed and sat opposite on its twin. He was wearing his 'mortified' face.

'I'm hurt.'

'I'm serious.'

'Fine. Fine,' he mumbled before his face suddenly brightened. 'How about humming? I'm pretty good at humming. Or whistling?' He pursed his lips and blew a few notes before a cushion landed square on his nose. Picking it up, he gave Ellie a wry brow raise. 'I'm taking it that was also a no.'

'You're tone deaf and dogs are beginning to howl, so yes, that was most definitely a no.'

*

'Wake up, Sleeping Beauty.'

'Hmm?'

Zak placed a mug of tea on the low table next to the sofa.

'What time is it?'

'Just after seven.'

'Really?' Ellie sat up. 'You should have woken me.'

'Why? There was nowhere you needed to be. Besides, I think a few snoozes are allowed after what you've been through. In fact, I'm pretty sure they're vital.' Zak was concentrating on dunking a biscuit in his tea.

Ellie smiled. He really was a sweetie. Why on earth she had picked someone like Carl over someone like Zak, she had no explanation for. Not that she and Zak would ever date. They'd just never felt like that about each other. It had been a familial relationship from the first time they'd met. And she was glad. Zak meant the world to her and she certainly wouldn't have wanted a relationship gone bad resulting in her losing both her lover and her best friend.

'I spoke to – oh bugger!'

'What?'

9

He held up half a biscuit. 'My biccie broke off!'

Ellie giggled at his forlorn face. 'Oh, poor Zakky!'

He stuck out his tongue and took another biscuit from the jar he'd plonked on the table alongside their drinks. Showing it to her first, he popped it whole into his mouth in an exaggerated motion.

'Zachary Benton! Just wait until I tell your mother!'

'What?' he asked innocently, chocolate brown eyes full of question, mouth full of chocolate biscuit.

'For someone with such a privileged upbringing, you have some appalling habits.'

'I don't know what you mean,' he replied, pretending to pick his nose.

Ellie stifled a smile, instead attempting to give the impression she was pointedly ignoring his actions. Zak knew her too well to be fooled but it was the principle. 'You spoke to whom?'

'Oh! Sandy. She rang this afternoon at the office as she's been trying to get hold of you. I gave her a very quick rundown – I didn't think you'd mind – and explained that your phone had got damaged.'

Ellie's phone had been in her pocket during Carl's last attack and had ended up, like so many other things, shattered into pieces. Zak had ordered her a new one to help take his mind off things while he'd waited in the hospital but it had just sat in the box after its arrival as Ellie told him she wasn't really in the mood to talk to anyone. Zak finally got it out and set it up anyway, partly as a way to keep his mind busy but also knowing that eventually she would want a phone.

'She was going to ring here but I thought you might be asleep so I gave her your new mobile number and said you'd call her when you woke up.' He saw her hesitation. 'I said you'd probably prefer a voice call for now, rather than your usual video chat and she was fine with that.' Ellie nodded, her eyes averted.

'Erm, El?'

She looked up at him. 'Oh no.'

'What?'

'You have that look?'

'What look? I don't have a "look".'

'Yes, you do. It's that look that says, "I know you're not going to like what I'm about to say but I'm going to say it anyway because I think I'm right."'

'Oh,' he said. 'That look.'

'Yes. That look.'

Zak let out a breath through his teeth. 'OK. Sandy and I were talking and we thought it might do you some good to go and stay with her for a couple of weeks. You know, help with the recuperation, get away from everything.'

'I don't need to get away from everything. In fact, I was planning to come back to work next week.'

'You can still work out there if you want. Your job is pretty portable.' She moved to reply but Zak stopped her. 'Ellie, I think this would really be good for you at the moment.'

'Well, I don't!' she snapped. 'I am coming back to work on Monday. The bruises will have healed more by then and I'm sure everyone already knows what happened anyway.'

'Ellie, come here.' Zak stood in front of the antique mirror that hung above a console table. Suddenly the bravado left her.

She shook her head. 'No. I don't think I want to.' Tears unexpectedly pricked the back of her eyes.

Crossing the room, Zak gently put his arms around his friend and led her to the mirror, his arms remaining solid, supportive and tender. Ellie studied his face in the glass – his floppy hair forever in need of a cut, the kind, soft brown eyes, and aquiline nose above a generous mouth. She then forced her gaze to move to her own reflection. It was worse than she had expected. Her left eye was still closed and a mélange of blue, purple and yellow shades. Butterfly stitches held together a cut on her temple about two inches long and her cheekbone was beginning to turn from

11

purple to green. Her lip was still partly swollen with a dark line showing where the split was starting to heal. Zak felt her breath hitch and knew that she had seen enough. He led her back to the sofa. She sat and he swung her legs up and laid the blanket back over them. 'What about all the people on the plane and at the airport? I don't want anyone to see me. They'll stare, even when they're pretending not to. You know what people are like. I'm like a human car crash. They can't help it.' She lifted her head and met Zak's eyes. 'I don't want to be stared at Zak. I feel hideous.'

'You are not hideous!' Zak's voice rarely took on a stern tone but it did now, derailing Ellie's panicky train of thought. She looked up into his face, its expression serious now.

Her eyes were wary and he had flashes of her looking at Carl like that. His stomach roiled at the fact that they'd nearly lost her this time at the hand of that...

He stopped himself, refusing to let his mind go down that road again. Instead, bringing his thoughts back to the present, Zak gently shuffled Ellie's legs up as he sat down on the end of the sofa.

'You underestimate me once again.' A mischievous grin tickled his lips. 'Have you forgotten that I am renowned for my cunning plans!' Ellie smiled in spite of herself. 'Wait here a moment. I shall return!' Zak disappeared, before making a dramatic swoosh of an entrance back into the room a moment later with a pair of stylish, oversized sunglasses and a baseball cap, the latter of which he popped on her head. 'There's a ticket to Dallas booked for you in business class and, if you want, you can just put the sleep mask on when you're snoozing and keep the glasses on at other times. They're dark enough to hide your black eye but not so dark you'll be tripping over things.'

'You are too good to me.'

'No, I'm not.' He gave his friend a gentle hug. As much as he would miss Ellie, he knew this trip back to see her childhood friend, and the place she grew up, was exactly what she needed right now.

Chapter 2

Ellie fastened her seatbelt and looked out of the window. She had a connecting flight to make in Texas but hidden behind the sunglasses and cap, she felt a little more relaxed, safer from peoples' enquiring eyes. Now that she was actually going, she couldn't wait to see Sandy.

Sandy Danvers was Ellie's oldest and dearest friend. When Ellie was seven, her father had been promoted which meant a move from London to Kansas. He'd worried initially how his shy daughter, their only child, would deal with the transition from their busy London life to one that would be far more rural, not to mention uprooting her from her friends. He needn't have worried.

The company found them a beautiful house with a huge garden – or yard, as his liaison had informed him it was called – and, apparently, the neighbours were quite delightful. Having dealt with plenty of sales people over his career, Andrew Laing had taken this with a large pinch of salt. But once they'd arrived, he'd had to concede that it hadn't just been good sales patter. The neighbours, Mr and Mrs Danvers, really were delightful. A family of six, their eldest two boys were at college so only home on holidays. The next one down was a boy, Ben, who would be going off to college in a couple of years' time and their youngest was a girl of Ellie's age, Sandy. She'd immediately taken his daughter under her wing, as her parents had done with him and his wife.

Eight years on, another promotion meant that the Laings would be returning home to England. Andrew knew that any job he took would be easier than telling his daughter that they were leaving Kansas – and so it had proved. Promises of long summer vacations and Easter breaks had done nothing to ease the pain for either of the distraught teenagers. They'd been inseparable almost since the day the Laings had moved in. Forcing them apart had given him more than one sleepless night, wondering if taking this new position had been the right thing to do.

Now, Ellie watched the little luggage trucks whizzing around on the tarmac outside the plane's small oval window as her mind drifted back to the time she'd had to tell her best friend her family was moving back home. It was funny. She remembered saying those exact words all those years ago. And yet, sitting on the Danvers' front swing with Sandy, she'd already felt like she was home.

As much as they knew their parents had hoped they'd come to terms with it, two weeks after the announcement had been made, Ellie remembered them still moping together on that same swing when Sandy's older brother, Ben, had returned home from a day out with friends. After finishing his music degree, he'd returned to the family home while pursuing his dream of becoming a professional musician. He played as part of a band that was popular at functions, and was always writing and recording songs, but over the past year he'd also been spending more time out in Nashville. Nine years younger than Ben, Sandy was the baby of the family and as such had always been a little protected, especially by him. Ellie knew her friend missed her big brother when he was away, but she was wise enough and had a big enough heart to know that was where he needed to be in order to follow his dream. Ellie, however, knew that they had both been thankful to see his kind, handsome face that day. She cast her mind back now to how he'd done his best to comfort them that day.

*

Looking ahead to the porch, Ben saw his teenage baby sister and her best friend Ellie resting against each other on the porch swing. A soft early evening Kansas breeze ruffled Sandy's dark, and Ellie's red hair as they sat in silent sadness. Ben mounted the steps, gave them another glance and took a chair opposite with a sigh. Two pairs of eyes flicked up to his. Sandy raised her eyebrows in a 'hey'. Ellie half smiled but her jewel green eyes remained sad.

'Hey.' Silence.

'I guess Mom and Dad already did the vacations and stuff speech, huh?'

Sandy gave a shrug with the level of indignation only capable of a wronged teenager. 'It's not the same, Ben.'

'No, I know, but sometimes we have to take what we get and make the best of it.'

The two girls looked up at him again. Sandy adored Ben but this didn't prevent her giving him a fifteen-year-old's disdainful 'What?' look.

'And don't give me that look either. It's just that things aren't always easy and I know this is really hard for you two but at least there are the vacations – think how jealous all the other kids will be when you tell them where you're spending yours! Pretty cool to have your best friend abroad. You'll get to visit each year, travel without your parents, have cute accents that boys'll like…'

His words percolated in their brains for a few moments and Ben saw the slightest flicker of change in their demeanours. The girls added a couple of their own thoughts and very gradually started to see a few possible upsides of the situation – though obviously they would still have preferred Ellie to remain in the States and thought it vastly unfair of everyone involved to tear them apart. That was a rock solid fact that would never change. Ben stood and left them to the plans they were now making about where they would go together in London. One hand on the front door handle, he threw a look back.

'Hey?'

The girls looked up.

'Don't say anything to Mum and Dad – or you, Ellie – about what I said about boys and cute accents. OK?'

Two grins full of metal braces were his reply – and reassurance.

Disappearing into the cool of the house, Ben smiled wryly to himself and shook his head. Those two were going to be heart-breakers, accents or not.

*

Ellie wearily took her seat in the jet that would now take her from Texas to Kansas, where Sandy would meet her. She didn't usually manage to sleep too much on planes but it seemed this time her body planned to take advantage of any opportunity it had to grab some extra rest, and she'd dozed on and off on the initial flight. At least Ellie had no worries of having to wait around at the airport for a while – Sandy was a stickler for punctuality. Always had been. Ellie laid her head back against the seat as the engines gained power and forced the jet into the sky. It was over a year since she had seen Sandy in person. The time just seemed to fly by and they hadn't been able to firm up any plans for visits. Not to mention that planning much at all hadn't been easy since she'd been with Carl. He'd never liked her seeing any friends or doing anything that didn't involve him. She swallowed and pushed him out of her mind. There was no need for him to be in her thoughts now. He'd already taken far too much from her. She steered her mind in a more pleasant direction.

With Sandy, for the moment, still living at home in the large family house, something Ellie knew both she and her parents were loving, Ellie would also get to see Molly and Ted Danvers, Sandy's parents. As the friends had last met up over in England, it was now over two years since Ellie had seen the people she considered her second family, and she loved hearing about the rest of the family, and the pride that rang in their voices as Molly and Ted spoke about Sandy and their boys.

Her mind drifted to the brothers. The eldest had already been at college and living their own lives when the Laings had first moved out to the States, but they had got to know them over the holidays and Joseph and Matt were both pleasant, witty and intelligent.

'Lovely manners,' her mother would always say after talking to any of the Danvers' offspring.

But Ben was different, and that special bond he and Sandy had made the relationship different too. This was no doubt helped by the fact that his easygoing manner resulted in his giving them rides all over town once he'd passed his driving test. Sandy idolised Ben and everyone knew the feeling was mutual. They were even closer in looks than their brothers. Although there was no mistaking the three men were brothers, Ben's colouring more resembled his father's and thereby Sandy's. Joe and Matt were both blonde-haired blue-eyed All-American boys, whereas both Sandy and Ben's hair was dark. Sandy had also inherited her father's soft brown eyes but on this the two differed, and Ben, as with his brother's, followed the maternal line of a pale ice-blue. The clear intensity of them combined with almost black hair made a truly striking combination.

Ben's dreams had also been far removed from that of all his siblings. Matt and Joe had both studied business and were now well established in the family company. Sandy had shown a keen business acumen at an early age and declared her intentions to study law, encouraged by Ben's best friend Tyler. Her wish was to then join the legal team at the family firm but she knew she'd have to prove herself worthy, and wouldn't just get a job there because of who she was. A bad lawyer could cost the business, and therefore her family, a lot of money. Sandy had approached her studies seriously. She'd been interviewed by the business' legal team along with other candidates for the position. Sandy had been top of her class, and had the quickest, smartest answers of all of them and was now part of the family firm, as per her dream.

The youngest son was the only one who'd never shown the slightest interest in business. Ben's heart had always been in music. He liked nothing better than to sit out on the porch swing quietly playing a tune he'd written or a favourite he'd heard on the radio. Although only next door, the girls were always sleeping over at one another's houses, and they would lie in their beds as the warm Kansas wind gently sucked the curtains in and out, listening to the quiet strums of Ben's guitar and the whispered lyrics as he unintentionally soothed them to sleep.

Ellie thought about Ben. Tall, kind, gorgeous and now married to a model he'd met at a charity function their band had performed at. She hadn't seen him for years. His devotion to music had paid off and he was now the lead guitarist in a successful country band. They'd already had two number ones in the US country chart and their current song was climbing both the country and the regular charts after being used in a huge box office success, which had brought them even more fans.

In the past Ben had told her that he knew he was lucky he'd been allowed to tread his own path and would be ever thankful to his family for that. Just the thought of sitting behind a desk all day had sent shivers down his spine. In turn, his family, and Ellie, were overjoyed for him. All he'd ever wanted was to play music and now that dream was reality.

*

18

Having checked her phone again for the hundredth time, Sandy's dark eyes scanned the travellers as she squeezed Todd's hand in nervous anticipation.

'Honey, you're going to break my hand.'

Sandy turned and smiled as she lessened the grip on her fiancé. As soon as she'd told him about Ellie coming to visit, and the main reason behind it, he'd volunteered to drive her to the airport, saying that it would let them catch up without having to worry about concentrating on driving. She was glad now that he had, as nerves and excitement and concern all bubbled within her while she continued to watch the gates for the first sign of her friend.

What Todd hadn't mentioned was that it was his concern for the woman he loved that compelled him to rearrange his day at the last minute in order to drive her to and from the airport.

Todd's family had been friends with the Danvers for years but it was only a couple of years ago that his and Sandy's friendship had deepened into something more. Every time he thought about that, he kicked himself for not seeing what an incredible woman she was sooner and at the thought of all the time he'd wasted not being with her. One night, after a couple too many beers, he'd confided this to his brother-in-law. Ben was, and had always been, as much of a brother to him as if they'd had the same blood running through their veins. Ben had just smiled, squeezed his shoulder and told him that sometimes people had to go through the things they did in order to appreciate the right thing – or person – when it was the right time.

Todd had met Ellie very briefly a couple of times when they were kids but not properly since he and Sandy had been dating. He'd seen her on Skype but if he was around when they called, he was usually shooed lovingly out of the room so that, as Sandy said, she could talk about him. But he knew how close the two women were and, if the information Zak had given Sandy was accurate, his fiancée was likely in for more of a shock than she thought when she saw her friend. She'd told him she was prepared but he didn't know if she was prepared enough. If he was right, the shock of seeing a woman as close as a sister bruised and battered was going to impact her harder than she thought. For Todd, offering to drive was a no brainer.

Beside him, Sandy was still scanning the crowds, jittering back and forth.

'There she is! Oh!' She squinted a little. 'She cut her hair.'

Todd followed Sandy's frowning gaze to see a slim woman, about Sandy's height, with a red, chin-length bob under a baseball cap. Her eyes were hidden behind rose-tinted aviator-style sunglasses.

'Ellie!' Sandy called, rushing to the end of the barrier and pulling her friend into a big hug.

Ellie stiffened involuntarily and eased away a little. Sandy pulled back. From a distance, Todd watched the concern on his fiancée's face. He had a feeling that was only going to increase once those sunglasses were removed.

'Ribs,' Ellie explained, an awkward smile on her face.

'Jeez. I'm so sorry, honey. You OK?' Sandy took her friend's free hand, closing both of her own around it.

'Yep. Fine. Fine.'

'I almost didn't recognise you. You didn't tell me you cut your hair.'

Ellie withdrew her hand and tugged at the hat, a shadow passing across her face. 'I hate it.'

'OK, so then we don't talk about it. Let's go home.'

Ellie nodded. Sandy had used the right phrase. It did always feel like coming home when she came back to Kansas. Seeing her friend at last, in addition to the emotional and physical roller-coaster she'd just come off, had made her throat tight. For a moment, she didn't trust herself to speak.

'Oh!' Sandy remembered her manners. 'Obviously this is Todd.'

Todd smiled and held out his hand. 'It's really great to meet you properly at last. Although obviously I wish it were under different circumstances.'

Ellie gave a smile, although to Todd it looked a little stiff and he guessed the make-up she wore hid more damage. 'Yes. Me too.'

He touched her arm very gently and briefly, silently adding to his fiancée's reassurance that she was safe now. 'Let me get that,' he said, reaching for the handle of the luggage trolley. Sandy took Ellie's arm and tucked it through her own as they walked to the car. As Todd busied himself loading the case into the trunk, the women got in the cab and made themselves comfortable.

'Can I see?' Sandy asked quietly.

Ellie paused then lowered her head. Slowly she removed the cap and carefully removed the glasses.

Behind them, Todd shut the cover of the pick-up. Hesitantly, Ellie looked back at Sandy.

'Oh, Ellie,' Sandy cried softly, tears welling in her eyes. Immediately, she pulled her friend to her once again, this time remembering the delicate ribs.

'All set?' Todd asked brightly as he got in, looking up from the ignition when he got no reply. Sandy was wiping her eyes on a tissue, and her friend's head was bent towards her, but Todd could now see the damage she'd been hiding. His mouth set in an angry line. Settling his breath, concentrating on driving rather than anger, he turned the engine over and pulled out. As he turned the corner, his peripheral vision caught Ellie's bruises again. He just couldn't understand guys that did that to women. Women they claimed to love! To Todd, those guys were the lowest of the low. There was no excuse to hit a woman. Ever. It really was that simple. Thankfully, Sandy had told him that at least this guy had now been arrested and Ellie was finished with him. For good. Glancing across again, Todd really hoped that was true.

The two women sat quietly in the car on the way to the Danvers' family home, their hands gripped in an unspoken gesture of friendship and support. There was so much to say but when she'd removed the sunglasses, the exhaustion in Ellie's eyes was clear for anyone to see.

After a few miles, Sandy brightened.

'Hey, want some music on? I have Ben's latest album on my phone.'

'That'd be great.' Sandy tapped her phone and scrolled for a moment. Soon the familiar sound of Ben's music filled the car. Ellie rested her head back against the seat, her hand still tightly within her friend's, and let the music surround her.

*

Molly Danvers was out on the porch before the car pulled up. As they stopped, she hurried down the driveway towards them. Ellie looked up, seeing Ted as he stood back by the house.

As much as Ellie wanted to be wrapped in the comfort of her own family, for the moment, she had kept the truth from them, having asked the Danvers to do the same. Still great friends with the Laings, they had been reluctant, but agreed to Ellie's wishes not to worry them, understanding her reasons.

Andrew Laing's blood pressure had always been fairly high. A career that he found both stressful and rewarding had only contributed to a genetic propensity to readings higher than was ideal. He'd been making changes and things had appeared to be going in the right direction but on a visit about eight months ago, Ellie had found her father looking grey and her mother looking worried. He'd laughed it off, saying that it was fine, his attention more focused on the bruise on his daughter's temple, something she had explained away as a tennis injury from a friend's wayward racket. Thankfully, they'd accepted it. She had wanted to tell them everything – how much Carl had changed since they'd moved in together and how she wasn't sure what to do now, that he'd promised it would never happen again, and had surrounded her with attention and gifts since it had happened – but couldn't.

She'd always valued her parents' opinions but looking at them both that day, she knew she couldn't ask them about it. Not right then. They clearly had enough to worry about. As Carl's behaviour got worse, so had her father's health and she'd had to time her visits to when any bruises she had were out of sight.

Six months ago, she'd been woken with a call from her mother who, in an eerily calm manner, had told her that they were at the hospital and that her dad had suffered a massive heart attack. Her mum's calm manner had frightened Ellie more than any hysterical crying could have done. It was almost as though she had already accepted something that her daughter just wasn't prepared to. She couldn't even remember the drive that day and had ended up with a fine in the car park as her mind had been on her dad rather than feeding a meter.

Andrew Laing's heart had stopped once in the ambulance as they raced to the hospital, but the paramedics had managed to resuscitate him, his distraught wife watching on. Having been informed at the nurse's station that her dad was still in surgery, Ellie had run to the waiting room and found her mum, and together they had just sat. And waited. Several hours later, the surgeon had come to them, his face unreadable. Ellie's mum's brave façade had crumbled before he'd even opened his mouth. When he told them that her husband was stable but critical, having once more arrested on the operating table, Ellie thought her mum's heart would break from sobbing. She'd held her as tightly as she could, almost as if by holding her so close she could keep her, and perhaps both of them, from falling apart.

She'd finally persuaded her mum to get a little rest but not until she'd been allowed to see her husband, just for a few moments. The medical team understood that she'd needed that moment, that reassurance that the man she loved was still here, at least for now and hopefully for a lot longer yet. After, Ellie had sat there holding her mother's hand as her head lay in her lap, a reversal of roles for the night.

Thankfully her dad had fought for his life and it had been the catalyst for her parents changing their lifestyle in a more dramatic way. They sold the large house in Surrey they'd lived in since returning home to England, cut down on their social commitments and found a small, but beautiful cottage in a tiny village down by the sea in Cornwall. It had recently been renovated to a very high standard so there was nothing to be done but relax and enjoy the life that had been spared. It had been a huge scare for all of them and, however much he told his wife and daughter that they were fussing, Ellie knew her dad had been scared too. The ease with which he'd agreed to her mum's plan of cultivating a much quieter life proved that. The change had been good for them and Ellie had no intention of putting any undue stress their way. She would tell them, in time. And she knew they'd be upset with her for not telling them – but she also knew they'd understand.

'Ellie, darlin',' Molly said, pushing the auburn curls back from the forehead. 'Oh, sweetheart,' she whispered, pulling the young woman to her.

'Mind her ribs, Mama,' Sandy warned, her own voice thick with emotion. Molly wrapped an arm around each of them and together they walked back to the house.

'Thanks for letting me stay here.'

'Don't be silly, honey. Of course you'd stay here.'

Ted Danvers studied Ellie's face as she walked up the steps. Leaning down, he kissed the unbruised cheek as he gently hugged her.

'You'll be alright now.'

Ellie nodded. He was right. She would.

'Right!' Molly said, discreetly wiping her eye. 'Let's get you people something to eat.' With that, she chivvied them all inside and Ellie was soon wrapped up in the warmth and love of the Danvers' family home.

*

A few days later, Ellie and Sandy were preparing dinner together in the kitchen, with the aid of a bottle of wine, when they heard a key in the front door. Ted and Molly had gone out earlier and weren't due back for a while yet, so grabbing another quick sip of wine, Sandy went to investigate. In the hall, she met Ben and his wife Cyndi slipping off their coats.

'What are you doing here?' she asked, her tone wary.

Ben pulled a face at his sister's unusually reserved greeting. 'Nice to see you too, kid.'

Sandy shifted her weight, before throwing a quick glance back towards the kitchen. When she didn't offer any further explanation for her lack of enthusiasm, Ben continued.

'We were just passing through. Thought we'd stop and say hi.' He bent and kissed her on the cheek, 'And see what's for dinner, obviously.' He grinned and Sandy smiled back. Ben's smile tended to make people do that – it was infectious. Plus, she loved the fact that, despite everything, he didn't change. His mum's cooking was still the best in his eyes. She noticed Cyndi standing serenely behind her husband, running a hand over her already perfect hair. Of course, Sandy pondered, he probably didn't have a lot to compare it to, excepting his own. From what she gathered, his wife was not a natural in the kitchen. And by 'not a natural', she meant 'had never cooked in her life and had no intention of starting now'.

Cyndi had apparently tried insisting on a cook and while Ben had always attempted to do whatever made his wife happy, he'd remained firm on that subject. The thought of someone else being in the house most of the day made him feel uncomfortable. He'd explained to Sandy as he had tried explaining it to his wife, that if he was writing and fancied a sandwich he wanted to be able to pad in and make himself one without feeling like he was in the way in his own home. While Sandy understood, Cyndi had merely pointed out that he would just be able to ask the cook to make him one, completely missing his point. He'd given up trying to explain but had insisted on no cook. If she wanted one when he was away and she remained behind – not that she ever tended to – then that was fine with him. But until then, either he'd cook or they'd get take out. Or see what his mom had in the oven.

'Hey, Cyndi.'

'Hello.' Cyndi gave the briefest of smiles as she stepped towards Sandy and did two air kisses. It was her latest habit. *Oh man!*

'Um, Ben.' Sandy began as she finished mentally rolling her eyes and took Cyndi's beautiful and very expensive coat. 'Ellie's staying for a few days. '

'Really? That's great! I didn't know she was coming over. I haven't seen her in years!' Ben cast his mind back, trying to remember when he'd last seen her, and couldn't, although he did recall the short telephone conversation they'd had after his wedding.

The painting that Ellie had sent as her gift had taken his breath away. He knew how much time that would have taken her and all the four- and five-figure gifts Cyndi had put on their list – an act that still made Ben cringe – couldn't come close to meaning what hers had.

Sandy had been chatting to Ellie on the phone when they'd dropped round after opening all the presents and, popping into the kitchen, he'd apologised for disturbing his sister as she'd sat on a kitchen stool with her feet tucked up, perched up like a gnome – a position that had always made Ben nervous. When his sister had told him who it was, he'd spontaneously taken the phone and said hi, wanting to thank Ellie personally having been disappointed she couldn't make the wedding.

What he hadn't expected was the reaction he'd felt on hearing Ellie's soft voice and gentle laugh after all these years. And, of course, that accent. Oh man, that accent! Passing the phone back to Sandy, he'd hurriedly got the glass of wine for Cyndi he'd originally gone into the kitchen for and returned to the living room. She'd pouted at the few minutes' delay as she took it, remonstrating as she did so. Across the room, he'd seen his parents drop their gaze and pretend not to notice his wife's nitpicking. He knew they weren't the only ones. Ben wasn't stupid. He hadn't expected the whirlwind of their romance to last forever, knowing it would transition into something even more beautiful. Everyone knew there was a honeymoon period. But he had expected the honeymoon period to at least outlast the honeymoon itself.

Things would settle in time, he knew, so he'd given his wife a gentle kiss, taken her hand and tried to forget that his kid sister's best friend was now no longer a kid and had a soft, unbelievably sexy voice.

That night, he'd lain in bed, guilt eating him up. Cyndi might not have been the woman that his family and friends would have chosen for him but he loved her, and he was, and always would be, a one-woman man. He'd put the phone call out of his mind and replaced it instead with an image of the two girls as annoying nine-year-olds. It had worked. Ellie had become just his kid sister's best friend again. But he'd always enjoyed her company and would be glad to see her again now.

'Ben, there's something you should know first,' Sandy began as she turned and hung Cyndi's butter-soft, full-length leather coat on the hook. 'Ellie's...' Sandy turned back to finish her explanation. Ben and Cyndi had gone.

'Damn!' She hurried after them, entering the kitchen just as Ellie responded to the call of her name.

'Jesus Christ!' Ben exclaimed.

Ellie's bruised face was a mixture of shock, horror and embarrassment. She wasn't expecting to see Ben or his perfect-looking wife – and certainly not unprepared like this. Heavy silence hung in the air for a second, all of them unmoving.

'Excuse me,' Ellie said, faintly, her head low as she fumbled for the back-door handle, trying to exit with as much dignity as she could, although right now she felt like the little she'd clung on to had just been totally shredded.

Walking almost blindly down the garden, she hurried along the path that wound through the large space towards the ancient, gnarled tree at the end. A rope swing hung from one of its thick branches. Ellie sat heavily on its wooden seat, worn and shiny with use. The wind rustled the leaves and gently creaked the swing to and fro. The breeze felt good on her face, exposed as it was now in this safe, hidden corner. In her mind, she saw again the shock and horror on Ben's face, the revulsion on Cyndi's, and closed her eyes. She felt ugly, her face hurt, and her whole body felt like she'd been run over by a truck. Right now, all she wanted was to curl up in a dark corner and stay there.

Back in the kitchen, Sandy had already exploded at her brother. 'Great! Thanks a lot, Ben!' Ben turned and stared at his sister, unable to think for a moment.

'What happened to her face?' Cyndi asked, her nose still screwed up in distaste.

Sandy was in no mood to be patient or polite. 'Her ex-boyfriend happened to her face. He had a bad day so he came home and beat the crap out of Ellie. Again! And right now, she's feeling pretty fragile and worthless and unattractive and both your reactions have really helped, so thank you so much!' she yelled, fury making her accent thick.

'Well, I guess she doesn't exactly look that attractive at the moment,' Cyndi blurted.

Sandy's eyes widened and she opened her mouth, about to unleash a torrent at her sister-in-law but Ben got there first.

'Be quiet, Cyndi,' he said softly, before heading to the door that Ellie had just left through. Closing it behind him, he left the two women alone in the kitchen.

Sandy stood staring at Cyndi for a moment, anger still flashing in her dark eyes. Keeping her thoughts to herself, for Ben's sake more than anyone else's, she stalked across the hall to the study and slammed the door, leaving Cyndi alone.

*

Ben had never felt so sorry in all his life. Just the bombshell of seeing Ellie like that, so bruised and battered, had stunned him. And then, as she'd looked from him to his wife and then Sandy, like a fawn caught in headlights, not knowing which way to run, he'd felt an overwhelming desire to pull her to him, kiss her battered face, and promise that no one would ever hurt her again, that he would always keep her safe. The shock of that unbidden thought had kept him entirely rooted to the spot. The picture he'd kept in his mind of the annoying nine-year-olds had now been totally obliterated by the image of the woman in front of him.

She was sitting on their old swing, bare feet dangling above the ground, head resting on the twisted rope support as one slow, sad tear rolled down her face. He stopped and watched her for a moment. Despite what his wife had said, Ben could see through the bruising, and, as he stood there, what he saw was a beautiful woman. And what he felt terrified him.

Ellie caught his presence from the corner of her eye and turned her head a little more towards the rope, away from him.

'Ellie? Ellie honey, I'm so sorry.'

'It's OK. Really.' She shook her head in forgiveness but declined to look at him. Ben felt worse.

'No. No it's not.' His voice was soft as he walked over and hunkered down in front of the swing. Still, she kept her head turned away. 'It was insensitive. I – I was just shocked, I guess.'

'That makes two of us then.' A ghost of a half-smile showed on her lips but she refused to meet his eyes.

'Hey, there's that smile.' Ellie didn't respond. 'Are you going to look at me?' he asked softly. He tentatively rested his hand on hers and, after a moment, she curled a single finger around it.

She shook her head and the salty tear dropped and landed on Ben's jeans, a dark blob on the faded denim.

'Why not?'

Her voice cracked as she whispered her reply. 'I don't even want to look at me.'

'Oh, sweetheart,' Ben whispered as he stood, gently pulling her up with him as he did so, wrapping his arms around her. 'It's OK. Everything's OK now. I promise.'

It was all that was needed to breach the fragile dam she had built in an attempt to keep back the flood of emotions bursting within her. Feeling secure in her friend's strong embrace, hidden from the world, Ellie began to sob. Great painful issues wracked her whole body as Ben curled his palm around the back of her head, holding her close as she let out the frustration and pain, the disappointment and fear that she'd been doing her best to hide from. Broken words filtered out every now and then, but she was so upset Ben couldn't make them out, so he just held her until she had cried herself out.

Ellie pulled away from him, searching self-consciously in her skirt pocket for a handkerchief. Finding one, she wiped her eyes and nose, keeping her gaze lowered.

'Oh no,' A look of concern furrowed her brow as she pointed at his shirt.

A large wet patch showed just below the shoulder where she had buried her head. Ben looked down and smiled, trying not to die a little bit at the worry he saw in her expression.

'It'll dry.' He shrugged.

'I'm so sorry. I—'

'It's OK,' he interrupted. 'Really. Needed a wash anyway.'

Slowly, gently, he placed one finger under her chin and tipped her face to his. 'I said it's OK.'

Finally, she lifted his eyes to meet his. Ben looked down into those startling green eyes, now swollen and red-rimmed. One was still half closed and surrounded by a rainbow-coloured bruise, as was her temple and jaw.

'How could anyone do this?'

'Please don't. You'll start me off again.'

He nodded, forcing a smile that thankfully, this time, received the smallest of ones in reply as she held the gaze momentarily.

Cyndi and Ben had stayed to dinner but Sandy had put Ellie to bed as soon as she returned from the garden with Ben, saying she'd bring her something to eat later. The tearstains on Ellie's face and her brother's shirt had told enough of the story.

'I'm not tired, Sands.'

'I know but you're having a rest anyway,' Sandy replied, ignoring the protest and pulling the cover over her friend.

'You're worse than my mum!'

'I'll check on you later.' Sandy smiled, kissing her friend on the forehead before leaving the room.

Ellie lay on the bed and watched the evening sun painting colours in the sky. She really wasn't tired but her head was pounding from all the crying. Maybe closing her eyes would make it go away.

*

Ben walked out with Sandy to collect their coats.

'I really didn't mean to upset her. You know I wouldn't have done that for the world.'

'I know.' Sandy hugged him. 'Ellie knows that too. Actually, although it probably wasn't the kindest way of going about it, I think it did her good. She's been trying to be brave and strong when she really needed to just give in and release it all. Start afresh from there.'

'I guess.'

'And your complete lack of tact seemed to do the trick!'

Ben looked pained. Then he caught the glint in her eye and pulled a face. Shoving the two coats at her.

'I'm going to say goodbye to Ellie. It could be another decade before I see her again.'

'OK. Don't wake her if she's still sleeping though.'

Ben tapped lightly on the door and pushed it when there was no response. She was lying, half on her back and half on her side, one arm cuddling a pillow. Her head was turned away from the window towards the door. Towards him. He knew he should leave but he couldn't. Not just yet.

'Is she still asleep?' Sandy poked her head around the door.

Ben flushed, glad of the low light. 'Yeah,' he whispered back

Sandy entered the room and stood at Ben's side, then looked down at her friend's sleeping form,

'She looks peaceful. That's good.' From the corner of her eye, she saw her brother's face twitch in anger. Nudging him, she derailed his thoughts. 'Come on. She wouldn't appreciate us spying on her.'

Ben looked back at Ellie, stepped across and momentarily covered her hand with his own. She didn't stir.

'Bye, Ellie,' he whispered.

Sandy quickly closed the shutters and then followed her brother out, shutting the door behind her. Ben hadn't moved.

'Why did she let him do this?' True confusion showed in Ben's clear blue eyes. Sandy couldn't help her surprise. This wasn't like Ben. Normally, he just dealt with things, fixed what he could and accepted what he couldn't. Taking things in his stride had always been his thing. However, his comment made her frown.

'I don't think she had much of a choice in the matter, Ben. It's not like she asked him to do it!'

'No, of course not. I didn't mean that. I just meant, why didn't she get out sooner. She was with him, what, over two years? He must have done this before. You said yourself that you think she had more trouble with him than she let on. Why didn't she just leave? She's bright and funny, and beautiful. Why'd she put up with it?'

'Well,' Sandy said slowly, 'she thought she loved him. And when you love someone, I guess it's easier to find excuses not to leave.'

'Ben?' Cyndi called up the stairs, that pout back on her face.

Ben looked down, startled. Molly, having returned, was stood behind her and the expression on her son's face unsettled her. He ran a hand through his hair before pasting on a smile on for his wife, then jogged down the staircase, lifting their coats from the banister on the way. After helping Cyndi into hers, Ben shrugged into his own and headed out into the night.

Chapter 3

'Hey.'

'Hi,' Ellie replied a little groggily, squinting against the sunshine streaming in to the bright kitchen.

'Sleep OK?' Sandy asked, pouring her friend a juice from the glass jug that stood on the table.

'A little too well, I think.' Ellie pulled a face as she inclined her head towards the clock on the wall. Sandy waved her hand. 'Don't worry about it. Looks like the rest did you good. You look brighter today.'

Ellie raised her one unbruised eyebrow in disbelief.

'Seriously.'

'She's right,' Molly said, bustling into the kitchen and taking charge of the pans on the stove. She paused for a moment and turned, meeting Ellie's eyes. 'Sometimes we want to keep everything inside when really it just all needs to come out so that we can start healing. Physically and mentally.' Ellie flushed and dropped her gaze. 'What a way to do it though,' she said, taking a sip of her orange juice.

Sandy and her mother exchanged a glance. Molly turned off the heat under the pan and crossed the kitchen, taking the seat next to Ellie. Reaching out, she took her hand, holding it within her own.

'What is it that you're worried about?'

Ellie felt the tears build in her eyes once more. Snatching a napkin from the table, she pressed it to them for a second.

'I just feel...'

Molly and Sandy waited.

Ellie took a deep breath before letting it out slowly. 'It's just that...Ben, of all people!'

'Ben cares about you. He always has.'

'Yes. But...it's not like I really know him anymore. I only saw him a couple of times after we moved back to England and I think the last time I actually even talked to him, apart from the quick thank you on the phone that time, was probably over ten years ago. And then I go and do a hysterical blubbing act on a huge music star's designer shirt.'

'He felt awful about upsetting you. Anything he could do to make up for that, he would have done willingly. Besides, Ben is still Ben. Just because more people know his name and face doesn't mean he's changed any,' Sandy replied.

'He didn't upset me. I just...I just wasn't expecting to see anyone else and it took me by surprise. Please explain that when you talk to him – unless they're due to visit again?'

Ellie wasn't sure how she felt about that particular circumstance. Sandy was right. She did feel better in a way, but not necessarily better enough to come face to face with the celebrity she'd noisily sobbed all over the previous evening.

Sandy nodded. 'He's heading off today on some promo thing so I don't think they'll be around for a little while now but I'll be sure to tell him. I promise.'

Molly smiled and patted Ellie's hand. 'Right. Breakfast!' she said, standing.

'I'll just get some cereal,' Ellie said, making to follow her. 'That's plenty.'

Molly laid a gentle hand on her shoulder. 'Not in this house. You should know that by now.'

Ellie sat back down and couldn't help smiling. She did know that by now. Her many visits, both when living next door and thousands of miles away, had taught her that. And when delicious smells began wafting her way as Molly sang to herself at the stove, she looked over at Sandy and gave a smile.

Across the table, Sandy returned it, seeing the beginnings of change and feeling her heart lighten just a touch at that glimmer. Last night she could have punched her adored older brother but right now, she would have hugged him. Whatever he did or didn't do, whatever he said or didn't say, had helped her best friend take another step in the right direction. For that, she would be ever thankful to him.

*

Ben had loved his house as soon as he saw it. Sadly, it hadn't been the new start with Cyndi that he'd hoped it would be. In fact, the day he'd taken her out there, not long after Ellie's visit, his wife had hated it on sight.

'You what?' Cyndi had snapped. Her perfectly made up eyes, complete with overlong false lashes stared up at him, the expression in them hard.

'I bought it.'

'Without asking me?'

'I wanted it to be a surprise.'

'Well! It's certainly that!' she snorted.

'There's stables and a garden and—'

'I know what's here, Ben.' Cyndi cut him off. 'We came before, but you said you were looking at it for a friend.' She gave a cursory glance around before meeting her husband's eyes. 'There's no way I'm living here.'

'You said it was nice when we came before.'

'That's because I didn't know you were thinking of buying it! I guess it is nice if you like this kind of thing.'

'Look, honey,' Ben had tried to reason, 'just give it a chance. I could even teach you to ride.'

'I don't want you to teach me to ride! Horses make me itch.'

Ben took a deep breath. 'OK…so how about this? We don't have to live here all the time. Just some of it. Have it as a place to come back to, away from the city and the noise and everything. A quiet retreat, you know.'

'So what I want doesn't matter? Is that what you're saying?'

Ben looked confused. 'Wait…what? No. That's not what I said at all.' He ran a hand through his hair, trying to figure how she'd got that from what he'd just said. 'You know that's not true.' He walked up to his wife and looked at her perfectly made-up face. A beautiful face and body in the perfect dress and shoes, with the perfect hair. She was everything he'd wanted. *Wasn't she?*

The late summer wind blew around them. Somewhere deep inside his head a little voice pointed out that, despite the breeze, not one strand of Cyndi's hair was moving. Ben lifted his fingers and touched her hair – it was almost rigid. She jumped back as though he'd burned her.

'What the hell are you doing?' she squealed, 'You know I hate people touching my hair!'

'I just…' Ben knew his answer would sound ridiculous so chose not to finish the sentence. Cyndi was still staring at him, an incredulous look on her face as she nervously patted her hair.

'Have you been drinking?'

'Nope,' Ben said quietly, lowering himself onto the steps of the porch before looking back up at his wife. She looked down and he noted that she seemed uncomfortable. Out of place.

'Sit by me?'

She raised an exquisite brow. 'It's filthy!'

Ben turned his head and glanced down at the steps. They were kind of dusty. 'It's only dust. It'll brush off.' Cyndi let out a theatrical sigh. 'Have you any idea how much this dress cost? Maybe if you ever wore something other than your jeans it might occur to you not to sit on the ground either.'

Ben didn't know how much it cost. Only that he had paid for it. Something that had never bothered him. He'd just wanted to make Cyndi happy. Unfortunately, that particular task had only got more and more difficult each day of their marriage.

'You never used to mind the way I dressed,' Ben said, as he made little piles of dust with the toe of his boot.

'Ben, sweetie,' Cyndi wheedled, crouching beside him. He took it as an offer of compromise and knew it was as near to sitting on the floor as she was ever going to get. 'I'm just saying that you're successful enough to wear nice things.'

'You mean I have enough money to buy a tie for ten thousand bucks and should wear it just 'cos it's designed by some guy who happens to be top of the fashion tree this month.'

'Well!' Cyndi stood up and began smoothing away imaginary creases. 'If you're not prepared to take this seriously—'

'Cyndi, I am taking this seriously, but this is me. This is who I am. I like my jeans and my boots and my hat. That's what I feel comfortable in and I can't change that. I don't want to change that. It's how you met me, and I'm sorry if you're now ashamed of me because of it.'

'Of course, I'm not ashamed of you, honey.' She touched his arm. 'I just think you have more potential.'

'Potential?' Ben looked back up in confusion.

'You know, the advertising contracts you've been offered and—'

Ben cut her off. 'Is it all about the money to you? Is that all we mean? All I mean to you?'

Cyndi looked taken aback. Ben never lost his temper with her. In fact, he rarely lost it ever. But she could see the anger – and maybe hurt – flashing in his eyes now. Inside she felt a little twinge that possibly she was responsible for that hurt. But still. She spent so much time and money on her appearance to look good for him and then he wanted her to hide out here in the back of beyond! And had the audacity to snap at her when she voiced an opinion on it!

'That's unfair!' Cyndi spat back. Her eyes were dry but she was working on that.

'Oh man,' Ben whispered under his breath.

'Sometimes I wonder if you even care about me at all! About what I want! What makes me happy!' Cyndi began, still endeavouring to force the waterworks. 'Trying to force me to live in the middle of nowhere when you know I'd hate it! All you care about is that you've got a pretty face hanging on your arm!'

Ben was stunned into silence. When he regained his voice, it was soft. 'Is that really what you think?'

'Yes! That's really what I think!' His wife spun on her five-inch, red soled stilettos and tottered off, the strut of her tantrum rather undermined by the insecurity of the spiked heels on the uneven ground. Ben followed her to the car.

'Do you think I don't love you?'

'I don't know!' She threw in a sniff for extra effect.

'You know I'd never try and force you – or anyone – into doing something they didn't want to. Surely you know that about me by now?'

She gave a shrug. Ben let out a sigh and shook his head.

'Cyndi.' He kissed her gently on the forehead. 'Look, you go back to the apartment tonight. I'll stay here and go see the real estate agent in the morning. We don't have to keep the house.' There was a pause. 'I just thought you'd like it. That it'd be a great place to bring kids up in.' He waited a beat, knowing that deep down, a part of him was hoping she would relent and say OK, that perhaps they would try living here for a while but the deal was done as far as Cyndi was concerned. She'd won. Again. As usual. She nodded as she fished out a compact from her Hermés crocodile Birkin bag and reapplied her lipstick. There was no trace of the tears.

'OK, I'll see you tomorrow then.'

He nodded then helped her into the Porsche and shut the door. She sped off down the unsealed drive, kicking up even more dust. As it lazily settled around him, Ben looked down at his jeans, removed his hat and beat at them half-heartedly with it.

Turning, he let his gaze settle on the house. His beautiful house. He'd fallen in love with it the moment he'd seen it and had been hopeful of a new start there. Walking back across, he took up his seat again on the steps and looked out onto the wheat fields that backed up to his land. The golden curtain danced and waved in the breeze. Soon it would be harvesting time and he'd been looking forward to watching as the huge machines worked their way along the crop. The process had fascinated him as a boy and still held allure for him all these years later. His eyes drifted over the rest of the landscape. There was so much space, so much land, so much sky. It was wonderful. He didn't understand how Cyndi couldn't love it. Couldn't get his head around why she would prefer to live in the city with the constant noise and people and traffic.

Cyndi was born in the city and had no desire to leave. He was born a country boy and would always stay one, in his heart at least. In that, it seemed, they would always differ.

A thought popped into his head. Now that Cyndi would be back at their apartment, he ought to ring Sandy and let her know she didn't need to go to the apartment and feed the cat. Housekeeping wasn't due in today and when Ben had told Sandy about his plans to take Cyndi out to the new house and surprise her, hoping that they would stay out there a few days, Sandy had volunteered to head over and see that their pet was fed.

'Well, I certainly surprised her!' He sighed aloud to himself, leaning his head back against one of the porch supports as he closed his eyes. The only noise was the wind as it played gently with the crop. He'd never felt so comfortable in a place. Never had such a feeling of being exactly where he was supposed to be as he did right now.

Opening his eyes, the reality hit him. There was no way Cyndi would live here – or anywhere like it. The moment she knew it was theirs and not merely a chance to see where someone else might be living – what someone else might have – she hadn't even wanted to set foot inside.

Ben knew his only option was to return to the city. He tried to push away the twist in his stomach at that knowledge. Tried to ignore the thought of how miserable he found constant city life, and how much more free and alive he felt when he was out here, in the wide open spaces he'd loved his whole life. He pushed a hand through his hair in frustration. He needed to leave. Staying at this house was only making him want it more. Better just to head back and call the real estate agent tomorrow.

Standing, he returned his hat to his head and walked down to the pleasant brick building that provided lodging for the farm-hands. Following excellent recommendations from the previous owner, he'd taken the workers on along with the property. The horses and land were in good hands with them. Ben made a mental note to specify that he wanted their interests looked after when he sold the property on.

'Hey Jed,' he called, addressing the head rancher as he held out his hand.

'Hey, Mr Danvers,' Jed replied, shaking it. 'You showing Mrs Danvers around?' Jed had seen them arrive in a shiny sports car that didn't seem the best choice for the tracks around here but then rich people tended to do things their own way from what he'd seen.

'Yeah.' Ben smiled. 'She got called back to the city though.'

'Oh, that's a shame. Still. Plenty of time.'

Ben smiled. At least Jed made the effort. When they'd visited before, they'd met up with Jed so that he could show them around the land. Cyndi's snobbery had shown its ugly head again then as she turned up her nose at the hat Jed had kindly offered her – a perfectly clean and acceptable one – in order to protect her from the heat of the day. She'd blanked him and walked off, dropping her designer sunglasses back in front of her face for the rest of the visit and asking Ben questions which would have been better directed at the ranch hand.

Her behaviour had caused Ben to cringe and, having made some lame excuse to Jed about her feeling out of sorts today, he'd called her out on it on the way home. She'd made a vague sort of apology and her behaviour had seemed to ease for a couple of days, but as soon as she was back with her friends, Ben saw the trait float to the surface again. Cyndi had been spoiled from day one by her parents and now by him. He knew he had to accept some of the blame. He'd been bowled over by her the moment he met her and swore then and there that whatever she wanted, he would give it to her. It was, after all, what she was used to and if he didn't, someone else sure would. But she definitely didn't want this house.

'Jed, do you think I could borrow the old truck for a couple of days?'

'Don't see why not? It might need some gas though.' Jed picked the keys off a hook and tossed them over.

Ben tried his sister intermittently as he drove back towards town but the line was constantly busy. Just as the apartment building came into view, it finally connected.

'Hello. You've reached Sandy Danvers. I'm afraid I can't take your call right—'

Ben hung up. She must already be on her way to the apartment, and rarely chose to connect her Bluetooth in the car, telling him that she enjoyed the feeling of being unplugged for once.

Parking behind Cyndi's Porsche, Ben got out and locked the door. A grin played on his mouth as he walked away. The battered, dusty truck looked so out of place among the sleek saloons, SUVs and shiny sports cars that decorated the apartment lot. He kind of liked it. Approaching the entrance, Ben punched in the code. The buzzer sounded and he pushed open the heavy glass door.

'Evening, Mr Danvers.'

'Hi, Jerry. I don't suppose you saw my sister go up this evening at all?'

'I'm sorry, sir, no. I just came on duty a minute ago.'

'That's OK. Goodnight.'

'Goodnight, sir.'

Ben bounded up the stairs two at a time. Cyndi always tutted and sighed at him whenever he did that. He was still upset about the house but maybe they could find some sort of compromise – he'd been right to come back tonight instead of sitting there, brooding over what could have been. Despite her faults, he loved his wife and knew that he was nowhere near perfect himself. He should have known not to buy something as major as a house without discussing it with her first. Although, he had a feeling if he'd have bought a place in Barbados, there would have been a lot less drama.

The elevator doors pinged open just as Ben walked past them and Sandy stepped out followed by Todd.

'Ben! What are you doing here? I thought you were staying at the ranch tonight?'

He bent and kissed her, before shaking Todd's hand. 'Yeah. Slight change of plan. I've been trying to call you.'

'Not to worry.' Sandy paused, studying his face. 'She didn't like it, did she?'

Ben looked up from the bunch of keys he was fiddling with. She could read him like a book. Always had. He could never lie to her. 'No.'

'I'm sorry,' Sandy replied, her heart breaking a little at the look in Ben's eyes – a look he was trying to hide. He shrugged his shoulders as he picked out the correct key. 'We'll be on our way,' she said, taking Todd's hand and turning to go as Ben opened the door to the apartment.

'No.' He raised a hand. 'We're fine. You may as well stay for a coffee, just so's it's not an entirely wasted journey. I'll go get Cyndi.'

Cyndi's shout of surprise made both Todd and Sandy jump. Exchanging a quick glance, Sandy moved a few paces across to peek towards the bedroom where the scream had emanated from. The look on her face made Todd follow, coming to stand behind her. Ben was leaning on the wall outside the bedroom door, his head tilted back, eyes raised to the ceiling, his skin pale, and looking desperately like he was trying not to throw up. 'Ben?' Sandy prompted, as she began to approach him. Suddenly she was halted by a man leaving the bedroom. Looking dishevelled, he hurried past them all, eyes lowered. The latch of the front door clicked loudly in the stunned silence. Ben pulled his head back, took a deep breath and then turning, looked back into the bedroom.

'Apparently we need to talk.'

'We should go,' Sandy stated as they stood in the living room, waiting for Cyndi to make her entrance. 'I think that's a good idea,' Cyndi agreed as she entered, tying the belt on a shimmering silk robe. Her expression was hard to read – she seemed neither embarrassed nor proud of being caught with a lover by her husband. But then she caught the look in her husband's startling blue eyes. For a moment, it shocked her. They were filled with such pain and such anger – something she'd never seen before. It unsteadied her haughty demeanour and her eyes darted to her sister-in-law. There, in brown eyes instead of blue, she saw the same pain and a whole lot more anger.

'How long, Cyndi?' Ben asked.

'Ben, I don't think this is a conversation we ought to be having in front of company.'

For once Sandy agreed with Cyndi. Moving across the room, one hand gripping Todd's, she stopped briefly and gave her brother's balled fist a squeeze and then let herself and Todd out of the apartment.

'How long?' Ben asked again after the door had closed behind his sister.

'How long what?'

'For Christ's sake, Cyndi!' Ben exploded, making her step back in shock. 'I know you're not as dumb as you try to make out so just answer the damn question. How long have you been sleeping around?' The slap took him by surprise.

'How dare you!'

'How dare I?' He felt a strange desire to laugh, as his hand touched the sting on his cheek. 'I wasn't the one caught with my panties down!'

'Oh, grow up! You can't tell me you didn't know.'

Ben sat down heavily, as though his knees could no longer support him. Cyndi hesitated and then sat opposite him. In a way it made it all so much worse. In the past when they rowed, she would storm off, slam the bedroom door and sulk for half an hour. Ben would potter around and then, after the set time had elapsed, he'd go in with a peace offering and they'd make up. But apparently Cyndi had no intention of stomping off this time. That fact meant that she wanted to deal with it, and that in turn confirmed to Ben it really was over.

He looked back at the beautiful face. There was little emotion to be read on it and he no longer knew how much of that was due to Botox and filler and how much was just due to Cyndi. In complete contrast, Ben's eyes were red, his hair was off in a bunch of different directions from where he'd been running his hands through it and his throat felt rough and constricted.

Cyndi looked back at the man she had loved.

'Nearly a year,' she said quietly.

'Why?'

'I don't know. I guess I was bored. The tour was great but then when that finished, I guess – it was just so...normal.'

Ben smiled but it was cold and didn't warm the ice of his eyes.

'Why are you smiling?' Cyndi asked, warily, unsure whether she truly wanted to know the answer.

'I suppose that answers everyone's questions as to whether you would have married me if I wasn't part of *Cheyenne*.'

Cyndi lowered her eyes. Ben had hoped for a denial, or at least an attempt at one, but she made none.

'I always told you I was just a regular guy, Cyndi, but I guess that wasn't enough for you?'

'I did love you, Ben.'

He looked at her and tried to believe it.

'Do you love him?' he asked, his fingers twiddling the gold band on his left hand

'I don't know.'

Cyndi could see the muscles in Ben's jaw working.

'So you threw our marriage away on a "don't know"?' She made no answer. 'What else is there, Cyndi?' Ben's uncharacteristic anger was bubbling up again. If she'd admitted to falling in love with someone else, he might have been able to understand it – in time at least. Ben was an old-fashioned romantic at heart and true love would win him every time. But this? This, he couldn't understand. He'd loved Cyndi with all his heart. He'd meant every single vow he'd made and the thought she had destroyed everything on a whim was beyond him.

'It's just sex then?'

'No.'

'So, it's not love and it's not sex. What is it, Cyndi? What else is there? Why else would you bring him into our house, into our bed?' He raised his palms to the ceiling. 'You're really gonna have to help me out here 'cause I'm struggling to find another reason.'

Hs wife noticed the strength in his accent. Ben rarely showed his temper but when he did, his accent always increased the angrier he got. It seemed to be a Danvers trait.

'Don't be sarcastic, Ben. It doesn't suit you.'

'Oh, really? Is that so?'

'Yes!'

Heavy silence filled the room as they glared at each other. Cyndi began to speak again. She wasn't used to feeling out of control and she didn't like it. She'd expected Ben to have started trying to win her back by now. Promising her something else – she wasn't sure what yet. She'd have to think about that. And she wasn't sure whether she wanted to be won back. But she certainly didn't like the fact that he wasn't even trying – just standing there glaring at her. Like it wasn't his fault too. Why should she take all the blame?

'I don't know what you want me to say.' She shrugged. It's not love and it's not just sex. I guess it's…something in between.' She tossed her now brushed-out hair. 'We just have a great time together – in and out of bed!' The pained look on Ben's face shocked her, and suddenly she knew she had gone too far. Cut him far more deeply than she'd realised. She also knew he didn't deserve this. Growing up, everyone had always said Cyndi Lawson was going to be a heartbreaker, and she'd been pleased with that description, knowing that it gave her power and got her attention, but right up until this moment, she had thought it was just a phrase.

Ben didn't have the energy or the words to respond to his wife. His stomach churned and his breath felt laboured as though he'd been punched. Cyndi moved towards him.

'Don't.' His voice was raw as he took a step away.

'Ben, please.' Ben looked down at the face that had captivated him from the moment he'd seen her. Stunning, like a Hollywood starlet, and he'd fallen for her completely. She'd been so sweet to him at the beginning and he'd loved her. Utterly. Completely. With everything he had. And now? What? He felt numb.

'I loved you so much,' he said.

There were tears in her eyes and this time he could tell they were genuine. 'I know.'

*

47

Ben drove around for hours, not seeing where he was, replaying things over and over again in his mind. *They had a great time 'in and out of bed'.* The phrase got louder and louder in his head until it was the only thing he could hear. At the next junction, he hung a U-turn and pressed the accelerator.

*

Todd opened his front door without checking the peephole and stood aside, already expecting the visitor. Sandy walked through from the kitchen, two beers in her hand and looked up at her brother, her eyes welling up as she did so. Despite his size, he looked small and broken. Crossing the room, she hugged him without a word, then handed him one of the beers.

'Here. I think you need this more than I do.'

'Thanks.'

Sandy returned from the kitchen with a replacement beer for herself and they sat in silence for a few moments.

'Man, am I stupid!' Ben said, eventually, shaking his head. He tried to laugh but a strangulated noise replaced the sound.

'No, you're not.'

'A year! Nearly a year and I never suspected a thing!'

'There was no reason you should have. You trusted her,' Todd countered.

'Yeah! Not one of my finer decisions apparently,' Ben replied as he got up and began pacing the floor. 'I mean, I know things weren't perfect but I just thought we'd work through them, you know? I didn't think she'd ever...' His voice cracked. 'I guess if I'm honest, it's been coming for a while. I just didn't want to see it. It's pretty obvious that we have nothing in common. We hold different values. Hell, she practically told me I don't even satisfy her in bed!'

Across the room Todd raised his eyebrows. He knew a few of the women Ben had dated over the years and that definitely wasn't

48

the impression he'd been given. Glancing over at his fiancée, he could tell she was just dying to run up and hug her brother, tell him he was way too good for that woman anyway, but she knew that wasn't the kind of support he needed right now. But Todd could see that inside she was raging with fury at her sister-in-law as her eyes burned with unshed tears at seeing Ben in so much pain.

Ben continued. 'You know what's funny, I went to touch her hair earlier today at the ranch. I don't know…stupid thing…the wind wasn't moving it and…anyway. Not important. But the thing was, she went absolutely nuts! Her husband goes to touch just her hair and she freaks out yet she's happy to roll around with God knows who in our bed! How messed up is that?' He took a swig from the bottle and wiped a stray tear away impatiently. 'Couldn't even go to a hotel. Takes him right there, under my nose!' Todd looked up from his beer bottle and studied his friend. Anger and frustration strained at Ben's emotional seams. Standing, he placed a hand on Ben's shoulder, gently steering him towards the garage. Ben looked perplexed at his friend as he took the beer from his hand and then opened the internal door to the garage. Todd nodded to the punchbag and tossed over a pair of gloves.

'Knock yourself out.' He gave him a half-smile. 'Though preferably not literally.'

The sweat was pouring off Ben when he returned half an hour later. His shirt was in a ball in his hand and the waistband of his jeans was damp from his exertions. Sandy walked past him on her way to the kitchen.

'Poo-eee!'

Ben smiled sarcastically and then hugged her.

'Ugh! No! Get off! Get off!' she yelled, pushing him away. His mouth attempted a smile.

'Feel better?' Todd ventured.

'Yeah. Yeah, I do.' He paused. 'Thanks.' Todd nodded in acceptance.

'Are you going to take a shower?' Sandy asked, having retreated to a safe distance.

'Is that a hint?'

'More of a demand.' She smiled at him. 'Throw out your stuff and I'll wash it.'

'OK, thanks.' Ben headed off to the guest room and shower and then poked his head back around the corner. 'For everything.'

Sandy smiled, kissed him on the cheek and then pushed him towards the bathroom.

Chapter 4

One Year Later

'Try to stay in one piece.' Sandy smiled and kissed her fiancé, before burying her face in his neck. 'I wish you wouldn't do this,' she whispered.

Todd turned his head and kissed her temple. Gently he took her face in his hands and kissed her, long and loving, before pulling back and meeting her eyes.

'Honey, I'm an old hand at this, you know that. I've been doing this since I was five years old. There's nothing to worry about. OK?' She nodded against his hands, unconvinced.

Pulling her to him, he wrapped his arms tightly around her, their bodies as close as he could make them. 'Besides, you think I'd do anything that would risk me not coming back to you every night?' She shook her head against his chest.

Stepping back, he took her face again. 'Ok, then,' he said, kissing her goodbye. 'I'll see you this evening.'

Sandy nodded and forced a smile as he brushed his fingers against hers, then jogged to the kerb. 'Come on, buddy, let's go!'

Todd said, climbing into Ben's truck as Sandy walked up to the driver's side and smiled at her big brother.

'Hey.'

'Hey.'

'Have a good time.'

Ben leant out of the window and kissed Sandy on the cheek. 'We will. Now stop worrying. I'll look after him. I promise.' She smiled and waved until they turned the corner and disappeared from sight.

Sandy read the same line of her novel five times before giving up and closing the book. It was always the same – she just couldn't concentrate when Todd went to the rodeo. Mostly she went with him but she had an appointment with the wedding reception venue this afternoon that they'd been waiting ages for. It was an extremely popular location and already had bookings three years in advance; although it was their dream choice, there was no way they wanted to wait that long. Thankfully a cancellation slot that worked for them had come up and Sandy didn't want to risk losing it by not seeming interested. Obviously, she'd rather they'd both been going but Todd had been doing rodeo ever since she'd known him and there were always dates that he wasn't available. As she hadn't been able to change the venue appointment, it was what it was. Todd had already told her that whatever she chose he'd be happy with, saying that all he wanted was to marry her and he'd happily do that in shorts and sneakers on the back porch so long as it meant he got to spend the rest of his life with her. Anything else that would make her happy was a bonus. Staring at the cover of the novel for a moment, she tossed it down and grabbed her car keys instead.

It was always an enjoyable drive out to Ben's ranch. There was an open offer to close friends and family to ride the horses whenever they liked and right then, she felt it might help take her mind off worrying about Todd.

As she pulled into the drive, she smiled. It really was a

beautiful house with its wooden slats and shutters, and the porch wrapping around it as though it was giving the house a big hug. Sandy parked the car out front and began walking down to the stables.

*

Ben and Todd had been coming to the rodeo for longer than either of them could remember. Todd had been fascinated by it from his very first visit and had been addicted ever since. He'd begged to be allowed to take part and eventually his family had relented. A natural talent, he was soon winning local and then national championships. The draw of it hadn't diminished as he'd got older and he'd been lucky, he knew. There was no denying that it was dangerous and he'd seen more than his fair share of injuries to both clowns and riders. He hated that it upset Sandy when he took part but they'd made a deal that once they were married, he'd stop. Their plan was to start a family soon after anyway, so he had a feeling free time was going be pretty scarce. Aside from which, why would he be here when he could be somewhere else that meant everything to him?

'Feels weird Sandy not being here today,' he said to Ben as he got ready for his first ride.

Ben nodded. 'She really wants that venue though.'

Todd smiled. 'That's true. She's had her heart set on it ever since we got engaged. I kind of feel bad I'm not there with her. Maybe I should have cancelled today.'

'You've visited that place before, right?'

Todd bent and adjusted his boot. 'Mm-hmm. We got a tour like the day after the engagement.'

'OK. So today's what? Just more details?' Ben asked.

Todd shrugged. 'I guess so.'

'Does any of that matter to you? I mean, would you even notice if the bows were satin instead of silk?'

He straightened and stretched his back. 'All that matters to me is marrying your sister.'

'So, stop worrying about it. If Sandy had really wanted you to go, she'd have told you. I think we both know that. I'm pretty sure you'd just be in the way today.'

Pushing on his hat, Todd grinned. 'Something tells me you might be right.'

Ben gave him a quick hug and then clapped his shoulder. 'Be good and be safe,' he said.

'But not in that order.' Todd finished off their pre-ride ritual, turned and walked across to meet his next challenge.

His friend left to find a good place to watch the next rounds, and sat comfortably chatting with a few of the regulars as they viewed the action, comments and applause mingling as the talent or technique of a particular rider was noted. Glancing over, he could see the top of Todd's hat as his friend braced himself, ready for the gate to the arena to open.

*

Ben had heard a rodeo arena go silent before and it always turned his blood cold. But this time he was completely frozen. Paralysed by the sight of Todd lying on the arena floor as rodeo clowns risked their lives to keep the still bucking animal away from the broken, unmoving body. And then Ben started to run.

They'd held him back, telling him that the last thing they needed was another person at risk and it had seemed like forever until he was able to see his friend. But Todd couldn't see him. He'd lost consciousness the moment he'd hit the ground and still hadn't regained it. As he was wired and tubed up in the ambulance, Ben sat across from him feeling useless and terrified. The siren screamed as they raced through the streets towards the hospital on the other side of town. His hand clutched his phone and he knew what he had to do.

Sandy was just leading Chancer out of the stables, chatting with Jed, when her cell phone rang. She checked the display and blanched.

'What's happened?'

*

Jed drove Sandy to the hospital. One look at her face had told him that she wasn't in any shape to drive herself. From what he'd been able to get out of her, Todd had taken a bad fall at the rodeo and still hadn't regained consciousness. She was almost out of the truck before Jed had pulled to a halt outside the hospital doors. He watched her sprint inside, waited a moment, then drove away, praying all the way home that Todd would be OK.

*

It had been four days since the accident, and now it wasn't only Todd's health worrying loved ones. Still swarming with wires and tubes, there had been no improvement in Todd's condition but neither was there any deterioration. Sandy had refused to leave her fiancé's bedside from the moment she'd been allowed to see him. She wouldn't eat and barely slept. Occasionally slumber stole over her, trying to embrace her in its warm comfort but she fought against it with a powerful vengeance and, so far, she was winning.

Ben studied his sister as he placed yet another cup of coffee on the table beside her.

'You really ought to try and eat something, sweetheart.'

'I'm not hungry.

'Even so.'

She didn't look at him. She'd barely looked at anyone but her fiancé for days. Her total attention was focused on Todd, hoping for a glimmer of movement, the faintest of signs that he was still in there, and would be back with her soon. Ben took in the dark circles under Sandy's eyes, the pale skin on her drawn and tired face, his guilt increasing as he did so.

I'll look after him, he'd said. *I promise*. And now look where they were. Machines beeping all around, tubes in one place, out of another, while his own sister could only watch, and hope and pray – no expression on her face, no tone in her voice, her entire being centred on Todd.

The doctors had been unable to tell them how long he could be like this. He could wake up tomorrow or it could be weeks… or more. God forbid it was either of the latter, or Sandy herself wasn't going to be in any fit state to see him.

'Honey, please eat something. You're going to make yourself ill.'

Sandy took the coffee cup and sipped at the hot liquid as Ben walked around to the other side of the bed and gazed down at Todd. Incredibly, all that showed externally from the fall was a broken wrist and a slight bruise on his temple.

'See ya later, buddy,' Ben said, closing a hand over his friend's for a moment. Crossing back, he placed a gentle kiss on the top of Sandy's hair, not that she noticed, then quietly closed the door on his way out.

'Any news?' Molly asked as soon as he entered the house.

He'd been staying at his parents since the accident as it was closer to the hospital. And maybe, if he truly admitted it to himself, because he didn't want to be alone right now.

'No change,' Ben replied. He hung his coat on the rack and looked back at his mother. 'What can I do, Mama? I feel like I should be able to do something!'

'There's nothing any of us can do but pray, sweetheart.'

'But—'

'Ben, it wasn't your fault. You can't keep doing this to yourself. Todd was going to that rodeo with or without you. Thanks to you he's getting the best medical treatment possible. All we can do now is wait. In the meantime, you can go wash your hands ready for supper.'

'I'm not real—'

'Ben, please! I already have one child who's barely eating. Please don't make me worry over you too.' Molly gripped the cloth she was holding, her knuckles showing white, the worry over Todd and Sandy etched into her face. He turned at her raised voice, seeing the panic and fear his mother was trying so desperately to keep inside.

With Todd being the son of family friends, they'd all been overjoyed when his and Sandy's friendship blossomed into something more serious. Whereas Ellie was their surrogate daughter, Todd was like another son and their joy at the news they were to gain him officially as their son-in-law had now been replaced by the fear that they might lose him altogether.

'It's OK, Mom,' Ben whispered. 'He's going to be just fine.' Molly issued a small sob that in turn released more. She began to shake under her son's strong embrace. Gently, he led her to the chair and sat on the arm beside her. He didn't really know what to say so he said nothing, and just held her.

'They were so happy!' Molly cried, 'They had their whole lives ahead of them!'

'And they still have! Nothing's changed that. Todd is going to be just fine and they're still going to get married and have seventeen kids and three dogs and then ask you to babysit!'

Molly smiled, fear in her eyes. 'Do you really think so?'

'Yeah, I really do,' Ben answered honestly. There was no other choice than to believe it.

'I'm so worried.'

'I know.'

'She won't talk to anyone.'

'I know. It's just her way of dealing with it. She's trying to be brave so we won't worry.'

'But she doesn't have to be brave, Ben! She's my baby girl! That's what I'm here for!'

'I know Mama, I know.'

Ben fiddled with the crystal stem of the wineglass, a thousand thoughts turning over in his mind. Through the window he could see his parents on the swing of the back porch, nestling against one another, exchanging fears and hopes in whispered voices. They'd asked him to join them but he'd declined, feeling that they should be able to say everything they wanted to to each other in private. As big as he was, and as old as he was, they'd still want to try and protect him – put him before themselves. But right now, they needed their own space and time as each of them tried to process the situation. Taking another sip, he set the glass back down on the table. He couldn't remember a time he'd felt so helpless. Or so alone.

As he sat back up, a picture on the wall caught his eye. It had been taken years ago. God! How young they all looked, he thought, smiling at the memory. Suddenly it struck him…

'The number you are calling…' Ben debated whether to leave a message as the automated voice continued on. 'Leave a message after the – Hello?' A human voice interrupted the answer machine. 'Hello?' it said again when there was no reply.

'Ellie?'

'Who's calling?' She sounded wary.

'Ellie? It's Ben. Ben Danvers.' The relief at hearing her voice was incredible. There was a slight pause.

'What's happened?' Ben started from the beginning and explained that he'd thought perhaps if he could get her to call Sandy, she might open up a bit. If she was going to talk to anyone, it'd be Ellie. They'd supported each other from their early years and Ellie was the one person Sandy wouldn't feel she had to be brave for. Her brother felt it had to be worth a shot.

'Truth is, I really don't know what else to try. You're kind of my last hope. She's just ignoring her phone mostly, but if she heard your ringtone…maybe…?'

'Yes, of course. Is there anything else I can do?'

'Hope and pray with the rest of us.'

'That goes without saying.' She paused. 'Ben, are you OK?'

'Yeah. Don't worry about me.' There was a lightness to his reply that he didn't feel.

'Well, I'm not entirely sure I believe that so I'm sending you a hug down the line anyway.' He smiled. Sandy and Ellie's standard phone hug.

She paused. 'Did you get it?'

'Yeah,' he said in a quiet voice. 'I got it.'

They said their goodbyes and Ben hung up.

'I got it,' he whispered again to himself. Suddenly he felt ashamed that in such a situation he was standing there wishing she'd delivered the hug in person.

*

Ellie made the call immediately after Ben hung up and thankfully, his hunch had paid off. Her best friend's distinctive ringtone had nudged his sister from her trance and she'd picked up.

'I'm so scared, Ellie!' Sandy had whispered into the phone.

'I know.'

'Everyone is so worried, I don't want them to worry about me too so I'm just trying to be brave when they're around.' Sandy paused. 'Ben always has fussed over me. I guess that's why he called you.'

'Something like that,' Ellie responded softly. Sandy could see her friend's face in her mind's eye, the gentle smile that accompanied the last statement. Suddenly a sob wrenched out.

'Oh Ellie, I wish you were here!'

'Oh, Sand! So do I.' Across the Atlantic, Ellie felt for her friend, the pain in her voice tore deep into her heart. 'I feel so useless. Is there anything I can do?'

'You've helped already, El. I'm so glad Ben called you.'

'Me too.'

'You'll call again tomorrow, won't you?' Ellie heard the edge of panic in the question.

'Of course.'

'I miss you so much.'

'I know. I miss you too.'

Chapter 5

Ellie lay awake, staring at the ceiling, turning things over and over in her mind. Letting out a long sigh of frustration, she rolled to face the window. Leaning over, she grabbed hold of the curtain and pulled it back. The sky was clear and a million stars hung suspended on the midnight blue sky. Looking out, Ellie reminisced how she and Sandy would lie out under the huge Kansas sky talking over their dreams for the future, who they were in love with that week, and all the latest gossip at school. Sometimes they would just lie there trying to count the stars or hoping to see a shooting star they could wish on.

Ellie sat up and hopped out of bed, grabbing her snuggly fleece dressing gown as she shivered in the cold room. Light from the full moon lit her way as she took her laptop from the dresser and scooted back across the room and into the warm bed. As she opened the lid, the machine came out of hibernation and its screen cast an eerie blue glow over her face as she connected to the internet and began a search.

*

'Zak? Are you awake?'

Her flatmate groaned loud before physically opening one eyelid with his finger and thumb to peer at the clock.

'Ellie, have you *any* idea what the time is?'

'I know,' she replied, coming into his room further, and sitting on the edge of his bed. After Carl's final attack, Ellie had moved into one of Zak's spare rooms. It had been intended as a temporary arrangement just until she got herself another place to live. She'd had to wait for the apartment she'd shared with Carl to be sold before she could do anything – all her savings had gone into that as she'd been determined to pay her own way, despite Carl almost demanding that he cover everything. At the time, she'd thought it was sweet, and his words had helped her believe that. And maybe with some men, that would have been true. But time and distance had shown her that Carl's persistence had just been one more way of him trying to exert control.

Thankfully, Ellie had stood her ground on that, despite her ignorance of his true character. The only good thing to come out of it was that the property, like everywhere in London, had increased in value and she now had more in her savings than she would have done had she just kept it in the bank.

She'd never gone back to the apartment. Between them, Zak and another good friend, Kate, had taken care of collecting the luggage she'd already had prepared, disposed of the furniture and items that had been broken in the attack and arranged for a cleaner to come in and have the apartment ready for sale as soon as possible. Ellie couldn't afford the mortgage on her own and had no desire to live there now even if she could. There were too many bad memories within those walls. She was doing her best to work through those with a counsellor – the last thing she needed was to go straight back to the place where everything had happened Carl was fired the moment his boss had found out what he'd done, and when Zak had spoken to him, he'd agreed, albeit reluctantly, that selling the apartment was the best option.

Besides, he knew he was going to jail. The only question left had been for how long.

The temporary arrangement of sharing with Zak worked well. It was him that taken her back to the hospital for the follow up they'd wanted. Kate, already having a friend in the field, had been recommended an excellent counsellor and between the two of them, they had taken Ellie to and from her appointments until she'd regained enough confidence to start doing things alone again. The Tube had been an option but as much as she tried to pretend nothing had changed, Ellie had to admit that things had. Of course, she had no intention of letting those changes win. She would overcome them but not having to travel alone for a while had helped her concentrate on the sessions, rather than being anxious about the journey. It had made her furious though – she'd been using the London Underground for longer than she could remember but her relationship with Carl had smashed her confidence into pieces, and she knew, frustrating as it was, that was going to take time to rebuild.

So her temporary living arrangements had gradually become permanent, and it was a situation that suited both of them. Although right now, it was possible Zak was having second thoughts. Flopping one arm out from under the duvet, he swiped at the bedside light. They both squinted in discomfort for a moment as their eyes adjusted. Zak had been out on a date when Ben had rung earlier. Quickly she explained Todd's condition, how worried Ben was, and how scared Sandy had sounded on the phone. 'I want to be there, Zak, with Sandy. I know it's really late notice to take time off work but I need to be there.'

Zak rubbed his eye with his fist and stretched. 'Do you have your ticket?'

She held up her phone in reply. 'E-ticket.'

'Then you'll need a lift to the airport.'

*

Zak parked on the short-term parking level, found a luggage trolley, then entered the terminal with Ellie. Once she'd checked in, they found a seat in a coffee shop to pass a little more time and help kick start their systems. After a while, Ellie glanced at her phone's lock screen to check the time.

'You'd better start getting back or you'll end up catching all the morning traffic. Zak looked down at his Rolex and nodded in agreement.

'You'll be OK from here?' he asked, a concerned look on his face.

You're so good to me, she thought. His concern was so genuine, she couldn't even tease him about it.

'Yes. I'll be fine,' Ellie answered, honestly. A year ago, she knew she wouldn't have been able to answer in the same way. It hadn't been an easy journey, but she'd been determined and she'd had the best support she could have wished for – both personal and professional. Zak and Kate had been there for her at her lowest ebb and helped her climb back up. For that, there were no words that would ever be strong enough to thank them. All Ellie could hope was that they knew how much their support had, and still meant. Carl had stolen enough from her but he didn't get to win. Not this time.

She gave Zak a huge hug. 'Thanks for the lift, and everything. I'm sorry again about the late notice.'

Zak shook his head. 'Some things are more important. You're doing the right thing and you know it. Take care and I really hope things turn out OK. Keep me posted, won't you?'

'Me too, and of course. I'll call you later.'

'Make sure you do.' Zak leant down and kissed his friend's cheek. 'Send Sandy my love,' he said.

'I will. Drive carefully.'

Ellie watched for a minute as he strode across the terminal, his navy, cashmere pea coat flaring out like a small cape with each long stride he took. Then she turned, pulling the small

64

case she'd hurriedly flung her belongings into, and headed for security.

*

The nurse on reception smiled kindly at the young English woman who asked directions to Todd Winchester's room. The poor girl looked exhausted and if Ellie could have heard her thoughts, she'd have agreed. The earliest flight she'd been able to get had involved two separate connections. Add that to the time difference and the fact that she hadn't slept the previous night and she was definitely beginning to feel a little frayed around the edges.

Her appearance, however, was the very last thing on Ellie's mind as she followed the directions the nurse had given her. Approaching the small waiting area, she glanced around, looking for the correct room number. It was Molly Danvers who saw her first.

'Eleanor…Ellie?' Her face was all astonishment as she held her arms out to the woman who felt as much a daughter to her as her own flesh and blood. 'What are you doing here?' Molly's eyes brimmed with tears as she stroked the soft curls, longer now than on her last visit.

'After I spoke to Sandy, I just felt useless and way too far away. I'm probably no help here either but—'

'Oh honey, I'm so glad you're here,' she replied, once more enveloping her in the embrace. She'd been thrilled at the slight hint of change she'd seen in her daughter once she'd spoken to Ellie on the phone. But having her here for Sandy now was more than she could have hoped for. 'Let's go see Sandy and Todd.'

'Is he – is there any change?'

'Sandy said she thought she saw his eyelids flutter early this morning, but there's been nothing since then. I think the doctors kind of believe it was just wishful thinking but she swears she saw it.'

65

There were all sorts of wires attached to him. Todd was a big guy but now he looked pale and small amongst all the machinery; so different to the man who had met her at the airport just over a year ago. Sandy hadn't turned when the door opened. Staff and visitors filtered in and out all day without her noticing. She just sat there, holding Todd's hand in both of hers, sometimes talking to him about their plans, sometimes just gently stroking the almost lifeless limb and watching the face she loved for the slightest sign of response.

'Sandy?'

'Yes, Mom?' Sandy's eyes never left Todd's handsome, still face.

'There's someone here to see you.'

Sandy half turned her head and saw Ellie's worried expression. A strangulated sob came from her throat as Ellie dropped her bag and wrapped her arms tightly around her friend.

Ben entered the room backwards, a coffee cup in each hand. Turning to place them on the cabinet, he saw his sister finally releasing all the pain she'd been storing since the accident. Her face was buried in the neck of a woman who was gently stroking the dark hair, making soothing noises as she would to a child. He didn't recognise the shoulder length red hair and a flash of panic bit through him at the thought a reporter may have got hold of the story and duped her way in. His eyes shifted to his mother but she looked calm as she gazed upon her daughter – calmer than she had in days.

Ben picked up the coffee for Molly and crossed the room, handing it to her. Standing next to her, he was now able to see the face of the stranger and his eyes widened in amazement as he recognised her, although he couldn't yet see those vivid green eyes, her head remaining tilted down in the comfort of his sister. Ben looked down at his mother, questions in his eyes. Molly smiled up at her son, simply squeezing his hand in reply.

Ellie felt Sandy's sobs subsiding and gently helped her sit back in the chair as she crouched beside her. Automatically, Sandy

66

reached one hand out to take Todd's while the other still clung to Ellie.

'I'm so glad you're here. I can't believe it,' she croaked in a sore and broken voice. There was a lump in Ellie's throat that prevented her from answering but her nod was enough of a reply. Molly Danvers' smile thanked Ellie again as she approached her daughter, and she released Sandy's hand into the care of her mother's. Exhausted in every way, Sandy barely noticed.

Moving out of the way, Ellie noticed Ben for the first time and gave him a little smile, noting that he looked almost as tired as Sandy. Crossing the room, she reached up and hugged him wordlessly as Molly finally managed to coax Sandy onto the cot the staff had made up in the room for her.

'That's the first time she's laid down in days,' Ben whispered after he reluctantly released her. 'Thanks so much for coming out. We'll never be able to repay you for this.'

She shook her head, her voice a whisper. 'You were all there for me when I needed you. There's nowhere on earth I'd rather be right now.'

Ellie turned to face Ben, and saw redness rimming the ice-blue eyes as he watched his mother fuss a little with the covers over Sandy. His baby sister's heart was breaking and a man he already considered a brother lay almost lifeless in the bed next to them and he couldn't help either of them. That fact, Ellie could tell, was killing him. Molly kissed the forehead of her now sleeping child and she motioned to the others. Quietly, they left the room, closing the door gently behind them.

Finally getting Sandy to give in to sleep seemed to have boosted Molly Danvers' own energy reserves and once outside the room, she took charge.

'Ben, why don't you take Ellie back to the house? You both need some food and rest. Todd's parents will be back soon, and Ted too, so it's going to get a little crowded anyway.'

'You sure, Mom?'

'Positive. Now,' she said, stroking Ellie's hair with one hand and resting her other on Ben's forearm, 'you two just look after each other and I'll see you at home a little later, OK?' She then hugged them both to her, Ben's arm reaching around Ellie as they each felt their own relief in being together.

'Now, off you go,' Molly chivvied, sending them on their way.

The two walked down the corridor, and Ellie stopped to pick up her case from the waiting area. Without words, Ben took it from her.

'It's alright, I can take it. It's got wheels and everything,' Ellie teased, not quite relinquishing her hold on the plastic handle. She looked up into the startling blue eyes and something in them caused her to relent to Ben's chivalry. Her mouth tipped in a small smile. 'Thank you.'

There was little conversation in the car. Not because conversation would have been awkward, but simply because both occupants were too tired, physically and emotionally, to speak much. A country station played quietly in the background and Ellie leant her head back against the seat and closed her eyes.

Ben glanced over at his passenger as they pulled up to a pizza place. He gazed at her slumbering face, noticing the way the late afternoon sunlight deepened the red of her hair, and cast shadows from long lashes onto her pale cheeks. The difference in her since the last visit was noticeable in so many ways, and not just the most obvious.

It still ripped him apart inside to remember that battered, frightened woman he'd startled that evening. If he ever got hold of the guy that did that to her…

The ceasing of movement woke Ellie and she opened her eyes to find Ben watching her.

'Sorry. I was just wondering what my next move was. I didn't know whether to wake you.'

Ellie rubbed one eye and looked to see where they were. Laughing, she turned back to Ben. 'We stop at a food establishment and you

don't know whether to wake me? How long have you known me?'
She pulled the catch and jumped down from the truck. Ben followed
her in and smiled as she watched a pizza being taken to a table.

'You know you're drooling, right?'

She nodded. 'That is entirely possible.' She casually wiped her
thumb and forefinger at the corners of her mouth, just to check.

'When did you last eat?' he laughed.

'God! I don't know. I ate on the plane but it feels like three
days ago.' She paused. 'When did you last eat?' she returned more
seriously.

'Oh. I…I've been eating stuff.'

'That's what I thought.' Her tone was sceptical as she turned
and headed off towards the counter. Ben was about to follow
when a hand on his arm stopped him.

'Excuse me, Ben?' The hand belonged to a middle-aged woman,
attractive and slightly embarrassed. 'I'm really sorry to bother
you but could I get a selfie?'

'Er, yeah…um…sure,' he stammered, caught unexpectedly, his
attention having been on Ellie. This was an aspect he still felt a
little uncomfortable with. It felt so odd that people wanted a
picture with him, or his signature on a piece of paper. And he'd
soon learned that paper was the easy option! He pulled his focus
back and realised the woman was saying something.

'—loved your last album! I play it all the time.'

Work was the last thing on his mind right now, but Ben chatted
to the fan for a few more minutes, making all the right noises
and trying to concentrate on the conversation, before her husband
joined them. He shook Ben's hand and they left, leaving him
finally free to catch up with Ellie at the counter.

'Sorry.'

'Not a problem.' She grinned, 'I keep forgetting you're a superstar!' Her voice was a theatrical whisper. Ben returned a sarcastic
smile, happy to see some of the confidence and humour he feared
she may have lost shining through.

'You're funny.'

'I know.'

'Where do you want to eat this?' Ben asked as they made their way back to the truck. Ellie shrugged her shoulders, as she sucked on the straw protruding from her Coke.

'I'm easy.' No sooner were the words out of her mouth than she looked up, flushing bright red. 'I mean…'

Ben was smiling with a mischievous glint in his eye. 'Hey, you match my truck!' Ellie pulled a tight smile but Ben could see beneath it. And he loved what he saw.

'Did you want to wear this pizza?' she replied, regaining her composure, a small smirk playing at the corners of her full lips.

'No, ma'am.'

They climbed back in and Ben drove for a short while before turning off down a dirt track. The pickup bumped along for a few minutes and Ellie clutched their dinner as they bounced in and over potholes. Curiosity got the better of her.

'Where are we going?'

'Here,' Ben said as he made a final turn and shifted the truck into park. Before them stretched land and sky and nothing more. There was no sign of man's interference. Here, it was just you and nature. No sounds reached them but the wind as it played over the landscape.

'Wow!' Ellie stared.

It was years since she had been out into the countryside of Kansas. She'd forgotten how huge it was and how it had the capability to show just how insignificant they all were in the grand scheme of things.

Ben let her soak up the view for a moment before taking the food with one hand and offering her the other. Ellie took it as she stepped down onto the uneven ground. Her eyes were still on the scenery but Ben's were on her. The joy and appreciation for their surroundings showed on her face, making him smile.

'We'd better eat this before it gets cold,' she said, pulling herself out of her reverie. Noticing a rug tucked under Ben's arm, Ellie took it and laid it on the ground. Then she knelt down and held up her arms to Ben to take the food from him. He sat next to her and they quickly devoured the food in companionable silence as the sky turned from blue to gold, streaked through with pink.

'I've never been here before,' Ellie said, folding the lid over on the now empty pizza box. 'It's stunning.'

'Not many people know about it. I brought Cyndi once.'

'Only once?' Ellie wondered in amazement, suddenly realising that the question had been asked aloud before she'd really thought about it.

Ben looked across at her as she leant back against the front of the truck. Her cheeks were tinged with pink.

'I'm sorry. That's none of my business. I—'

'No, really it's fine.' Ben replied, a little distractedly, 'You know, that's...um, that's pretty dusty.'

'Sorry?'

'The truck. You're gonna get dirty.' His face showed genuine concern.

Ellie studied him for a moment, trying to reconcile this man with the laidback character she had always known, but she couldn't. Instead she started to laugh.

'Oh Ben, I've been in these clothes for far longer than is usually thought polite. I really don't think a bit of dust is going to make much difference at this point in time.' He nodded and lowered his lashes.

'Thanks anyway though.' Her companion looked a little embarrassed. 'And do remind me to brush off before we get back in. I don't want to make your truck grubby.'

'That's not why I said it,' he answered quickly.

Ellie shook her head, smiling. 'I know.'

Ben hesitated for a moment before returning the smile.

'You know, that does look kind of comfy.' He shifted, settling himself next to Ellie. Orange swirls now joined the pink and gold

71

in the huge sky. 'I tend to forget that every woman doesn't have the same hang ups as Cyndi.'

Ellie was unsure as to whether she was expected to make a reply. Watching him for a moment from the corner of her eye, it didn't seem as if he was expecting one so Ellie remained silent. 'I only brought her here once but I don't think she appreciated it too much. Complained the whole way. Didn't like the dust and couldn't see the point of sitting on lumpy ground when there was nothing to see.' His eyes scanned the painted sky as it threw its colours over the landscape. 'She couldn't see it.'

Ben's voice was soft and slightly hoarse. Todd's accident and the uncertainty of his fate were heightening emotions that still caught him out from time to time. The divorce had been final for months now and Cyndi had moved straight in with the guy Ben had seen leaving his bedroom that night. He knew he and Cyndi weren't meant to be together – that was pretty obvious to him now and he tried not to kick himself too much that he hadn't seen it before he'd given her his heart. But what was done was done. And he would move on. He had moved on. Just a heck of a lot slower than Cyndi had.

'Why don't we go back now?' his dinner companion suggested. Ben sat up from the truck, level with Ellie.

'Jeez, I'm sorry Ellie. I didn't mean to embarrass you. You're right, we should go.' He stood and held out a hand, helping helped Ellie haul her tired body up from the blanket. It was probably just as well as she'd have easily sat there all night, looking out across the landscape and letting the sound of the wind lull her to sleep.

'Thanks,' she said, letting go of his hand. 'But just so you know?' Ben looked down at her. 'You didn't embarrass me. Please don't ever think you could do that.'

He gave a shake of his head, then tossed the empty pizza box in the rear of the truck and slid behind the wheel as Ellie got in the passenger side of the cab. The engine gave a low burble and

Ben pulled smoothly back out on the track. Bouncing back down the way they had come, they sat companionably once more, headed in the direction of the Danvers' family home, the country station again keeping them company.

Before long, Ben pulled up in front of the large house and switched off the engine. 'Well, here we are.'

Ellie got that same familiar feeling as she stepped down from the cab. A feeling of comfort. She'd been here so many times, it really was like coming home. Looking down the quiet street, she could see part of the house she had once lived in. Apparently, it was still owned by the same family the Laings had sold it to and Ellie found herself wishing again that they'd never left. But they had, and there was no point looking back.

Turning, she noticed Ben standing a few feet away, waiting patiently as she reminisced. She gave him a soft smile as she walked up the path to meet him.

'Neighbours OK?' Ellie teased, indicating their old house with an inclination of her head.

'Yeah,' Ben replied. 'Improvement on the last lot anyway.'

'Oh, ho ho.'

They entered the house and Ellie made her way to the guest bedroom. Going straight to the en-suite bathroom, she began to run a much longed for bath. Having set the water running, she wandered back out to the bedroom, moving to the window to pull the shade, stopping to gaze momentarily on the once familiar view. A knock at the door pulled Ellie from her memories.

'You decent?' Ben poked his head around the door.

'Near enough.'

'Thought you might want this.' Entering the room, he held out a cold beer to her.

'Ah perfect! Thanks.'

'Pleasure.' Ben glanced in at the rising bubbles as he took a swig from his own bottle. He nodded to Ellie, indicating the direction of the bathroom. Frowning, she followed his glance just in time to see the bubbles almost to the rim. 'Oh crikey!' Thrusting the bottle back into Ben's hand, she rushed in to turn off the taps. 'The water pressure in the flat is so low, it takes ages to run a bath,' she called out before re-entering the room. 'Pressure is a bit better here apparently.'

'Apparently,' Ben agreed, the hint of a smile showing a flash of white teeth against the dark, unshaven jaw. Ellie's face was a little flushed from the steam and a stray damp curl had loosened from the tie she'd shoved it back in when they were eating earlier. It now bounced softly in front of her face and her attempt to blow it back resulted in it returning almost immediately to the same place. Ben gripped his beer tighter in order to stop his hand going to her face and sweeping the hair back from it – something his whole body was urging him to do. He returned the bottle.

'Have a good soak.'

'Thanks. I'll see you later.'

*

The forceful water pounded over Ben. It pummelled his back and shoulders but did nothing to relieve the tension that had been there since the accident. And now there was a new source. Ben knew he was the one whose actions had brought Ellie back to Kansas, and he'd never regret that. Something had told him that she would want to be with them at such a time, and that her presence would help his sister. It had been clear from Sandy's reaction at the hospital that it had been the right thing to do.

What he wasn't sure of was whether he had done this for Sandy alone. Thoughts turned over and over in his mind, and he closed his eyes against the strain. His body and mind were so tired. Entirely exhausted. But sleep was something that had eluded him for anything more than a couple of hours since the accident. His mind turned to Todd lying in that hospital bed, hooked up to so many machines. The man he'd promised the sister he adored he'd keep safe. Tears mingled with the water as Ben gave in to guilt – and fear.

It was some time later that he made his way downstairs. Hearing a sound, he turned towards the kitchen to find Ellie bustling about, pouring warmed milk into two mugs. Ben watched her for a moment, the casual scene of domesticity making him smile. She was dressed in a T-shirt and shorts style of pyjamas and the dressing gown that usually hung on the back of the door in the guest bedroom. Her hair was loose, her face free from make-up – and she took his breath away.

'Hey.'

His bare feet had made no sound and the greeting made Ellie jump, a little of the milk spilling onto her hand.

'Bugger!'

'I didn't mean to startle you. I'm really sorry!' Ben apologised, rushing over to where she was standing, blowing on her injured hand. He tried to take it.

'No, really, it's fine.'

Ben's look was kind but it broached no argument. She released her hand to him. Leading her over to the tap, he placed the burn site under the cold running water.

Ellie grimaced. 'I always think this is worse than the actual burn.' Ben nodded in agreement. 'I was beginning to wonder where you'd got to actually,' Ellie said through half-gritted teeth, in an attempt to take her mind off her now painfully numbing hand. 'Thought you'd disappeared down the plug-hole.' She slid her hand away from the water.

'You should be so lucky,' Ben replied quietly, smiling as he gently took hold of her hand again and held it in his own under the tap for a few more minutes.

They sat in the TV room and sipped their drinks. It was a great room – small and cosy with squashy chairs and a sofa. Ellie sat in a chair, with her legs tucked under her whilst Ben stretched his long limbs across the sofa. Having finished his drink, he placed the mug on the low table in front of him. 'You know, you're the only one who hasn't told me this wasn't my fault.' His eyes remained on the empty cup.

Ellie looked out at him from the rim of her mug as she finished the last of her own drink. Getting up, she set her mug down next to his then tapped Ben's leg so she could sit on the other end of the sofa. He swung his legs round and watched as she sat down, folding one leg under her as she did so.

'Would it make any difference if I did?' she asked.

'But what if he doesn't wake up, El?' His voice was soft and raw. 'What if...' He ran his hands through his damp hair, his mind going places he didn't want to think about. Ellie couldn't bear to watch his pain. Moving closer, she gently pulled Ben towards her, wrapping her arms around him and he clung to her as though he would drown. She said nothing, just held him close as tears filled her own eyes.

It was in this position that Molly and Ted Danvers found them when they returned from the hospital later that night. Both of them having finally yielded to the demands exhaustion made on body and mind, Ellie's arms encircled Ben protectively as he clung to her through tortured dreams. Molly silently picked up a blanket, laid it over the sleeping pair, switched off the light and went to bed.

Chapter 6

Ellie had told Zak that she would try and get some work done, and although he'd appreciated the offer, he'd also told her that it shouldn't be her main focus out there. If she did, then great, but if she didn't, not to worry about it. They would cope. Sometimes there were far more important things in life than work.

He'd been right. Focusing on work was proving to be much harder than she'd thought. Her thoughts kept reverting to how cruel life could be as she looked on the pale figure in the bed. Several days had now passed since Sandy had professed to see a flicker of movement on Todd's face and, although she hadn't voiced it, Ellie knew that even Sandy entertained doubts as to whether she might well have imagined it.

'That's lovely!' Molly said, peering over at the pad resting on Ellie's knee. On it a small posy of flowers was detailed in pencil. Ellie looked at Molly in surprise and then down at the paper, almost as though she were seeing it for the first time.

'It's just a doodle.'

Molly smiled and took her hand. 'Then I wish I could doodle half so well.'

Opposite them, on the other side of the bed, Sandy slumbered fitfully as she rested her head on her hands, they in turn clasping Todd's. 'Thank you again so much for coming out. It means a lot to us.' There was a pause. 'To all of us.'

Ellie nodded without looking up. She understood Molly's meaning and that her thanks were directed not only from her daughter but also from her son. She'd woken before Ben the morning after she'd arrived, dawn just beginning to break across the eastern sky. Her hand had been resting on his chest, his arms loosely encircled around her and a blanket over both of them.

She'd gently extricated herself, desperate not to wake and perhaps embarrass him. He'd looked peaceful for the first time since she'd arrived and, although she wanted him to stay that way for as long as possible, she knew it was best if she left and crept back to her own room. One of the main reasons for that being she had an overwhelming desire to remain exactly where she was but she realised it was all just the heightened emotions of the whole situation. The last thing she, or Ben, needed right now, was for her to develop a teenage crush on her best friend's celebrity brother!

Molly retained Ellie's hand as they sat in shared support, the silence broken only by the sounds of the various machines helping keep Todd alive.

*

Ellie made her way back towards the waiting area next to Todd's room. A stroll around the hospital gardens had refreshed her and relieved the slight ache in her lower back from having sat for so long. Entering the rather full elevator, she glanced to check that the button for her floor was lit, then leaning back against the wall she watched as the numbers increased on the display. From the corner of her eye, she saw a familiar face. Turning her head, she found herself looking directly into the striking blue eyes of Ben Danvers who was rammed into the far corner. He gave a brief brow raise and smile, acknowledging her across the heads of their fellow passengers.

'Any change?' he asked her after exiting the lift. Ellie shook her head as they turned the corner of the corridor. Ahead, a commotion could be seen near Todd's room. A doctor ran in, quickly followed by two nurses. For a moment, the two were frozen as the possibilities of what all this could mean raced through their brains.

After what felt like hours had passed, though Ellie knew it had only been a few seconds, she automatically followed when Ben took her hand and began hurrying towards the scene. He gripped tightly, and she in turn did the same – both of them knowing on some level that it was more from fear and a need for support for themselves than from any altruistic intention.

Approaching the door to Todd's room, they briefly saw the small nursing team crowding around the bed before a nurse exiting the room asked them to wait outside.

'What's going on?' Ben asked, but the nurse was already walking away. He was unsure as to whether her lack of reply was because she hadn't heard him or because she wanted to avoid answering.

Ellie looked up at him. His face had paled under his tan, contrasting with the ice blue of his eyes, now shining with emotion. Ellie steered him to the nearest sofa and sat down.

'I could still hear the machines beeping. That's got to be a good sign, hasn't it?' he asked.

Ellie had no comforting answer for him but nodded anyway. Their combined grip remained strong and without thinking, she wrapped her free hand around Ben's bicep and waited.

They sat for what felt like an age, Ellie staring at the door, Ben's eyes focused on a patch of floor a few yards in front of them. Eventually the door to Todd's room opened and several staff moved off in various directions. Ellie watched the nurse who had ushered them away earlier speak briefly with a doctor then point him their way before heading off towards the nurses' station.

The doctor approached, and Ellie desperately tried to work out whether the news he was about to bring was good or bad, but his expression told her nothing.

Dr Martin Travis studied the couple as he walked towards them. The woman was watching him, her green eyes riveted. He was used to it – friends and relatives eager to talk to him, desperate for news but fear paralysing their movement. She held, and was in turn held, by a man he knew to be Ben Danvers. Travis had been braced for the possibility of difficulty once he'd discovered his patient, Todd Winchester, was the future brother-in-law of the country star. Travis had had his fair share of dealings with celebrities and other wealthy types, and though some were fine, there had been a handful who felt that they, or their relatives, deserved better treatment, or more staff attending to them, or should be recovering quicker just because they were rich. Much to his relief, Danvers had been no problem, apart from nearly wearing a patch in the floor from his constant pacing. Although, interestingly, since this woman had arrived on the scene about a week ago, he'd paced far less, content to sit as long as she was near.

The doctor was now in front of them. Ben looked up suddenly, as though surprised to see him there.

Quickly he stood, a battle raging inside of him. There were so many questions but he couldn't bring himself to ask even one. Ellie, standing alongside, tightened her grip. And then Dr Travis smiled.

'I thought you'd like to know Todd has woken up. It looks like he's going to be just fine. All the scans are clear and there's no sign of any permanent damage from the accident.' The doctor paused briefly. He'd seen a lot of head injuries but not all of them ended this way. 'He's a very lucky guy.' Tears were already flowing down the woman's face.

'Thank you,' Ellie said, her voice hoarse, 'Thank you so much!' she repeated as Ben too thanked the doctor, pumping his hand furiously. Travis couldn't help the grin that spread over his face. These were the moments he did the job for. Finally, Ben released the doctor's hand.

'Todd's parents and fiancée are with him now but you can go in for a few minutes when you're ready.'

At that moment, Sandy's dark tousled head appeared at the door, her eyes searching the room. Seeing them, she ran across the waiting area and flew into her brother's arms and he hugged her tightly, relief at last flooding his whole mind and body. Finally, Ben released her and she turned to Ellie, almost stifling her with the force of her embrace.

'Thank you,' Sandy whispered in a voice raw from emotion, and exhaustion. Ellie made a restrained nodding movement, her friend's hug preventing her from making any larger actions. Sandy eventually stepped back. 'Why don't you come and say hi?' She smiled, tears of joy and relief still running down her face. Dr Travis nodded to the group who thanked him once more before entering Todd's room.

*

'I can take you to the airport.' They were waiting for the elevator at the hospital. Ellie had wanted to stop in on her way to the airport, just to see everyone for a few more minutes, trying to squeeze every last moment out of a trip that had begun traumatically but, thankfully, had ended on a high.

'Thanks, but it's fine. Really. I've already booked the cab and this way I can sleep on the way. If you drove me, I'd have to be polite and make conversation.' She grinned mischievously.

Ben really wished she wouldn't do that. Since Todd's recovery, Ben realised how much he'd relied on Ellie during the nightmare and now it was over, all those feelings he'd tried to stifle before were desperately trying to push their way through. The past fortnight had given him a cold, hard wake-up call. Nothing was certain in this world and sometimes you just had to grab life before it was too late.

OK, she hadn't shown any interest in that direction towards him but, hell, the circumstances had hardly been conducive to romance. But she'd been there – for Sandy, for his parents and for him. Ben had always felt protective of women, especially those he dated. Maybe it was a little old-fashioned but that was fine with him. But now he realised that sometimes he needed someone to rely on too and, excepting his family, Ellie was the first woman who'd ever done that for him. Or she was the first woman he had let do that for him. He made his decision. This was it. *Tell her how you feel,* he prompted himself. *Tell her now. Tell her that you're in love with her.*

'Ellie—'

'No, Ben,' Ellie laughed, cutting him off. 'The car will be here any minute and you're supposed to be writing anyway, aren't you? I'm not going to be responsible for you bunking off work.' She giggled again.

Ben forced a smile, knowing he'd missed the moment.

Standing on tiptoe, Ellie planted a light kiss on his cheek. 'Bye.' She studied him for a moment, her hand on his forearm. 'And get some proper rest now, OK?' She stepped into the elevator and punched the button for the ground floor. As the doors began to close, a large man hurriedly pushed past Ben, almost launching himself into the car. He was partially obscured by the largest bouquet Ellie had ever seen.

'Maternity's next floor down,' he mumbled, a sheepish grin on his scarlet face. The doors began to close again. Ellie looked past the flora at the handsome face of Ben as he raised a hand in a silent farewell. She waved, hoping he would take her advice to get some well-deserved rest as she reflected on the fact that the recent strain had resulted in his parting smile looking almost sad as he'd disappeared behind the closing steel doors.

Chapter 7

One Year Later

'So,' Kate asked as she took a sip from the white wine the air hostess handed her. 'Is Zak billing this upgrade to the company?'

Ellie looked across at her companion sharply and caught the twinkle in her eye.

'No. It was a present.'

'Should have married him years ago.'

'Kate!'

'What?' she shrugged. 'You should have.'

Ellie took a sip from her wine and reflected on her previous relationships. It had taken her a long time to trust men again after Carl. Well, except Zak and Ben, but they were different. She knew neither of those would ever do anything to hurt her. It had taken a long time and the support of her friends, including Kate who, in the past few years, had grown to become one of her closest friends. She'd stepped up without being asked when Ellie's life fell apart and had been there for her ever since, making her laugh and letting her cry. It just proved to Ellie that it wasn't until you needed them that you really knew who your true friends were.

'Maybe you're right,' Ellie shrugged. 'Except that it's never been like that between us; it's more of a brother and sister thing.'

'That doesn't seem to stop some people. Especially in some of those trailer parks from what I hear.'

'You can't go around saying stuff like that!' Ellie burst out laughing, half choking on her wine as she tried not to spray the entire business class section.

Kate laughed as she passed Ellie a napkin and pointed to her chin. 'I can't take you anywhere!'

Her friend widened her eyes at her in blame. A member of the cabin crew passed by them and Kate nudged Ellie at the slightly disapproving look she pretended not to give them.

'Oops. Looks like we might have to stay behind after class again.'

*

The credits rolled on the movie and Kate and Ellie removed the headphones, tucking them in the pocket beside the seat. Ellie glanced over at her companion.

'What?' Kate asked.

'What are you thinking? You always chew your lips when you're thinking.'

'Do I?'

'Mm-hmm.'

'Oh.'

There was a pause. 'So?'

'We're staying at Ben's ranch, right?'

'Right.'

'And he's Sandy's brother.'

'Yes. One of them. She has two more, both older than Ben. He's a great guy. You'll like him, although I don't think he's going to be there very much, hence the free run of the house. Kind of a house-sitting favour, although from what I hear of this house,

I'm pretty sure we're getting the better deal out of it all. Sandy says it's absolutely beautiful. '

'Great. So, this Ben. He's the country and western star one, isn't he?'

'I think it's just called country now really. And he doesn't think of himself that way. Or act it. But yes, he's part of the group Cheyenne.'

'Right. Not really my kind of thing but, you know me, I'm always open to options!'

Picking up her wineglass, she proposed a toast. 'Here's to country and cowboys!' Kate wiggled her eyebrows in mischief. 'And to the gorgeous Mr Danvers for putting us up for three weeks free of charge which should give us plenty of time to rope a few cowboys for ourselves!'

'You're incorrigible!' They chinked glasses.

Kate took a sip and then turned to Ellie. 'No, not really. Just hopeful. You've not seen anyone seriously since Carl.'

'That's not true. I saw Will.'

Kate raised an eyebrow. 'Three dates is not seeing someone seriously.'

Ellie let out a sigh. 'What's your point?'

'No point.' Kate's tone was kind and concerned. 'Apart from the old "all work and no play" adage.'

Ellie smiled. 'Are you calling me dull?'

She knew Kate meant well. It was true that relationships weren't exactly top of her priority list and she also knew that concerned her friends. But she'd made mistakes before, one of which had nearly killed her. If she ever got serious with someone again, it would have to be with someone she trusted implicitly.

Someone who would accept her for who she was and love her as a person, not a possession. And it wasn't like she hadn't tried. She'd made the effort but those dates had been exactly that – an effort. Shouldn't being with the right person feel effortless?

Anyway, she'd had other demands on her time, including one

that felt more important to her than any more dates with men she wasn't interested in. A local gallery had just taken a few of her paintings, and things were already looking promising. It had been hard work and nerve-wracking but the owner had been incredibly enthusiastic about the results. One had even been sold the same day it went on display, and he'd already asked for two more. Ellie was thrilled but, with Zak's business also growing, she'd been incredibly busy and was definitely more than ready for a holiday.

'No, I'm not calling you dull,' Kate said, 'I just think that maybe you should have a little more fun – at least for the next three weeks.'

'OK, it's a deal.' Ellie held up her hand in a boy scout salute. 'I promise to have a good time.'

'Good!'

'I have another toast,' Ellie proposed. 'To Sandy and Todd, for giving us the best excuse and opportunity for a good time!'

'Cheers!'

'Cheers!'

*

The house really was beautiful. Although only a few years old, it was built in a traditional style, and already had a well-loved feel to it. Its freshly painted boards glowed in the late afternoon sun, and a swing on the wraparound porch creaked gently in the warm breeze. Surrounded by golden wheat fields on three sides, it was like a welcoming oasis, shimmering in the afternoon sun.

Ellie loved it. Unexpectedly, she felt tears begin to burn in her eyes and chided herself for being so ridiculous. A combination of jetlag and the emotion she always felt being back in Kansas was sending her system haywire. That and the feel of the sun on her face after the grey drizzle they had left behind in

London. Todd and Sandy had been letting their guests take in the view when Sandy suddenly noticed the tears in her friend's eyes.

'El, are you OK?'

Ellie looked round, startled for a moment. 'Yes!' She laughed and looked a little sheepishly at them all. 'It's so beautiful.'

'Well, thank you, ma'am.' A deep voice behind them made her start. Ellie whirled round as Sandy grinned and hurried over to hug Ben.

'Where did you sneak up from?'

'I've just been down checking on one of the horses with Jed. Midnight caught his hoof in a rut a few days ago and stumbled. Picked up kind of a nasty cut on his leg but it looks like it's healing well now, so it's all good.'

As Ben spoke to Sandy, Ellie was busy feeling an idiot and trying to hide the fact that she'd been ostensibly getting all teary over his home. Casually she ran her shirtsleeve across one eye and then the other.

Sandy led Ben over to the others, and he smiled widely at Ellie as she wrapped her arms around his neck for a hug. She had worried that it might be awkward when she saw Ben again. A little over a year ago, when Todd had been lying in a hospital bed, none of them knowing if he would live or die, she and Ben had become close, supporting each other – maybe even attracted to each other. But it had been such an intense, surreal situation and between her gallery work and him going straight back into the studio with the band to begin writing and recording a new album, as well as promoting their next tour, a year had flown past without them even speaking. Now she was back and feeling hugely relieved that it wasn't awkward at all. They were just Ellie and Ben, friends from childhood once again.

'It's good to see you,' he said softly, before standing back and studying her for a moment. 'Your hair's longer.'

Ellie touched her hair automatically. 'Yes, I...I'm growing it.'

Kate privately raised an eyebrow, taking in the handsome cowboy's smile.

'And this is Kate!' Ellie said, suddenly aware that everyone was watching and desperate to shift the attention away from herself.

'Pleasure to meet you, Kate,' Ben said, shaking her hand.

'And you. And thanks for the offer of letting us stay here. It's a beautiful location.'

'You're more than welcome. Besides, it'll be nice to have some company. Now, let's get you all settled and you folks something to drink. I'll get your luggage.' Ben approached Todd's SUV to help unload it, slowing as a truck ambled down the driveway. Dust flew out from the tyres despite the slow speed, and it rolled to a halt next to Ben. As the driver got out, Ben greeted him warmly, laughing at a comment apparently meant only for his ears.

The new arrival's eyes then fell on the assembled group, his laughing gaze fixed on Sandy as he bent to give her a hug before placing a kiss on her cheek.

'Still marrying him then?'

'Sure am.'

'Well, no harm in asking.' He grinned at Todd who returned it, shaking his hand as he did so. Tyler Marston was Ben's closest friend. They'd been roommates at college and he'd always been there for him, always would be, expecting nothing in return. Ben knew that that wasn't true of everyone who wanted to become his friend or rekindle an old friendship these days.

Tyler had been out of the country on business at the time of Todd's accident and had later berated Ben for not calling. He would have dropped everything that moment if his friend had needed him. He'd been relieved, if a little surprised, to hear that Ben had, after a few days, been able to manage the stress and guilt better – a change that had apparently occurred when Ellie Laing, the redhead his kid sister used to hang around with, came out from England to be with her. He hadn't seen her since he and Ben were at college but he was glad she'd been of help to Sandy – and apparently her brother.

Ben hadn't said anything but Tyler had known his friend a long time and he'd had a feeling there might have been more to it than Ben had told him. At least on his side. Now, as he was introduced to Ellie properly, one look at Ben's face told him he'd been right. Ben was already in deep. As for Ellie, he didn't know her well enough to judge the answer to that particular question. Maybe the next few weeks would give him more of an answer. In the meantime, his attention was drawn to her friend, Kate.

'Hope you ladies don't mind me staying here too. It's just that when Ben told me his plans had changed and he was going to be home after all, well, I just didn't think it was fair to let him shoulder the responsibility of hospitality all by himself!'

Kate smiled widely at him. Never one to hide her feelings, she already liked this smart talking cowboy with the twinkle in his eye.

Ellie looked up at Ben, confusion showing on her face. 'You're staying here?'

As far as she knew, the plan was that, apart from the wedding day itself, Ben was going to be out of state. Sandy knew that Ellie had been saving for a holiday and had suggested to Ben that she and Kate stay at the house as it was going to be empty, enabling her to extend her visit for the wedding into a proper, relaxing break. Ben had apparently been more than happy with the arrangement and everything was settled. Except it appeared that the plan had now changed.

'Oh no!' Sandy's hand flew to her mouth. 'With all the planning I must have forgotten to tell you. Ben's arrangements were postponed. He's not going…yet.' She flushed a little and then giggled at the others who were all staring at her. 'We'll get the drinks.' Sandy grabbed Todd's hand and they disappeared inside the house to fix refreshments, and escape the now rather awkward silence.

Kate and Tyler were grinning, clearly unmoved by this new piece of information. Ben, meanwhile, was highly embarrassed that the women hadn't been made aware of the changes before they arrived, knowing that they may have preferred to alter their accommodation arrangements. Ellie caught sight of his stricken face.

'That's OK,' she said, misreading his discomfort for something else. 'I'm sure we can find something in town—'

'No!' Ben and Tyler replied in unison, startling themselves, each other, and their guests.

'I mean, there's plenty of beds. Rooms! Bedrooms,' Ben corrected himself, blushing furiously.

Tyler grinned even wider. He'd definitely been on the money before and whatever feelings Ben had had for this woman previously clearly hadn't dulled over time.

'Look. Let me show you around and, well, I understand if you'd rather not stay but it'd be an honour if you did.'

'Well, that's settled then.' Kate beamed, grabbing her case handle in the back of Todd's car. Tyler took it from her immediately, staggering slightly as he lifted it out.

'Don't believe in any of that travelling light stuff, huh?' Kate raised her perfectly shaped eyebrows at him.

Tyler grinned then tipped his hat to her. 'Shall we?' he proposed, indicating for her to lead the way. Her wide grin received one from him in reply as they began strolling towards the house.

'I think this is going to be great fun!' she enthused. 'And Ellie could certainly do with some of that, couldn't you, sweetie?' Kate tossed a loving look at her friend. 'Bless her, she's been working so hard and barely ever goes out. I've told her it's not healthy. A couple of dates and that's it! All work and no play and all that...' Kate's voice faded as the screen door closed after them. Ellie rolled her eyes.

Ben lifted out the remaining suitcase, a faint smile tugged at the corners of his mouth at Kate's relaxed manner. He had already known he would like her, having heard from his sister how much she had done for Ellie after the whole thing with Carl, but now, having met her, he liked her even more. Although, clearly as not as much as Tyler did.

Ellie felt the need to break the silence. 'I do actually go out.'

Ben flashed a smile. 'I'm sure.'

The silence returned as Ben stood the case on the driveway and swung the rear door of the SUV closed.

'Look. Are you sure it's alright for us to stay here? I mean, now that you're going to be here and won't have the house to yourself?'

'I'm sure. Positive, in fact.'

'Well, you know, we wouldn't want to cramp your style or anything.' Ellie was well aware she was on the verge of babbling now but seemed unable to stop herself.

Ben laughed as he wrapped his fingers around the handle of the suitcase. Perfectly even, white teeth contrasted against his tanned skin.

'I mean if you…we…if you wanted the house to yourself or anything, you know. You can just tell us to get lost.' *Shut up, Ellie.* She looked up at Ben who hadn't said a word. His hat shielded the bright blue eyes from the sun, but under its shadow Ellie saw they were smiling.

'And it was three dates. That's more than a couple.'

'OK.'

'You're not going to let me pull that suitcase, are you?'

'Nope.'

Ellie shook her head and followed the indication he gave with his hand to head inside and catch up with the others. They chatted easily for a while as they sat around the large wooden table in the heart of the kitchen, Sandy's homemade lemonade refreshing them all.

'Shall I show you to your rooms?' Sandy said after a while. Without waiting, she took charge, asking Todd to bring up the girls' luggage.

'Yes ma'am!' Todd replied, saluting.

She paused a moment with a hand on her hip, a brow raised at his cheeky reply but no one could miss the smile accompanying it. Tilting her head at him, she walked back across the room and kissed him. A full, sensual, lingering kiss which drew a loud whistle from Tyler and a 'whoop whoop' from Kate.

'Please,' Sandy whispered.

'Anything you say, ma'am,' Todd replied, aware of the stupid grin now plastered on his face. She gave him a wink before rejoining the girls waiting on the stairs in order to continue the tour of the house.

Tyler downed the remains of his cold beer.

'Man!' he exclaimed. 'You sure I can't persuade you not to marry her?'

'Absolutely. Totally. One hundred per cent.'

'Damn.'

Ben grinned as he handed his friend another beer. Tyler had been teasing Todd about Sandy ever since they had started dating.

'Anyway,' Todd countered, 'you've barely taken your eyes off Kate since you got here!'

'Yeah, I know. She's pretty hot! You kept that a bit quiet, buddy,' Ty directed at Ben. 'Thinking about keeping her all to yourself, were you?' He began walking around Ben in mock interrogation.

'Nope.' Ben smiled, relaxed. 'I've never met her before.'

'Yeah, yeah. This is to get me back for kissing Jessica Simmons in fifth grade, isn't it?'

Ben blinked. 'You kissed Jessica Simmons?'

Ty stopped pacing and met the questioning faces of Todd and Ben. He coughed, moving on swiftly. 'Well, sorry to break it to you, pal. You may be famous and fabulously wealthy but I, my friend, am irresistible!'

At this the other two roared with laughter.

'What?' Ty did his best to remain serious, 'Hey! I don't see what's so funny.'

*

The house had six bedrooms, four of which were en-suite, plus a further two separate bathrooms upstairs and a third downstairs. Additionally, there was also a study, dining room, games room, an outside pool, plus an indoor one, a light and airy living room and a cosy snug, and of course, the beautiful kitchen with its handmade limed oak units and sparkling granite counter tops. It was here that Sandy's tour concluded and the women joined Ben, Tyler and Todd. All three were now on their second beer and they retrieved more cold ones for the girls.

'It really is the most beautiful house, Ben.' Ellie smiled, running her hand over one of worktops.

'I'm in love with that pool!' Kate indicated with a nod of her head to the pool around the back that she had seen from an upstairs window, its coolness glittering invitingly.

'Hope you brought your bathing suit then!' Tyler wiggled his eyebrows. 'Or maybe I should hope that you didn't.'

Kate threw her head back in laughter. 'Are you always this cheeky?' she asked, glowing at the attention.

From others it might have sounded odd or creepy, but after just a few minutes of talking to this man, Kate already felt completely relaxed – as though she'd known him for years.

The group moved out to sit on the porch and enjoy the late afternoon sun. It was Ellie's favourite time of day, and she never tired of the beautiful light it produced. Ben pointed Tyler in the direction of some potato chips as he grabbed a cooler and dropped in some beers and soft drinks. Outside, Sandy and Todd sat snuggled together on one of the sofas, and Ellie moved to sit next to Kate on its partner but stopped when she pulled a face. Ellie stared blankly at her for a moment as Kate frantically directed with her eyes, a mischievous smile playing on her face. Suddenly Ellie understood.

'Oh!' she mouthed, and instead crossed to the wooden swing as it creaked gently in the late afternoon breeze, leaving the seat next to Kate free for Tyler.

Ellie plopped down onto the swing and sunk into the squashy cushions piled onto it. She gave herself a little push off then tucked her legs up under her. As the friends sat, the warm sun worked its magic on them all, and they chatted easily and lazily about the wedding, work and trivia. Ty soon joined them.

'Ben's just on the phone. Said he'd be out in a minute. Is this seat taken?' He indicated the space next to Kate, who flashed him a brilliant smile and motioned for him to sit.

Ellie watched the proceedings, smiling. *Poor guy. He doesn't stand a chance!* Kate was a great friend – loyal, funny and always ready for an adventure, like this holiday. The timing couldn't have been better. Kate was a broker in the City whom Ellie met through Zak at a work function, and she'd been talking about getting out of it for a while now. She'd made her money and wanted to walk away before she felt that she couldn't and ended up burning out, as she'd seen so many of her colleagues do. When Ellie had suggested this trip, a long holiday that included a romantic wedding, it seemed the perfect way to begin her new start. Sandy and Kate had met when Sandy had been over in England visiting, and they'd really hit it off so she'd been more than happy for Kate to accompany Ellie and attend the wedding, especially if it meant that it would encourage her friend to take that holiday she'd been promising to. Ellie watched as Kate and Tyler shared a joke, their body language relaxed and contented, not to mention a little tactile. Her smile grew. Yes, she thought, she was very glad Kate had come.

Ellie turned her attention to the bride and groom. Both now had their eyes closed and were basking in the warm rays, looking happy but exhausted. The wedding was to be a big affair and Todd and Sandy had done much of the planning and arrangements themselves. Ted Danvers was a wealthy man and the fund for his only daughter's wedding was more than substantial. A wedding planner's fee would have been a drop in the fiscal ocean, but it was the one thing that Sandy had been adamant on. This was to be their day and they would arrange it. She couldn't bear the thought of a stranger arranging something so personal. Todd's accident had only reaffirmed that feeling. So that was that, and in two days all of their hard work would pay off. The three-week Caribbean cruise booked for the honeymoon would be well deserved, and well required, once it was all over. Ellie smiled at their obvious happiness, knowing it was all the sweeter having nearly lost it.

Resting one of the fluffy cushions on her lap, she began to stroke it absent-mindedly. It was kind of soothing, like stroking a pet. She gazed out across the wheat fields, now glowing in the soft, golden light of early evening. Above them the sky was a deep, rich blue and together they formed two beautiful swathes of colour as perfect and simple as if a child had painted them. In her appreciative trance, Ellie failed to notice that Ben had come out from the house and she looked up as a shadow fell across the swing. 'Kind of like stroking a dog, isn't it?' he said, easing himself down onto the other end of the swing. His voice was soft and low in deference to the others who now all seemed to be dozing.

Ellie noticed that Ty had tipped his hat down over his face, as his chest rose and fell with the slow, steady rhythm of sleep. She giggled.

Ben looked across at her, a half-smile on his lips. 'What?'

Ellie nodded at Ty. 'I thought they only did that in the movies!' Suddenly she jumped up, balancing on one leg, her face screwed up in pain.

'Ow! Ow! Ow! Oh God!' It was very hard, not to mention inconvenient, trying to express the pain quietly.

'What's wrong?' Ben's face was full of concern as he shifted forward, perching on the edge of the swing.

'Cramp!' Ellie's face creased again as she gritted her teeth to prevent yells of anguish escaping.

'Try putting some weight on it,' Ben suggested.

Ellie attempted to, but the affected leg kept seizing up and she hobbled from one foot to the other before trying again. Ben held her arm as she over-balanced and she caught his expression. Although his features were full of concern, Ellie thought she glimpsed a hint of something else.

'Are you laughing at me?' she whispered crossly. Ben was the last person she had thought would enjoy her discomfort.

'No!' His reply, at least, seemed genuine. Ellie let him help her gently back to sit on the swing.

'It's just that it looks real painful…'

'Which, apparently, is hysterical to some people!' she griped in a whisper. Jet lag combined with her current discomfort was not a great combination.

'No! Honest! I'm not laughing at your pain, honey, I promise. It's just that I thought it was, well, it's kind of sweet that you were trying to be so quiet about it all.' His face was honest and open. Letting out a sigh, she shook her head in apology, a shy smile accompanying it, but its appearance was brief as she once again clutched at her leg in agony, the relentless cramp tearing at her muscles. Ben winced in sympathy before tilting his head at her.

'May I?' he asked, softly.

She wasn't sure what he was asking permission for but as she trusted him implicitly, she agreed.

Ben reached down and gently lifted Ellie's affected leg on to his lap. She shuffled in her seat to accommodate the change in position. Carefully he began to massage the cramped limb, and the strong but tender action brought much welcome relief.

'Ellie?'

'Hmm? Oh, sorry! Pardon?' Ellie flushed. Ben's touch had brought a rush of unexpected feelings, and caught up in them, she hadn't realised he had spoken.

'I said does it feel any better yet?'

'Yes! Yes, it does. Thank you,' she said, retracting her leg and distractedly copying the movements Ben had performed on it moments before.

'No problem. Sandy used to get it all the time when she was younger.'

Ellie smiled, then looked back to the wheat fields, away from him. The daylight was fading now but she could still see the crop outlines dancing in the evening wind. Suddenly she felt odd and she didn't know why. Of course Ben only thought of her as a kid, just like his sister would always be a kid to him.

She'd been strong for him a year ago, and they'd felt like equals then but that was then – an almost unreal and incredibly tense situation. Things like that often made people act in ways they wouldn't ordinarily.

It was stupid feeling…what was it that she felt anyway? Disappointed? She wasn't sure. Anyway.

Whatever it was, it was pointless. She and Ben were friends and she loved that. She felt comfortable with him which now, more than ever, was something she placed an incredibly high value on. She wasn't even sure why she was feeling this way. Mentally, she took a deep breath and put it down to being over-tired, jet lag, and the emotional reason she was here in the first place. But deep inside, Ellie knew there was something else. A fear that she might never feel as comfortable and trusting of a man as she did when she was with Ben. Of course, it wasn't Ben that she wanted – which was just as well as she was sure the last thing on this particular music star's mind was dating his little sister's best friend. Ellie and Sandy shared everything and if there had ever been an indication of Ben showing anything more than a polite interest in Ellie, wild horses wouldn't have kept Sandy from calling her. He'd pretty much just spelled that out for her anyway, perhaps already worried that she might have interpreted the healing massage as something more personal.

Besides, according to Sandy, Cyndi had done such a good job on Ben that he had pretty much avoided any sort of relationship ever since the divorce, claiming he preferred things that way these days. Her friend, however, had her doubts. In her opinion it was more that her brother was so scared of getting hurt again, he'd sooner avoid the possibility entirely. Suddenly feeling tired and self-conscious, Ellie curled up into a ball.

'You ought to keep them out straight for a while. Help the blood flow.' Ben indicated her legs with a nod of his head.

Ellie didn't reply but she did take his advice. Before long, he had also closed his eyes and begun to doze along with the others.

Ellie sat next to him in the swing, absentmindedly stroking the cushion and listening to the soft swish of the evening wind. Although tired, the afternoon nap everyone else seemed able to grab continued to elude her, leaving her to her thoughts and trying not to remember how good Ben's hands had felt on her leg, even though they had been placed there in the most innocent of manner. She felt the heat rush up her chest and face as her mind suddenly took hold and, unbidden, raced ahead, imagining those hands moving further. Ellie fidgeted on the swing, sneaking a glance at her companion as she pushed the thought firmly out of her mind. Yes, Ben Danvers was one of the most good-looking men she had ever seen and she'd yet to meet anyone with a smile to beat his... but still. She was not about to start lusting after him like some lovesick teenager – she'd made enough messes in her love life without adding unrequited love to the pile, thanks very much. Ben was just Ben. And that was all she needed, or wanted, from him.

The noise of a vehicle crunching its way slowly down the drive made her look up, and she watched as the dust curled out from the tyres and floated in the low light from the house and the car's own headlights. She glanced across at Ben but he hadn't stirred. The porch light was soft and cast shadows on his cheeks from his long eyelashes. Gazing upon them for a moment, Ellie wondered at the unfairness of creation that resulted in men being born with eyelashes that they didn't appreciate and that most women would kill for and many paid good money to fake.

The closing of vehicle doors woke the others from their slumber and Ellie was thrilled to see Ted and Molly Danvers emerge from the car's interior. She was always delighted to see them, but especially this time as her reason for being here was such a joyous one.

'We brought pizza!' Sandy's father called, holding up a stack of boxes.

Ted Danvers was still a handsome man, the grey touching his temples only serving to lend an air of distinction to his character. His wife followed him up the porch steps, greeting everyone in turn and already making Kate feel as if she had been part of the friendship circle for years.

Molly was one of those people who never seemed to age. On Ellie's previous visit, her friend's mother had looked understandably tired and drawn, so Ellie was pleased to see her normal radiance and easy smile not only back in place, but magnified.

Kisses and hugs were exchanged all round and Ben grabbed two more chairs for his parents before retaking his position on the swing next to Ellie. As they all chatted together, her gaze flicked back to the strong, handsome face of Ben. He resembled his father a great deal, even down to the mischievous twinkle in their eyes – both men had a fine ability to retain a straight face whilst teasing. Ellie had learnt this quickly growing up next door and would search their face for the smile in their eyes that would give the joke away. And it would always be there. Even in those trying, formative teenage years, Ellie had never felt affronted by them which, she appreciated, was quite an achievement.

As the others talked, Molly leant over to and spoke softly to Ellie. 'Sandy tells me you're still working too hard and not playing enough.'

Ellie smiled. 'Why does everyone keep saying that?'

Molly gave her a look that only a mother could. 'Perhaps you might need to consider the truth of it then?' she said, taking Ellie's hand.

Ellie laid her own on top of Molly's. 'It's not like I've been locking myself away entirely. I have actually been out on a few dates.'

Suddenly she wondered if she was trying to convince Molly or herself?

'No one special yet, then?'

She shook her head. 'No. But that's OK.'

And it was OK. Of course it was. Ellie smiled a big smile but even to her own ears, the words sounded false, the tone too bright. Molly didn't respond and Ellie knew the older woman could see straight through her, just as her own mother could.

Ellie had learned her lesson the hard way and she wasn't about to take up with a man just to be with someone. That wouldn't have been fair on her or him. She'd worked hard to get back the confidence and self-respect that Carl had stripped from her but there were still scars. Internal as well as external. She knew in time those would fade, even if they never went away entirely.

That first date had been a big step, and thankfully it hadn't been a disaster. The guy was a friend of Zak's and Ellie got the feeling he'd been set up as a kind of practice run for her. He'd been kind and funny and it had been a pleasant dinner, but there was no special attraction on either side. With Will, the guy she'd seen a few more times, she had tried but it still didn't feel right. As nice as he was, and as keen as he was, Ellie just didn't feel fired up in the way she ought to. And, if she was honest, she knew that if it had been right, she shouldn't have to try – those feelings should just be there.

Of course, now they'd decided to spark in the most inconvenient situation. Ellie was, however, convinced that this was a one off – just the result of a tired and overwrought body, the warm summer evening, and everyone around her either being madly in love, or, judging by the looks of Kate and Tyler, madly in lust. But it was still a little awkward, nonetheless. Glancing at the others as she did her best to escape Molly's searching look, she felt a tightness in her chest. This. This was what it was supposed to be like...but would she ever have that? And would she ever let herself have that, even if she found it?

'Ellie, sweetie? Are you OK?' Molly's concerned voice called her back to the present.

'Oh, yes. Yes, I'm fine. Sorry. Just a little tired.' She smiled at her, all the while knowing that no one pulled the wool over this woman's eyes. Emotions bubbled up inside and Ellie pushed them back hard. This time was about Todd and Sandy and she wasn't about to spoil it for them or herself by getting upset.

'I'll take these in. Help earn my keep.' Her tone was light as she collected the empty glasses but Molly wasn't fooled. She caught her arm and gently pressed it, the gesture saying more than words ever could. Her kindness only made it worse.

Ellie placed the glasses in the dishwasher then leant against the sink and pushed the lever. Cool water flowed and she held her wrists under the stream, slowing her racing pulse and cooling the hot blood hurtling around her body. Ellie leant forward and splashed water onto her face.

'You don't have to do that, you know. Clear glasses, I mean.' Ellie spun round in surprise as water dripped from her face. She ran a hand under her chin to catch the worst.

'You OK?' Ben asked when she didn't reply.

'Uh huh.' Ellie smiled brightly, unleashing a few more droplets as she tried to lean nonchalantly on the sink.

Ben nodded and walked from the kitchen. Ellie held the pose for a couple of moments before turning back to face the sink and hanging her head.

'Great, El. Very cool,' she chided herself aloud.

A towel appeared in front of her face. She looked at it for a second as it hung there.

'Thank you.' Swearing internally, she remembered her manners and took the towel, wiping her face as Ben returned outside.

From the corner of her eye, she didn't miss the grin he'd made no attempt to hide.

*

Revived by food and laughter, the evening passed in an easy, relaxed manner as the group swapped news and stories. Eventually the subject predictably swung back around to the imminent wedding.

'So…' Molly looked across at Kate. 'Is your dress upstairs?'

'Oh yes! Let's go see it!' Sandy jumped up in a state of excitement that had only been increased by the champagne they'd shared. As she passed, she grabbed Ellie's hand, pulling her from her seat too. What Sandy hadn't noticed was her brother's legs stretched out under the table in front of them over which she promptly tripped. In an attempt to remain upright, she grabbed onto Ellie, who immediately went straight down too and a yelp sounded as an elbow connected with a shin. For a few minutes, their laughter prevented them from moving at all and it was only with help that they finally managed to untangle themselves and stand up.

'Oh man, what am I letting myself in for?' Todd exclaimed as he helped the pair up.

The girls stood with their arms linked and giggled, feeling for all the world that they were eleven years old again. Ellie looked down at Ben who was rubbing his shin.

'Whoops. I think that was my elbow. Sorry.'

'No problem. Just an old riding injury. Don't worry, it'll be back to normal in a few weeks.' Ellie's smile faded as she glanced down at the long leg encased in dark denim.

'Stop it!' Sandy admonished with a laugh as she batted her brother's hat off his head. 'You have no such injury. Don't be so mean!'

Ben looked up into Ellie's concerned green gaze and grinned,

102

swigging the last of his beer. She narrowed her eyes at him and he gave her a wink and laughed.

Mrs Danvers followed the three younger women up the stairs as they giggled and laughed. Sandy instructed them that if Ben or Tyler teased them like that once she'd left, they both had full permission to retaliate.

'Isn't that right, Mama?'

'Oh sure. You give it right back to them. Don't let those boys get away with anything,' Molly agreed, her smile as wide as her daughter's. Her mind, however, was on something else as she reflected on the fact that just now was the first time in a long time she had seen her youngest son smile like that – a smile that was clearly from the heart. He'd looked genuinely happy for the first time since his marriage had ended. And even before that, if Molly was truly honest.

They filed into the bedroom and Molly sat on a chair as Kate's garment hanger was found and opened and a chorus of oohs and aahs, including her own, accompanied it. Smiling, she watched the three women caught up in their joy and excitement, but her gaze lingered on Ellie. That girl had certainly had her troubles, but she seemed determined not to let them ruin her life. But was she working too hard at it all? Was her determination to win becoming a problem in itself as she filled her hours almost completely with work? Maybe this vacation was just what she needed. As Sandy held Kate's dress up against her new friend, commenting on how perfect it was for her colouring, Molly's thoughts drifted back to her youngest son – a man who had closed his heart for the fear of ever having it shattered again.

Yes, she thought as she rose to join the girls, maybe it was exactly what they all needed.

Chapter 8

The following day dawned bright and sunny but neither Ellie nor Kate saw it. They'd sat out on the porch until gone two in the morning, blankets having been brought out when the night air began to cool and the conversation continued. Ellie now rolled over and focused blearily on the clock. Four o'clock. She lay there for a while trying to get back to sleep, and just as she was finally drifting off, the door flew open. Kate stood there looking as bleary-eyed as Ellie.

'It's four o'clock.'

'Shhh!' Ellie held a finger to her lips. 'I know,' she whispered. 'But I don't think everyone needs a wake-up call.'

Kate stared at her and frowned. 'It's four o'clock,' she stated again, slower this time. Receiving nothing but a blank look from her friend, she added some clarification. 'In the afternoon!'

'Oh my God!' Ellie sat bolt upright in the bed. The two looked at each other in embarrassed horror as grins began to form.

'Oops.'

'I'm going to have a shower,' Ellie said, pushing herself out of the comfy bed and pulling back the blackout curtains to see that it was indeed late afternoon. 'I'll see you downstairs in a bit and we can apologise for being such terrible guests together.' Kate laughed and left her to it as Ellie headed for the en-suite. The shower pounded muscles stiff from travelling and she stepped from the cubicle feeling refreshed and far more awake.

Ellie snuggled against the soft warm cotton of the bath towel wrapped around her body and sat on the edge of the bed. Tipping forward, she towelled her hair dry, her mind drifting until a knock at the door disturbed her thoughts. Kate had obviously changed her mind about going downstairs alone and had called on her for back up. And, having now recovered from her shock of waking up in a stranger's house in the middle of the afternoon, this time she'd remembered to knock.

'Come in.'

'I thought I – oh! Excuse me.'

The deep male voice surprised Ellie.

She flipped her hair back hurriedly just in time to see the door closing.

'Ben?'

His face appeared around the door, a slightly bashful expression showing. 'I'll come back.'

'No, it's OK. Hang on a minute.'

He entered the room more fully as she disappeared into the en-suite, re-emerging moments later wrapped in a silk print robe. Her damp hair looked darker as she deftly wound it around her hand and pinned it up.

'Hi.'

'Hi.'

'I'm so sorry about the time. You should have woken us.'

Ben grinned and waved his hand in a gesture of dismissal. 'No problem. Best to catch up on sleep now rather than in the middle of the ceremony on Saturday.'

'I think we can safely say that this would be my last trip to the States if I did that.'

'Well then, I'd definitely better make sure I keep my eye on you.' Ben's thought was voiced before he had time to censor it, but Ellie didn't seem to notice or take the comment as anything other than friendly assurance. She probably just saw it as brotherly concern, Ben thought grimly.

'Thanks! I'd appreciate that.'

'Coffee?'

'Lovely, thanks. I'll be down in just a minute.'

He smiled and pulled the door closed behind him. Ellie looked across at the view from the window. The sun shining in the biggest blue sky, contrasting perfectly with golden wheat dancing in the breeze. Hurrying across the room, she pulled open the door again.

'Ben?'

He was a few feet from her, one foot on the top stair.

'I just...' Now she felt foolish. Ben remained silent but his smile was gentle and the blue eyes held a questioning look. Ellie took a deep breath. 'I just wanted to say thanks again for letting us stay here. It really is so beautiful.' She waved her hand to indicate a similar view through the landing window to the one she'd just been studying.

Ben's smile grew. 'Yes, ma'am. It certainly is.'

'Afternoon!' Kate emerged from her room and quickly took in the scene. 'Sorry about the time,' she apologised breezily to Ben, who remained at the top of the stairs as she passed. 'Tyler downstairs?'

'Sure is. Been waiting for you.'

Kate beamed and exchanged a happy look with her friend before descending the stairs. 'Ellie? You do know you can see straight through that robe from the landing,' she called back.

Ellie looked back to Ben whose grin and helpless shrug confirmed that Kate was indeed correct. Mortified, she hurried back inside the bedroom and closed the door. Ben heard the muffled laughter from within before carrying on down the stairs, considering what a pleasant afternoon it had turned into.

*

Ellie wandered around the land that belonged to the ranch while Kate took a trip with Tyler into town. She had been hesitant to leave Ellie, insisting that it was her she'd come on holiday with, not Tyler.

'Even if he is gorgeous, witty, intelligent…' She'd smiled but her heart was serious. 'I don't want to abandon you.'

'Don't be silly, Kate. You're only going into town!'

'You'll be on your own with Ben out as well.'

'It's OK, Kate. I'm a big girl now.'

'I know. It's just that—' Ty emerged from the house, and Ellie grabbed the opportunity, calling to him. 'Tyler, please take this woman away.'

'With pleasure,' he'd said with a smile.

It was so peaceful here. So perfect. She carried a sketchbook in one hand and a pencil tucked into the loose knot of her hair. A soft, oversized cotton shirt flapped gently on the breeze, protecting fair shoulders from the sun. Denim cut offs showed off her legs, toned from the walking she'd begun doing a couple of years ago as part of her therapy, and that she had continued once she discovered how much she enjoyed having that time to herself, discovering new routes and occasionally making sketches of scenes she found appealing.

The rays warmed her skin and relaxed her mind as she strolled, occasionally removing the pencil from her hair like a pin and taking down the scene in front of her in shades of grey. As Ellie passed the stables, she chatted to the ranch hands who, in turn introduced her to the horses.

'Can you ride, ma'am?'

'Yes. Well, I used to but it was a long time ago. I think I'm probably quite rusty now.'

'It'll all come back to you once you're back in the saddle.'

Ellie glanced at the Western saddles hanging in the stable and moved to run her hand over the soft leather of one of them. She'd always thought they were far more comfortable than the traditional English ones. Her parents had arranged for her to ride when they got back to England, desperate to try and make her happy after the move, but she hadn't kept it up for long. She'd much preferred the more relaxed position of the Western saddles, borne out of years of cowboys spending uncountable hours in them, to the poker straight stance required by the English ones.

'Mr Danvers loves to ride. Why don't you get him to take you out sometime?'

'Oh, I'm sure he has things to do,' she said, moving back over to stroke the nose of the nearest horse. 'We're really just staying here on the proviso that we make our own entertainment.'

Jed gave his gum a thoughtful chew. He already liked this woman a whole lot more than Ben Danver's ex-wife, and he had a feeling that his boss would happily take some time out to go riding with her. But that was his business. Jed resumed brushing the stallion's coat, watching Ellie from the corner of his eye as she smiled at the photographs on the wall, and touched the polished tack, talking to him about his job and the horses and the upcoming wedding. She was easy to talk to and seemed genuinely interested in his answers. Jed wasn't sure what the real deal was with Ben and Miss Eleanor, but with that soft voice and pretty laugh, not to mention the cute accent, if his boss had any leanings in that direction, he'd be crazy to let her get away.

After a while, Ellie thanked Jed for the introductions and his time and continued with her exploration.

Rounding an old outbuilding, she came face to chest with Ben.

'Hey! I was just coming to find you.'

'You found me.'

'That I did,' he laughed.

Ellie stepped back from him a little in what she hoped was a nonchalant manner, embarrassed with the feelings his sudden closeness stirred in her.

Come on, Ellie. Pull it together.

Suddenly she laughed to herself, as she cringed at what Ben

would say if he could read her thoughts right now! If she was certain of one thing, it was that 'seduce Ellie' was most definitely not on his to-do list.

'What?' Ben tilted his head at the expression on Ellie's face but she shook it off, her face clearing. He looked at her for a moment, squinted up at the sky, then returned his attention to her. 'Come with me,' he said, and held out his hand.

For Ellie, taking it felt like the most natural thing to do. Her hand now gently resting in his, he led her back the way she had come to the stable buildings.

Jed was still there, and he and Ben exchanged small talk for a few moments before going on through to an anteroom. The ranch hand returned to his task, smiling as he noted that his boss had kept hold of Miss Eleanor's hand throughout their conversation. It was also the most relaxed and happy he'd seen him in a long time. If they didn't take that ride he'd mentioned to her earlier, he'd be pretty surprised.

The smaller storeroom that Ben led his guest through to held an assortment of clothes, both men's and women's.

'Spares,' Ben explained. 'For when people want to ride but aren't properly attired.' The last part was spoken in a surprisingly good English accent.

Ellie raised an eyebrow. 'Watch it.'

Ben grinned at the warning and reached up, pulling a black Stetson from a shelf. He plopped it down on Ellie's head and laughed as it covered her eyes.

'A little too big.'

'Really? Are you sure?'

Replacing the hat on its hook, he grabbed another. It was pale with an almost flat brim. Ellie remained in position, hands by her sides as Ben placed it on her head. He bent his knees so that he was under the brim and looking into Ellie's emerald eyes.

'Perfect,' he said softly. Ellie smiled and he quickly straightened before he could pull her to him and kiss those full lips like he'd been dying to do ever since the moment he'd seen her standing on his driveway wiping her eyes, he'd guessed from the dust, looking for all the world – or to him at least – that she belonged there completely.

'Wait here a second.' With that, he disappeared back into the main part of the building, leaving Ellie to nose about the room a little more.

'OK. C'mon,' Ben said, having returned.

'Where are we going?' she asked, rejoining the mystery trail, once more attached to Ben's hand as they walked back to the main body of the stables. Two horses stood waiting, fully prepared for a ride. One had small pack bags resting on its hindquarters.

'Ready?'

'Now?' Ellie asked, her pitch a little higher than usual from the nerves that were currently coursing through her body.

'Sure. Why not?' Ben asked. Glancing over from checking his tack, he caught the expression on his companion's face. Emotion rose in him briefly before he buried it again. He stopped, facing her. 'We'll just walk, OK? Save all the good stuff until you get your confidence back.'

Ellie nodded, a hint of uncertainty still showing through as she looked up at him with those clear green eyes – eyes full of trust and honesty. Suddenly he felt that fire and fury he'd experienced on seeing her that evening, bruised and fragile, and he tried not to remember the other emotions that had almost engulfed him as he'd held her sobbing in the low light on his childhood home's garden swing.

He hadn't realised it was going to be so difficult having her staying here for the wedding and beyond. Although he'd been happy to go along with Sandy's plans initially when his own had changed, he'd debated making rearrangements. But that was stupid, he'd told himself. Ellie was just a friend. He'd known her for decades, and those feelings from before? They were just a mixture of a natural inclination to protect and a reaction to his own unhappy marriage. It was nothing more than that. He definitely didn't need her like his mind and body had been trying to tell him he did. He didn't long for her to be the last sight his eyes took in at night and the first they saw in the morning. And he certainly didn't want to stroke his hands and mouth over every inch of that smoking hot body. Ben rested his head against his horse's nose for a moment, his expression hidden from the others, and rolled his eyes. The horse whinnied a little and Ben took that as a sign that even his mount was telling him to get a grip.

'Thanks,' Ellie said, looking down to where Jed now stood, having given her a boost into the saddle. 'Ready?' she asked, looking across to her host who was now settled on his own horse.

Ben nodded, indicating the way. Jed led her horse to the gate as Ben followed behind, giving her a moment to get used to the sensation of being in a saddle again after so many years. Handing the reins over, he wished them both a pleasant ride and headed back into the stable.

'I'm not sure about this. I don't think Sandy's going to be too pleased if I turn up in a plaster cast to be her maid of honour.'

'So don't fall off then,' Ben teased, merriment flashing in his eyes.

'Gee. Thanks for the advice.' Ellie's face was serious but he could see the glint in her eye.

Ben edged his horse close to hers. 'You're going to be just fine. We're only going to walk. I promise to look after you.' His face clouded as he remembered the last time he'd promised to look after someone he'd cared about.

'Promise?' Ellie teased.

'Promise,' Ben replied. He'd never meant anything more in his life.

'OK. So long as I can blame you, that's fine,' Ellie teased, nudging the animal into a walk.

Ben let her go for a minute. He'd promised to look after her but God knew he wanted to do so much more than that. He wanted to love her – and her to love him. But there was no way that was going to happen. No way he would even let that happen. Ellie was the gentlest soul he had ever met but that was no guarantee she wouldn't break his heart and once was plenty, thanks very much. Besides, who was he kidding? Someone like Ellie could have her pick of guys, and the more her confidence grew, the more she'd meet. He knew he could never be in the running – divorced, chasing forty and living over four thousand miles away. Yes, he was wealthy but for the one woman that mattered to him, that didn't matter. Pushing everything but the moment out of his mind, he moved his heels against the side of his mount and trotted to catch up to Ellie and Merlin.

'OK?'

'Mm-hmm.'

They walked on in companionable silence, allowing Ellie to gradually regain some confidence at being in the saddle again. Watching, Ben could see as she finally began to really relax back into it.

'Better?' he asked.

'Yes,' she answered simply, turning to him with the most beautiful smile. She was happy and genuine and relaxed. It was the first time he'd seen her smile like that since she was a kid. He knew that everyone assumed that easy, relaxed smile had disappeared along with braces and pigtails but there it was. It had just been buried under pain, fear, stress and the day to day business of living but it had been unearthed again out here in the middle of nowhere by a handsome cowboy and a jet-black stallion named Merlin.

They walked side by side for a couple of hours until Ben spotted a shady spot for a rest. A creek ran nearby and they steered the horses towards it. Ellie watched the water as it made its way across the landscape, glinting in the sun.

'Isn't it amazing how it sparkles like that? It's like it's got diamonds in it.' The comment was more addressed to herself, but Ben heard and looked across, an expression she couldn't make out clouding his handsome features. Looking out at him from under the brim of her hat she smiled, embarrassed, before looking back at the water. Ben dismounted and flipped the reins before moving across to assist Ellie, who was halfway down. She wrapped a hand around his forearm as support.

'Thanks. I think I forgot what a long way down it is!' she said, laughing as she looked up at him. 'I guess you have an advantage.'

'Advantage?' Ben queried as she released his arm. He moved across and began emptying some items from the saddlebag.

'Long legs,' she replied, patting Merlin's flank as the animals drank greedily from the cool stream.

Ben turned back towards her, the contents of the saddlebags now cradled against his chest. 'If it makes you feel better, yours don't look too bad from here either.'

Ellie turned and looked into blue eyes full of laughter and mischief. 'Hmm.'

She took a blanket from the top of the pile he was carrying and bopped him on the arm with it. 'That reminds me, I have a bone to pick with you about the other morning.'

'What?' he asked, distractedly, trying not to stare as Ellie leant on her hands and knees and spread out the rug on the ground.

'You know exactly what!' she replied, leaning back on her heels. 'I thought you were a gentleman?' Ben frowned, concentrating on getting his mind back in to PG territory.

'On the landing?'

'Ohhh. That.'

'Yes. That.'

'OK. For clarification purposes, I am a gentleman. But I'm also a guy, and believe me, no guy in his right mind would have acted any differently.' He opened the wine and poured some into two plastic glasses, then handed one to Ellie. 'Besides, what was I supposed to say?'

Ellie thought about that. 'Good point. I hadn't got that far.'

Ben had got a lot further but he was doing his best not to think about any of that right now.

'Cheers,' he said, holding up the glass.

'Cheers.'

All was quiet as they savoured the wine and the weather, the combination of warmth, wine and perfect company relaxing Ben more than he could remember in a long time.

'What are you smiling about?' Ellie asked after a while, catching his smile.

There was the barest hint of a flush on his face as he shook his head, and he could only hope the shade from the brim of his hat was hiding it. 'Not much.'

Ellie tilted her head. 'Why don't I believe that?'

Ben pulled an innocent face that was so bad both of them burst out laughing.

'What?' she asked again.

'I just wondered if you might be thinking of taking any more lie ins.'

'Why?'

He started to grin. 'Because I enjoyed the view last time.'

Ellie looked across at him, eyes wide in surprise but laughter making them shine. Leaning over, she grabbed the hat from his head and pushed it in his face.

'Stop it!'

'Hang on, just give me a minute…' He made a thinking face and Ellie made another grab for the hat but he moved, catching her arms as she tipped off balance. She landed with a bump against his broad chest, and her half-parted lips were so close, so tempting, he could almost taste the sweet red wine on them.

Laughing, Ellie pushed herself back from him, turning away so that he wouldn't see the heat soaring through her show in her eyes. Oh, how she wanted to kiss that sexy mouth! 'What's in here?' she asked, burying her face in one of the brown paper bags from the saddle pouches. Ben collected himself and listed a simple lunch of bread, cheese and pate.

'Ooh! How very European!'

'Yeah, I know. Not very "cowboy", is it? The guys keep a stock ready for impromptu rides.'

'It might not be very cowboy, but it's great and I promise I won't tell anyone,' Ellie enthused as she broke off some of the fresh bread and spread the soft cheese over it before handing it to Ben.

'Thanks,' he said, in love with her enthusiasm and joy at the simple things, watching as she prepared some bread for herself.

'So, you up for this cookout tomorrow?'

Ellie bobbed her head up and down in agreement as she chewed her mouthful. 'Is that what Kate and Tyler went into town for?'

'Amongst other things,' Ben said without thinking.

Ellie raised her eyebrows at him as she bit off another mouthful. He lowered his eyes and she smiled at his reaction. He was such a contrast sometimes. Shy at the thought of hinting at what Tyler and Kate might be doing and yet teasingly brazen about enjoying the view of Ellie's naked silhouette against the window. She took another bite and leant back against the pack, closing her eyes and enjoying the simple stillness of the moment.

*

Sandy, Kate and Ellie caught up on the gossip, mostly about Kate and Ty as they leant against the hay bales.

'It's weird,' Kate pondered, 'He's so unlike the type I tend to go for.'

'Well, to be fair, there aren't that many cowboys in London. '

'No, but there are plenty of lawyers and not one I've met is like him. Anyway, you know what I mean. He's just, well, so different from anyone I've dated before.'

'Wow.' Ellie smiled.

'What?'

'You really like him, don't you? I mean…really like him.'

'No!' Kate laughed it off, her normal bravado returning, but it didn't fool either of her companions. She became aware of them both watching her. 'OK, yes. No. Oh, I don't know. It's ridiculous. Anyway, why are we talking about me? The Big Day is nearly here – we should be talking about Sandy! In fact, I demand we talk about you now!' Kate grinned, laughing as she linked her arms around her two friends.

As the women caught up on all the last-minute wedding plans, Ty, Ben, and his elder brothers joined in the baseball game that had begun. Spectacular, unnecessary dives became the norm as each one tried to outdo the player before. The others sat, rolling their eyes and laughing, Sandy advising that if one of them ended up breaking an arm before the wedding, then they should start running because she'd be breaking their other one!

Before long, the girls were persuaded to join in. Both Kate and Ellie scored a home run, garnering extra cheers for their efforts in true honoured guest style. Eventually the game ended and the food began. Chicken, pork and beef were in endless supply along with a mountain of fresh bread, potatoes, salads and of course, beans. These were no ordinary beans though. These were Mrs Danvers' special recipe, unlike anything you could buy and totally delicious. The evening wore on, the temperature dropped and darkness began to envelop the gathering in its slumbering embrace. Children snuggled down in blankets as they slept off the excitement of the day and voices became softer in deference to them.

Ellie was sat next to the wife of Joe, Ben's eldest brother, who held their ten-month-old baby whilst a toddler slept curled on her lap. Suddenly the toddler jumped in her sleep, waking herself, the little girl's face creasing as a small, tired and disorientated grizzle escaped. Ellie's neighbour leant down to soothe the startled toddler, but she refused to be placated by a gentle stroke, and the cry increased. Her mother turned to Ellie.

'Would you mind holding the baby for a little while?' she said, already holding him out to her.

'Of course not!' Ellie smiled, taking the precious bundle gently and looking down at him as he slumbered on, tucked against her body. She wrapped her own blanket lightly around him and gazed in wonder at the miniature features.

'So, after Saturday, there'll just be you left to sort out,' Ben's brother teased him. 'I don't suppose you'd consider taking him off our hands, would you?' Joe asked of Ellie. In the twilight, she blushed furiously.

'Thanks for the offer,' she replied lightly. 'But I'm pretty much content with just borrowing ones this size for the moment.' She indicated the snoozing bundle in her arms.

Ben shifted in his seat, prodding the campfire with a long stick. 'Yeah, I did that whole relationship-marriage thing before, remember, Joe. I think we all saw that it's definitely not my forte.' His smile made light of his heartbreak.

'You know, honey, not every girl's the same,' his mother cautioned him softly.

What Molly didn't know was, at that moment, Ben was thinking the exact same thing as he gazed across at Ellie cuddling his nephew, relaxed, happy and looking as if it was the most natural thing in the world. Or maybe she did.

As they sat talking in hushed tones, the child in Ellie's arms snuffled a little and issued a small cry. She rocked him gently, making soft soothing noises then looked up as his uncle rested his guitar on his lap and began to sing a lullaby. Tyler, comfortable against the hay bale, both arms wrapped loosely around Kate, harmonised perfectly. His new lover smiled up at the unexpected talent he had kept hidden.

They sang another and various members of the group joined them, uninhibited. To them, Ben was just Ben – their brother, son or friend. They loved him for who he was and had no worries that they would be judged on their vocal talents by a professional.

It was so clear to her why Ben loved it here, refusing to move closer to Nashville permanently, as many others in his position had done, or back to the city. It made things more tiring for him with the extra travel, but his view was that it was a price he was more than willing to pay for the knowledge that, after all was done, he got to come back here.

Ellie shivered a little against the chill of the night. Her charge looked so comfy and peaceful she hated to move but she kind of wished she'd put a jacket on before she'd got him settled. And then Ben was in front of her, bending down on his haunches and wrapping another blanket around her. She breathed in. He smelt of soap and hickory wood smoke from the fire.

'Better?'

She nodded, not trusting herself to speak. He looked into her eyes and, for a moment, she thought he was about to say something but there was nothing, save a short smile. Ben pulled his eyes away from hers and looked down at the child in her arms. As if sensing he was being admired, a pair of sleepy blue eyes opened, staring back into the matching pair of his uncle's. Bored, he closed them again and snuggled into the warm body holding him. Ben had never thought he'd ever be jealous of a baby.

'Cute little guy, huh?'

Ellie nodded. The light was low from the fire and a scattering of storm lanterns, but she thought she saw a glisten in Ben's eyes.

'Must take after his uncle,' he joked.

'Well then, let's hope he inherits his modesty from someone else.' He smirked at her riposte.

'Hey, Ben, play us something else.' A neighbour handed Ben's guitar across and he sat down on the hay next to Ellie and his sleeping nephew, settling the instrument on his leg. Softly, he began to strum a familiar chord before his deep voice brought in the vocals. Ellie turned to look at him but his eyes were lowered. She swung her gaze opposite at Sandy and Todd, and Sandy returned the smile. The song her brother was playing had been her and Ellie's absolute favourite 'slowy' growing up and they used to bug Ben to play it all the time. As a sweetener for having to move back to the UK, Ellie had been given piano lessons and the song had been the first thing she had learnt to play by heart, much to the disappointment of her classically trained piano teacher. Ellie caught the smile he gave across the firelight to his baby sister. For all the success and the millions of adoring fans Cheyenne had, Ben's truest fans were still those closest to him, and in return, it was their favourites he would always remember to play. The song finished and it was Ty's turn to entertain. Ben handed over the guitar and leant back against the hay, looking at Ellie.

'I haven't heard that in years,' she whispered.

'Well, Sandy would have kicked my butt if I hadn't played it but...' He paused. 'I thought you might enjoy it too.'

'I did. Very much so. Thank you.' He didn't look up but she saw the smile as he sat listening to his friend play.

It was late and people were exchanging warm embraces and kisses before disappearing home. Ellie was relieved of her charge and rewarded with a big hug.

'Maybe I can return the favour someday?' The baby's mother offered, a gentle smile on her face.

'Oh!' Ellie laughed. 'I don't think you have to worry about that!'

The older woman studied her for a second, before squeezing her hand. 'We'll see.'

After the last guests had gone, Ellie and Kate helped their hosts clear away the remaining evidence of the gathering.

'Thanks,' Ben said. 'We can move the bales back in the morning.'

'Y'know? I really wasn't planning to see all that much of the morning.' Tyler chuckled. 'Thought I'd take a tip from our guests here.'

'Oi!' Kate punched him on the arm, 'That was once and we were jet lagged.' Tyler was laughing and rubbing his arm as Kate demanded an apology.

'Fine. OK.' He put on a solemn face and took both her hands in his. Ben tried to hide a smirk. Ty was up to something.

Tyler cleared his throat dramatically and took a deep breath. Then, quickly, he bent and threw Kate over his shoulder in a fireman's lift and set off at a run for the house. The stillness of the night carried Kate's laughter and screams on the air as she begged Tyler to put her down. They watched the figures disappear into the darkness and after Kate's final threat that she was about to throw up apparently did the trick, silence reigned over Ben's land once more. He and Ellie stood in the pale light from a quarter moon.

'I hope he listened in time.'

'His own fault if he didn't.' Ben shrugged, smiling. 'Ready?' He held out an arm and Ellie linked hers through it and together they returned to the house at a far more leisurely pace.

Chapter 9

'Oh my gosh! I can't believe it's actually here!' Sandy was buzzing.

The wedding day had finally arrived and preparations had been well under way since a little before six that morning. All the girls' hair had been done and final touches were just being applied to made-up faces. The bride, three bridesmaids, maid of honour, hairdresser, a make-up artist and the mother of the bride all currently resided at the Danvers' family home. Ted Danvers had sensibly decided to escape the female mêlée and was spending the morning with his paper on the porch.

'OK girls, off we go.' Molly ushered her daughter's attendants out to the waiting car. Having already hugged her several times, she turned back for a moment to look upon her little girl, swathed in ivory silk, proud father stood beside her.

'Y'know, honey. When you used to dress up and pretend to be marrying that big old teddy bear, I thought it'd be a long time before the actual day came. Now it all just seems like the blink of an eye.'

'Oh, Mama, please don't. If I start crying now, I'm not sure I'm going to be able to stop.'

Molly smiled bravely and Sandy pointedly avoided looking at

her father. If he had tears in his eyes too, then she was gone for sure.

'I love you.'

'I love you, too.'

Molly kissed her daughter and hurried into the waiting limousine. Ellie reached out and held her hand as they all waved excitedly to Sandy.

*

At the church, Todd was like a jack-in-the-box, popping up and down in excitement until his older brother and best man finally warned him that if he didn't stay still, he was going to sit on him. Todd chuckled, the huge smile refusing to leave his face.

The ushers were at the door of the church doing a fine job of ensuring all the guests were seated on the correct side and happily installed with a service sheet and hymn book. Joe noticed the limousine draw up and tapped Ben on the shoulder, nodding at the approaching vehicle.

'Want to go see what kind of state Mom's in?'

Ben nodded, checked his pockets for Kleenex, and led the way to the car, arriving just in time to assist his mother and the attendants to alight.

Molly exited first and gave each of her sons a huge hug. Joe passed her a tissue and continued to help the other occupants of the car out into the warm sunshine. Bouquets came first, minded by Ben as Joe gallantly assisted the women, who then collected their flowers back from Ben. Ellie stepped elegantly from the vehicle, thanking Joe for his assistance. She turned to Ben to retrieve her bouquet.

'Hi.'

'Hi.'

'Suits you,' she teased, nodding at the flowers when he failed to return the bouquet. 'Oh!' He started, suddenly thrusting the posy back towards her.

'Thanks.' She took them and quickly joined the others, Ben watching her every movement.

'Hey, buddy.' Joe prodded his brother with another bouquet.

Ben took the proffered posy, passing it back as the final attendant exited the limo. Joe shut the door and stood back to await the arrival of his sister and father. A grin played around his lips.

'Why don't you escort Mom inside?' he nudged Ben, 'I can wait here for Sandy.' Joe stood near Sandy's attendants and threw his mother a knowing look.

Molly smiled at the tease and looked expectantly at Ben, who offered his arm. Stopping to give Ellie a quick hug, she retook her son's arm and together they walked sedately into the building, enjoying the moment and the weather.

'Ellie looks beautiful, doesn't she?' Molly said, her conversation casual.

Oh God, she did. She'd taken his breath away when she'd stepped from the car. The dress, the hair, the make-up. Sandy had chosen the perfect look for her attendants. Understated, but stunning. He tried not to think about Ellie's full mouth, treated to a soft, rose-coloured lip gloss, glistening in the sunlight, just waiting for him to…

'I said Ellie looks lovely.'

'Yes, Mom. Yep. They all look real pretty.' Her son might think he was being non-committal but she was his mother. And like the others, she had seen the look in his eyes.

Her smile widened as she patted Ben's arm. 'Yes, they do.'

Sandy looked amazing. As she entered the church, Ted puffed up with pride beside her, Todd's breath caught in his chest. Tears filled his eyes and choked his throat. She looked so beautiful, so perfect, so…Sandy. His Sandy.

*

123

Ellie was in full control until the reverend began recounting the couple's story and how Todd's accident a little over a year ago had very nearly prevented this happy event from ever transpiring but that God had blessed them all. That was it. She'd lost it. Mopping up what she could with her fingers, while trying not to ruin her make up completely, she motioned to the others for a fresh Kleenex. All hers had gone to Sandy's cousin who had been crying ever since she'd stepped foot in the church. 'I'm sorry. Weddings just do this to me. Even on TV,' she'd explained as she'd taken Ellie's last tissue.

None of the other attendants had any spare tissues so she turned discreetly to the pew behind her where Joe, his wife and children sat. Ben sat at the end, his three-year-old niece cuddled on his lap. Ellie motioned again for a Kleenex as Ben watched from the corner of his eye. Joe rummaged in his pockets and produced one, which Ellie took, making a relieved face at him.

'Thank you!' she mouthed, before returning her attention to the service.

The bells rang out as the couple prepared to leave the church and begin their new life as Mr and Mrs Winchester. Sandy had asked the ushers to escort the attendants out as the number was even, and she thought it would be a nice touch. The bride took her new husband's arm, followed by two sets of proud parents, who in turn were followed by Ellie and Todd's brother and the three other couples. Ben's cousin practically bounced up and down on his arm, as he watched the couple in front of him.

'How are we getting to the reception?' Cousin Lizzie asked, clinging to Ben's arm. 'Lord, I just love weddings!'

'Really?' Ben laughed. 'I'd never have guessed.' A stretch limo pulled around the corner.

'Oh my! Is that for us?'

'Sure is,' Joe stated, glancing behind him to see the fleet of town cars pulling up that had been hired to ferry the guests around so no one had to drive. The eight attendants filed in to the limo and each took one of the crystal glasses already set out. The car glided off and Ben opened the champagne, expertly pouring each glass.

'To Sandy and Todd,' the best man toasted.

'Sandy and Todd,' they all echoed.

A few minutes later, Joe peered out of the tinted window to see where they were.

'Still time for another!' he declared. Caught up in the joy and giggling, they all accepted. 'I have another toast.' The group waited expectantly for Joe, their glasses poised in readiness. 'To happiness,' he toasted. Unseen by the others, Joe's eyes met his youngest brother's above the glasses.

Ben gave the tiniest shake of his head and then tilted his glass towards his brother. 'To happiness.'

*

The reception was huge and extravagant as befitted the only daughter of a successful CEO and the son of a highly respected banker. After the dinner and speeches, the band began to play and called upon the newlyweds to take the floor for their first dance.

Ellie watched as Todd and Sandy gazed into each other's eyes, lost together in their happiness, oblivious to the hundreds of guests watching. For the moment, they were alone in the world, and Ellie felt almost as though she was intruding just by watching them. Pulling her gaze away, she studied the roof of the huge marquee that played host to the joyous occasion. Inky-blue swathes of luxurious fabric covered the roof, to which were attached hundreds of tiny, twinkling fairy lights. As the main lights had dimmed after the meal and speeches, a magical transformation occurred and the appearance was given of a venue open to the night sky.

'Would you honour me with a dance?' Ellie's eyes shifted from the make-believe sky to the handsome face of Ben Danvers. He was gazing down at her, showing that trademark smile, and looking dangerously attractive in the required black-tie dress code. He glanced over at the bride and groom as another song began.

Ellie followed his glance. 'They look so perfectly happy.'

He nodded in agreement, a sparkle in his eyes. Ellie wasn't sure whether it was there from happiness for his sister and his friend, the large quantities of champagne that they all seemed to be getting through or a combination of both. Whatever the reason, she was glad to see it.

'Y'know, people are watching – I was really hoping you wouldn't be mean enough to turn me down and leave me standing here looking stupid.'

Ellie considered him for a moment, a playful look in her eyes. Ben fought inwardly to control his desire.

'The way you look tonight, I don't think you'd be left standing alone for very long.'

The smile widened. 'Was that a compliment?'

Ellie blinked. 'Umm…' Her boldness deserted her as quickly as it had unexpectedly arrived.

'Well, if I look halfway decent, then maybe you'll dance with me?' he said, gently pulling her from the seat, before placing a hand on the small of her back and guiding her expertly through the throngs of people to a space on the dance floor. Ellie felt the heat of his hand through the soft silk of her dress, its touch causing longings she had never expected, and dare not admit to.

Reaching a spot on the floor, Ben moved, taking her hand with one of his as the other shifted slightly on her back. Together they began to move to the music. Ellie kept her eyes focused just above his shoulder, her gaze averted from his. With the joy, not to mention the champagne, of the day, Ellie was having a little more trouble corralling her emotions and the last thing she wanted to do tonight was make a fool of herself in front of Ben by showing them. She knew they'd pass…in time.

Ben looked down at his partner. She was quiet and seemed to be gazing off to a point in space.

'Hey?' he asked softly. 'Everything OK?'

Ellie looked up into his eyes, seeing the concern on his face. Concern for her. Without thinking, she squeezed his hand briefly and smiled the smile she'd been holding back. Relief flooded his face. 'Yes. Absolutely. So?' she began, directing him away from asking any more questions about her. 'Were you instructed to ask me to dance? Or is it that I'm the only one you don't think is mean enough to turn you down for a dance in front of people? I guess that's nice. Isn't it? I think? If that is the case though, what I said earlier is true. Pretty sure anyone you asked would say yes. I think you'd have to agree.'

'I think you think too much,' Ben laughed. 'And, no, that wasn't the only reason I asked you. Although, always a bonus to be able to use friendship as a preventative to getting shot down in flames in a room full of friends and family.' Ellie leant back a little to look up into his face.

She arched an eyebrow enquiringly. 'I see. And the other reason?'

'I asked you because I wanted to dance with a beautiful woman who wasn't mean enough to turn me down in front of everyone.'

*

OK, so he'd told her. Now she knew that his view of her was far more than just as Sandy's friend. He watched her reaction. She didn't look pleased. Actually, she looked kind of shocked…

Oh crap. Who was he kidding? Why the heck would she be pleased? Damn champagne! Right. He needed to rectify this, and quickly.

'And obviously, my sister would literally kick my butt if she discovered that I saw you sitting out and hadn't asked you.'

*

Ellie quickly pasted the smile back on her face. 'Oh! Ha! Yes! Yes, I think you're probably right.' She laughed and did her best to make it sound natural. For a moment, she'd thought – oh, what did it matter what she'd thought? He'd just clearly stated that she was a charity case. Sandy would indeed go nuts if her brother had left her friend sitting out, so he'd asked her to dance. Simple story.

'No probably about it.'

But wouldn't it have been lovely if he'd actually wanted to ask me, she thought to herself as they continued the dance. The orchestra finished the song and she began to pull away.

'Where are you going?'

'I'm going to sit down before I get my eyes scratched out for hogging you,' she laughed. Ben, as always, was completely oblivious to the many admiring glances he was drawing. She began to walk off but he caught her hand.

'Hey! So you are mean enough to turn me down?'

Before she could make a reply, an elegant blonde was upon them.

'Hello, Ben.'

'Binky?'

Ellie's eyes widened at the nickname. At least, she assumed it was a nickname.

'You remembered!' The woman laughed, laying a hand familiarly on Ben's arm.

'Hard to forget.'

Ellie took in the fabulous figure and beautiful face and could see why it would be hard for any man to forget her. Binky flashed him a million-dollar smile, as she turned to Ellie.

'Always the charmer,' she laughed.

Ellie smiled in agreement, gently pulling her hand from Ben's as the new arrival asked to be introduced.

'Excuse me.' Ben gave a shadow of a bow. 'Eleanor Laing, Bianca Jacobs. Known affectionately as Binky. We were at high school together.'

Ellie shook the offered hand. 'Actually, it's Bianca Meadows again now. Marcus decided he preferred a younger model so...' She left the sentence unfinished.

There was a moment's silence and Ellie suddenly felt rather awkward, aware that she herself was the younger model of this particular group.

'Well, if you'll excuse me.' She smiled. 'I'm sure you both have a lot to catch up on. It was very nice to meet you.'

'Aren't you going to ask me to dance?' Bianca asked when Ellie had left. Ben looked at the woman who had been his high school sweetheart. She was still beautiful, and, judging by the diamonds, a heck of a lot wealthier.

'Sure.'

'She seems very nice,' Bianca said.

'She is.'

'I didn't know you were dating a Brit.'

'I'm not,' he said, smiling down at her as he changed the subject.

Ellie grabbed another flute of champagne from a passing waiter and joined Ty and Kate at a table. They were sitting close and talking quietly to each other.

'Hello!' She plopped down heavily on the seat next to them. 'I've come to be a gooseberry and spoil all your fun.' A big grin was plastered onto her face as she took another big swig from the crystal.

'Oh, darling! You're not spoiling our fun!' Kate laughed, hugging her friend.

'Well, you know what they say,' Ellie began, keeping her tone

129

light and trying not to look back towards the dance floor. 'Three's a crowd and all that!'

'Nope,' Ty stated. 'Pretty sure three is a threesome.'

Kate's mouth dropped open and Ellie began to choke on her drink. Ty's attempt at a straight face failed abysmally.

'You're so bad!'

'I was kidding!' He laughed as he fended off Kate's abuse. 'Honey, believe me, you're more than enough for any man!' Kate coloured briefly and stopped trying to whack him with her clutch.

'What's so funny?' The trio looked up to see Ben and Bianca pulling up chairs to the table.

'I just—'

Kate placed a hand over Tyler's mouth. 'You do not want to know.'

Ty pondered a moment before grabbing Kate's hand. 'Actually, I think Ben might be interested.' Kate said nothing but her look said it all.

'OK. OK.' He sat back in his chair, still holding her hand and grinned.

'I see you haven't changed a bit, Tyler.' Bianca smiled down at the mischievous, handsome face.

'Nor you, Binky. Still as pretty as ever. Ladies—' he took in Kate and Ellie in his gaze '—please welcome the Prom King and Queen of senior year.' Ellie forced her smile to stay in place.

'Oh my! That was a long time ago!' Bianca laughed.

'And you don't look a day older,' charmed Tyler, his tongue planted firmly in his cheek, as she took the compliment just as light-heartedly. Ty turned his attention to his oldest and closest friend. 'It's just such a shame that time hasn't been so kind to you, buddy.'

Ben rewarded the insult with a thin smile.

'Oh, I don't know,' Binky interjected. 'I think he's looking pretty good.'

Ellie looked at Ben following the compliment. She couldn't

have agreed with his ex-girlfriend more. He did indeed look pretty good. Unexpectedly, he suddenly met her eyes and shrugged in embarrassment, a big smile creasing the handsome features. Ellie raised her glass, inclining it towards him with a slight movement and drained the remaining contents. She could only hope the pink tinge on her cheeks was put down to alcohol, rather than anything else.

'Ladies and gentlemen, the bride and groom are about to depart.'

Men and women bustled in different directions to form the leaving line. Slowly, Todd and Sandy made their way down, saying goodbye to all the friends and relatives who'd made the journey to celebrate their special day. As they got to the end, Ellie held out her arms and Sandy fell into the hug. Pulling back, her eyes glistened with tears and the gesture said more than a whole page of words ever could.

'I love you,' she said finally, a distinct wobble in her voice.

'I love you, too.'

'I'll call you when we're back.'

Ellie nodded as her throat tightened with emotion, seeing her friend's hand held in her new husband's, knowing how easily this happiness might have been snatched away. The newlyweds made their way to the limousine that was to take them to a luxury hotel for the night before they embarked on their cruise the next morning. A few close friends and family members hovered around the car to see them off, the rest of the guests remaining a respectful distance back.

'Take care of her,' Ben instructed Todd.

'I intend to.'

Ben nodded, pulling his new brother-in-law into a hug. He'd never quite been able to relinquish the blame for Todd's accident and still now just the thought of it made him feel physically sick. Having said her goodbyes, Sandy walked over to where her brother and husband stood chatting.

'Hey, Mrs Winchester.'

Sandy giggled, the name still sounding unfamiliar but also perfect. Her brother held out his arms and she went to him, wrapping her own tightly around his waist as she'd used to when she was little. Finally releasing him, she pulled back, eyes sparkling from the day's emotion and excitement, and champagne.

'Now,' she began, taking hold of Ellie's hand whom she had beckoned closer, while still retaining her brother's. 'I want you two to look after each other for the next two weeks, OK?' They nodded, smiling somewhat indulgently at her.

'I'm serious!' Even in her champagne-and-happiness-fuelled fuzz, Sandy saw through the look. 'You are two of the most special people in the world to me, and I need to make sure you're both going to be alright whilst I'm gone.'

Todd now joined his new wife. 'Honey, we'll only be gone three weeks.'

'I know, but I still have to make sure. You're know what they're like. They're both…vulnerab…able,' Sandy explained in a loud whisper, struggling a little with the last word. Todd met Ben's eyes over Sandy's head and shrugged, half in resignation, half in agreement.

'Now, you have to promise me.'

Ben leant down and kissed his sister

'I promise that we…' He swallowed, choosing his words. 'We'll look out for each other while you are gone.'

Sandy considered them both for a moment, accepting that this was the most she was going to get out of either of them. She rolled her eyes, gave them both a smile and let her husband help her into the limo.

The bright day had turned into a clear and cool night. Ellie's shoulders were bare against the chill and she shivered slightly as they awaited the departure of the limousine. Ben had shifted his position in order for others to have a better view and was now stood behind her. Suddenly, his arms were around her.

'My jacket's inside so this is the best I can do for the moment.' He leant close and, without turning, she could hear the smile in his voice. Ellie was glad of the low lighting so that the blush of pleasure she felt remained her secret. Placing a hand on his forearm, they both waved the car's occupants goodbye before watching it disappear into the night.

*

Kate slept on Tyler's chest and he draped an arm protectively around her in the back of the car as they travelled back towards the ranch. Ellie couldn't help the little pang of envy that crept over her – she looked so relaxed and happy. Kate was notoriously difficult to please when it came to men and she really seemed to like Tyler. Sneaking another glance, it was clear that the feeling certainly appeared to be mutual – his face and body looking as relaxed as her friend's. Ellie knew she should be happy for her friend – which she was! More than happy. It was just…was she jealous? Was that why she felt so uncomfortable? Her insides twisted at the ugly feeling, sensing it was partly true. Not of Kate and Tyler, as such. Tyler was lovely but he didn't set off any sparks for Ellie…not like someone else did. And perhaps that was the real problem. The moment Ben had wrapped his arms around her earlier, she had stopped shivering from the cold but a new sensation had replaced it, causing her nerve endings to tingle and respond in a way she knew could only lead to trouble. But for that moment – that one delicious moment she had allowed herself to just be – it had been wonderful. But she knew that was all it ever would, or could, be. A few moments to pretend.

God, she had a headache. The window was cool on her face as she leant on the smoked glass.

From across the seat, Ben watched from the corner of his eye as a frown creased Ellie's face, before she leant her head against the cool window and closed her eyes.

Chapter 10

It was half eleven when Ellie wearily padded downstairs the following morning. Although her body and pounding head told her to stay in bed, manners won over and she forced herself from the comfort of the duvet and into the shower. Pulling on a shirt and well-worn, faded jeans, she went downstairs to face the world.

The world, however, appeared to still be asleep – at least this little corner of it. Ellie mumbled to herself and debated about returning to bed. Deciding against it, she made a cup of instant coffee and headed out to the porch, taking a deep breath full of the fresh morning air. A small stack of blankets remained on the chair from the cook out and Ellie took one from the pile as she passed, laying it loosely over herself as she snuggled into the cushions on one side of the swing. Sipping the hot liquid, she waited for the caffeine to start hitting her system, in the meantime letting her mind wander freely. Eventually it found its way to Ben.

For some reason, Ellie's tired and slightly hungover brain seemed to decide that this was a good time to ponder, and maybe rationalise, why she was experiencing feelings for him now, after all these years. Ellie wasn't sure it was the best use of her time – and definitely not the safest for her heart – but right now she didn't have the energy to change the subject so she just let go and went along for the ride.

On the face of things, Ben's attraction was pretty cut and dried. One look at him could tell you that. He was utterly gorgeous and extremely sexy with both attributes magnified by the fact that he had absolutely no idea the effect he had on women. But then he'd always been like that, so why was she just now succumbing to his charms?

Aside from the few dates she'd conceded to go on, Kate was right in her comments about Ellie having been working all hours. Although the excuses she made about deadlines weren't lies, perhaps Kate and the others were closer to the truth than she wanted to acknowledge when they told her that she was hiding from reality in her job. Her painting and illustrations led her into another world. A world where she never had to think about violence and pain, a world that was gentle and peaceful where nothing and no one could hurt her. She took another sip of the coffee, wrinkling her nose as she realised she'd spent longer than she'd thought turning things over in her mind, letting the remains of her drink go cold. Placing it on a small table that stood to the side of the swing, she pushed herself off into a gentle rock with one foot before tucking it back under the blanket again. Quickly she stopped the swing again, the movement doing no favours for her hangover.

Looking out across the dancing wheat, golden in the morning light, Ellie felt relaxed and comfortable – even if she couldn't figure out why she seemed to be developing a crush on her host after decades of knowing him. Or perhaps that was the reason, pure and simple. For the first time in years, she felt at home – and the fact that it was Ben's home she'd finally felt able to relax in automatically tied him to the experience.

Or maybe it was simply that she was more than overdue a break and her brain was so exhausted it was just working out the kinks. Zak had been trying to get her to take a break for ages

135

and although she'd wanted to, and had even begun saving, something had held her back. Was it that she'd have time to think? Was is that very thought of not being immersed in something, allowing her mind the time to wander, that scared her? She'd come a long way, Ellie knew that, but there was still work to do. Did she hesitate because secretly she worried that a step away from her routine might result in a step, or even two, backwards? Whatever it was, she knew that Zak had been right when he'd insisted that taking more time off around the wedding was a good idea. Ellie sighed as she remembered how grouchy she'd been about it. She knew that her bad temper had partly been masking her concern and, as she cast her mind back to their conversation, could only hope that Zak knew that too.

*

'Ellie, you can't keep doing this,' Zak had said, a few months ago, having just heard her turn down the offer of a long weekend break to Barcelona.

'What?' she'd asked, already suspecting the answer.

'Hiding.'

'Hiding? And what is it that I'm supposed to be hiding from?'

'I don't know exactly.' Zak had shrugged. 'But you're doing a pretty good job of it.'

'Zak, I am not hiding. From anything! I just happen to enjoy my job. I would have thought that should please you.'

'Oh, El. Of course I'm happy you like your job, but I'd be even happier if you took a bit more time to enjoy yourself.'

Ellie had started to say something.

'Outside of work,' he'd clarified. 'You know. Take a holiday, get out a bit more, find a boyfriend.'

Ellie had looked up at him sharply, her skin pale but with two points of high colour on her cheeks. Zak knew the look and had winced as he waited for the explosion.

'Get a boyfriend?' She'd practically spat the words. 'I would have thought that you, of all people, would understand why that's not exactly a top priority on my list of things to do. And besides, contrary to popular male belief, it is actually possible for a woman to be happy without a man.'

'Oh, for Christ's sake, Ellie!' Zak had retorted, rolling his eyes. 'Don't go all bloody Germaine Greer on me. We're not talking about women in general. We're talking about you.'

'Well, I'm finished talking about me.'

'I'm not.'

'So that's it then, is it? You're giving up on any possibility of happiness. You get a couple of knockbacks…' He'd stopped for a moment. 'Sorry. Terrible choice of words. But…that's it? You're never going to try again?'

She'd opened her mouth to point out that she had actually been on a few dates but Zak had stopped her.

'I mean really try again – and mean it. I thought you were a true romantic?' Ellie had sighed, the fight leaving her. 'So did I.' She'd plopped down heavily on Zak's big comfy sofa. 'But when you're lying in a hospital bed, black and blue, with a tube up your nose, all those romantic notions seem just that little bit harder to keep hold of.'

Zak had sat down next to her then. 'El, Carl was an arsehole. But that doesn't mean every man you meet is going to be the same.'

'No, you're right. Another man might move on to Life Size Barbie.'

Zak had winced. Having persuaded her to come with him for a rare, quick drink after work recently, they'd run into Will who was now apparently dating a woman who definitely had a lot in common with the aforementioned doll, and looked a lot happier and relaxed than he had on his few dates with Ellie. It wasn't that she wanted him back, and she was truly happy that he'd met someone who could make him laugh and smile as she hadn't been able to do. But it was hard not to feel a jab of insecurity. Perhaps she would never find what he, and so many others, seemed to be able to. Whether that was because it just wasn't written in the stars for her, or because she refused to look up at those stars, she wasn't yet sure.

Zak held her gaze for a moment, before his shoulders slumped and he'd looked back at her, deflated. 'I'm making a bit of an arse of all this, El. All I'm saying is that you're too special a person to be on your own. You've got too much to give and you deserve to have someone who realises just how wonderful a woman you are, and knows how lucky he is that you choose to be with him.

'But all that aside, I'm worried about you. You need a break. Time to get away from work and relax. Totally. Why don't you take up Sandy's offer and stay at her brother's place for a while after the wedding? Must be pretty nice if he's a rock star. Probably got hot tubs in the bedrooms and mirrors on the ceiling!' He'd waggled his eyebrows.

Ellie had smiled at his silly faces but remained quiet. Zak was right and they both knew it. But knowing and admitting were two different things. Of course, she didn't want to give up on her dream of finding love – but then again, she wasn't sure if she could face the thought of meeting someone only to have it all go wrong again.

'He's not a rock star,' she'd said.

Zak had smiled, knowing that she'd go.

*

And so here she was. Sat on the "rock star's" porch, trying desperately not to give in to having a crush on him! Still, another couple of days and she was sure her feelings about Ben would be back to normal. And what a relief it would be to have everything just as it used to be, because that was most definitely what she wanted. Wasn't it?

'Penny for them?' Ben's deep voice jolted Ellie back to the present.

'Jeez!' She jumped, her hand flying to her chest.

'Sorry, didn't mean to startle you.' His voice was husky and raw from a mixture of alcohol and the late night. Ellie did her best not to notice it, or the melting effect it was having on her stomach. He was dressed in a plain white T-shirt, well-worn Levis, and bare feet, and looked just as hot, if not hotter, than he had last night in full black tie. 'You were miles away,' he observed, sitting down opposite her. She smiled at him briefly, wary of letting on that his observation couldn't have been further from the truth.

*

Ben sipped at the black coffee he had brought outside and wondered what she'd been thinking about. Sometimes, when she thought nobody was looking, he saw those big green eyes almost swim with sadness, and no matter how he fought against it, every day he was finding it more and more difficult not to pull her to him and tell her that she didn't need to be sad or frightened anymore. That he would do everything he could to make sure she never had to feel that way again. There was no denying it for him anymore – all he wanted was to love her, protect her, take care of her, and make her laugh. Most of all, he wanted to wake up every morning and look into that beautiful face, and see that same love reflected in her eyes. Ben took another mouthful of hot coffee and told himself to stop dreaming.

'Anything I can do?'

She shook her head. 'I'm fine.'

Ben nodded, although he remained unconvinced. He thought again how fragile she looked sitting there, wrapped up on his swing. Her hair, still damp from the shower, had made patches on the white shirt and a recalcitrant curl kept falling across one eye until she finally pushed it firmly behind one ear. Ben's mind wandered back of its own accord to the thought of Ellie in the shower. He forced a change of subject.

'Want another coffee?'

'That sounds perfect.' Ellie pushed off the blanket and padded back into the kitchen behind her host.

*

As Ellie smiled in return, the realisation hit her with a thud in her chest. Ben had just illustrated perfectly why she was suddenly falling for him. He was simply being nice to her. That's all it was. Bloody Zak! She'd been quite happy with her head stuck in the sand until he'd forced her to pull it out. And now, here she was, thousands of miles away, trying very hard not to fall in love with someone totally inappropriate just because he was kind and gentle and really, really sexy.

'How's your head?' Ben asked, battling with a filter paper, as they'd both agreed that instant just wasn't cutting it.

'Absolutely pounding. How's yours?'

'About the same.'

'Really?'

'You sound surprised.'

'I am!'

'I'm not,' he laughed, a deep and raw throaty sound which sent a shiver of heat through Ellie's body.

'I think we cleared the county of champagne last night. I expect nothing less.'

'I know, it's just that…' She stopped, suddenly feeling foolish.

'What?' Ben had been concentrating on pouring fresh coffee beans into the machine, their aroma filling the air, but he paused as he looked back at her, raising a brow in anticipation.

'It's just that I thought you'd be more used to all this, champagne, partying all night, that kind of thing.'

140

Ben laughed that laugh again. 'I'm afraid not. We're pretty boring when it comes to the party scene. None of the band are really party animals, much to my ex-wife's disgust.' He pressed a button on the machine and sounds of the water percolating filled the quiet. He leant against the counter and grinned. 'Besides, that's what happens when you get old. You want to be in bed by ten.'

'I guess that depends who you're with.' Ellie laughed then blushed immediately. The thought had popped into her head but she'd had no intention of it popping out of her mouth. And then it did.

Ben laughed and waggled his head in agreement as he watched the steaming, rich, black liquid begin to filter through.

'Besides, you're not old! Nothing like it.'

'I am compared to some of them out there.'

'So? Everything's relevant. You have experience that they could never have. Anyway, you're as young as you feel, and all that.'

'Or as young as the woman you feel according to some,' Ben replied, laughing. She raised an eyebrow and tried to look severe but Ben could see a smile tugging at the corners of that luscious mouth.

'That sounds like something Tyler would say,' she stated.

'It is something Tyler would say.'

'I hope you're not taking my name in vain.' A rough-edged voice came from the doorway. Kate appeared from behind Tyler, smiled a hello at Ben and went to stand by Ellie, linking her arm through her friend's.

Ellie studied her. 'You look like I feel.'

'I feel like I look.'

'Do you want something to eat?'

They all tried not to laugh as Kate visibly changed colour at the mention of food. She shook her head gingerly.

'Come on, let's get you some fresh air.' Ellie led Kate onto the porch and sat her on the sofa. Kate laid down and curled her legs up, snuggling in against the soft cushions as Ellie placed the blanket she'd been wrapped in earlier over her fragile friend. Bending down, she tucked the comforting, fleecy material around her friend. 'So, how was it?'

Kate opened one bleary eye. 'What?'

Ellie grinned. 'Don't even try to "what" me. I know you too well. You have that look and so does he.'

'What look?' Kate forced open the other eye in an effort to convey innocence.

'Kate.'

Kate paused before closing her eyes again, and smiled a lazy, satisfied smile before answering.

'Wonderful.'

More coffee arrived courtesy of their host, and Ben handed Ellie a mug before taking his own and sitting down next to her on the swing. Absentmindedly, he stretched out one long leg and began to rock the swing gently as Tyler tenderly woke Kate, who'd already dropped back off to sleep, and coaxed her into drinking some water. Ellie tried to ignore the movement of the swing. No good. Suddenly, she placed a hand on the leg causing the motion in the hope of ceasing it. Ben looked round at her touch.

'Would you mind not doing that just at the moment?' Her voice was soft, eyes closed in concentration as he felt the warmth of her hand on his thigh. She moved her hand to her stomach and opened her eyes to find him looking at her.

'Remind me never to drink that much champagne again. Ever.'

'I think we should make it a two-way pact,' he replied, holding out his hand to shake on the deal. Smiling, she took it.

'Agreed.'

'Why don't you go back to bed?' He paused, considering his words. She caught the look as he did so.

'What?'

'You look kind of green.' He chuckled as he said it.

'Wow! You really know how to sweep a girl off her feet, don't you?' Ellie said, pretending to be affronted. 'And anyway, did you look in the mirror today? You're hardly a pin up yourself!' she continued, knowing she was blatantly lying.

'Technically, he is,' Tyler reasoned, from opposite, his eyes closed.

'Well, there's no accounting for taste,' Ellie fired back and Ben laughed even harder. She grinned, confirming the tease before closing her eyes again.

*

Ben leant back and tried to think of a time with Cyndi when he was this relaxed, when she had teased him, or he had teased her and she hadn't taken offence. He couldn't. In fact, teasing wasn't really something Cyndi had known how to do – and she definitely hadn't known how to take it. Ellie rose from the swing, bringing him back to the present.

'Where are you going?'

'To sit on something that doesn't move,' she replied, looked pointedly at his leg, which had once again begun the gentle rocking motion as he'd drifted off into his thoughts.

'Oops. Habit.'

Ellie sat and tucked her feet up on the chair as Tyler roused himself once more.

'So, you going to see Bianca again?'

Ben and Ellie both looked up at the question. Quickly, Ellie returned her attention to finding a comfortable position in the chair, hoping that no one had seen her unintentional show of interest. She squidged herself around a little more before settling, tucking her knees under her chin, keeping her eyes averted and doing her best to give the impression that the current topic of conversation held little interest for her. Ben, however, still hadn't replied.

'Are you?' Tyler asked again, lazily opening his eyes just in time to catch the flash of annoyance Ben shot him.

Ellie fidgeted in the chair.

'You want to swap seats?' Ben asked, turning his attention to her, ignoring the question for a second time.

'No, I'm fine. Thanks.'

Ben watched her pretending to be comfortable on the chair in order to prove her point.

Tyler watched both of them, sure now that Bianca Meadows was most definitely not the woman at the forefront of his friend's mind. Ben had closed his eyes and turned sideways in the swing, his breathing soon becoming slow and steady as he caught up on sleep. Even Ellie seemed to have dozed off in what looked to be an extremely uncomfortable position.

Tyler worried about Ben when it came to women. Ever since Cyndi, he'd understandably become fiercely protective of his own feelings. Nobody could blame him for that – the woman had shredded the guy's heart. He'd told Tyler that he'd never leave himself open to that kind of treatment again, and Tyler believed him. For a while at least. But the irritated look Ben had just flashed him when he'd mentioned Bianca confirmed Tyler's suspicions of the last few days. Ellie Laing had found a chink in Ben's armour.

What bothered Ty though was that he wasn't sure she'd been looking for it. Hadn't they all heard her the other night at the cook out saying she wasn't looking for a relationship with anyone or anything, aside from her work. From what he'd heard of her history, Tyler didn't blame her. He had seen Ellie around as a kid but had only really got to know her this past week. She was kind, funny, intelligent and real pretty. And the effect she had on Ben was amazing. Tyler couldn't remember the last time he'd seen his friend relax and laugh like he had in the past days. Everyone – except perhaps the two in question – could see the reason. The question now was, would Ben admit it?

Ellie fidgeted and woke. Standing, she stretched her back, looking with a hint of envy at the happily sleeping figures of Kate and Ben. The latter had swung his legs up onto the swing and was now dozing with his feet hanging over one arm and a half-full cup of coffee resting on his chest. She leant over him, gently releasing his fingers from the mug. Collecting the other used cups, she stepped quietly into the house. As the screen door closed silently behind her, Ty wondered as to how she truly felt about Ben and whether she had spoken to Kate about it.

He returned his attention to the sleeping form resting her head on his lap and stroked away a stray strand of hair from her face. There was no reaction, and she slept on peacefully. Tyler smiled knowingly. Truth was they'd both been up pretty late last night, but, oh man, the lack of sleep had been worth it! Stroking Kate's hair, he smiled contentedly to himself and drifted back into a pleasant dream.

Chapter 11

'Elephant,' Ellie stated.

'Where?' She and Kate had just taken a swim in the warm pool and were now lying on perfectly cushioned hardwood steamer chairs, staring up into the deep blue sky of a Kansas afternoon.

'There.' She pointed. 'Look. There's a trunk, his ear's there, a tail and legs.' She paused for a moment, studying the cloud creation, its form changing slowly but constantly. 'You have to squint a little bit.'

Kate was unconvinced. 'A little bit?' she snorted. 'That leg's not even attached!'

'It's clouds.' Ellie turned her head, dropping her sunglasses momentarily down her nose. 'They're not known for their exact, scientific shapes.'

Kate grinned. 'I can't remember the last time I did this.'

'I can. Hyde Park last summer.'

'I guess sometimes it pays off to have a flaky job you can do in the park,' Kate teased.

In truth, she was in awe of Ellie's artistic talent and had often told her she envied her for being a member of that small, elite club of people who adored their job.

'Oh, ha ha. Actually I was on my lunch break.'

Kate looked over the top of her sunglasses at her companion. 'You never take lunch breaks.'

'I know. I don't think I was feeling well that day.'

'Either that or Zak physically locked you out of the building. Hey look, your elephant's turned into a hippo.'

'With a severe limp.'

'Anybody home?' Tyler's disembodied voice called.

'No,' Kate called back.

'Great. So it's OK to take Betty-Sue here upstairs and indulge in an afternoon of hot, steamy passion then?'

'Absolutely. Go right ahead.'

'Great. Thanks! See you in a few hours.'

Kate grinned, shaking her head. 'Daft sod.'

Ellie opened her mouth to say something, changed her mind and closed it again. Kate saw it.

'What?'

'What?'

'You did your "fish face" thing.'

'Excuse me?' Ellie spluttered with indignant laughter. 'I do not do a "fish face" thing!'

'Oh, sweetie. You totally do. When you're thinking whether to say something or not, or how to say it, your mouth opens and closes a little.' Ellie stared at her friend as she did an impression.

'Like a fish.'

Ellie was still staring.

'A very cute fish,' Kate tried helpfully.

'I do a fish thing and you never told me?'

'Well, then you might have stopped doing it.'

'My point exactly!'

'But if you stopped doing it, I wouldn't be able to tease you about it.'

'You're supposed to be my friend.'

'I am. That's what gives me the right to tease you about your funny habits.'

'You know, I'm really beginning to think I should have asked Zak to come with me instead.'

'Rubbish.' Kate dismissed the comment. 'We both know that you made exactly the right choice.'

'We do?'

'Of course we do. If I hadn't come, I wouldn't have met Tyler, which by the way, I am forever indebted to you for, much to my disgust. You know how much I hate owing anything to anyone.'

'So your coming here has been good for you. And Tyler, obviously. Enlighten me again as to why, from my own point of view, I made the right decision?'

'Sweetie. Gorgeous as Zak is, I really don't think he would have made such a good double date partner as me.'

Ellie rolled her head on the lounger to look across at her friend.

'Double date?'

Kate pushed herself up onto one elbow and peered down at Ellie. 'You can't tell me you don't like Ben.'

'Of course I like Ben. Just not in the way I'm assuming you mean.'

'Really?'

'Really.'

'You know I don't believe you for a minute, don't you?'

'Not my problem.'

'El—'

'Anyway,' Ellie broke in, 'even if I did like him, in that way, which I don't—' Kate gave a brief eyebrow raise which seemed to indicate she'd yet to change her belief '—we've been here over ten days and he's not done anything to suggest – to indicate – anything else on his part.' Ellie struggled with her reasoning words, desperate to keep her tone light even though she knew in her heart they masked disappointment. 'He's been the perfect gentleman. I'm still just his little sister's friend to him. Nothing more.'

'So why was he enjoying the view so much when you stood

in front of that window in your dressing gown the day after we got here?'

'Because…' Ellie hesitated a moment before finishing. 'Because he's a bloke!' Kate cracked into laughter.

'Oh God. Did I just do that thing? I did, didn't I?' Ellie said as Kate began laughing 'Oh!' Ellie responded before shoving the cowboy hat Ben had given her the day of the ride over her face.

It was in this position that Ben and Tyler found them, having unloaded the provisions they'd bought in town.

'She taking a siesta?' Tyler inclined his head towards Ellie as he settled himself next to Kate.

'No. I think she's trying to sulk but she's not terribly good at it I'm afraid.' Kate leant across, removing the hat to find a broad grin hiding beneath.

'Do you mind?' Ellie grabbed the hat back, 'I'm trying to be in a huff here. It's a very fine art and takes a great deal of concentration.' Her voice was muffled beneath the canvas.

'Why is she sulking?' Ben's voice joined the conversation.

'I took the mickey out of her for that fish face thing she does when she's thinking sometimes.'

'Oh, the…thing?'

Ellie snatched the hat off in time to see Ben also doing an impression of her thinking process.

'Ben!'

He stopped mid-fish. 'Oh, honey,' he chuckled, perching next to her, his hip close to hers. 'You've been doing that for as long as I can remember.'

'I have?'

'Yep.'

'I'm going to have serious words with your sister about this. Honestly. I can't believe that I have a habit of making fish faces and nobody even thinks to tell me I look ridiculous!'

Ben smiled down at her. 'Actually it's kind of cute.'

At Ben's words, Kate put on her best 'I-told-you-so' face and gave Ellie a teasing, smug look. Ellie ignored it and went back to hiding her embarrassment behind the hat.

'Did you get everything you wanted in town?' Kate asked.

'Oh yeah! And more besides. Ty's worse than a woman when it comes to shopping.' The grin Ben was sporting disappeared as he turned to see Kate's steely glare fixed on him.

'No offence,' he said, flashing a trademark smile.

'Yeah, yeah. I bet that smile gets you anywhere.'

Behind her hat, Ellie blushed as the thought of where it would get him with her pounced unbidden into her mind.

'Honey, can I talk to you a minute?' Tyler's voice was unusually serious.

Ellie peeped out to see Kate looking at him, catching the brief flash of uncertainty on her friend's face.

'Of course.'

Tyler helped Kate to her feet, and they walked slowly down the garden, and out towards the paddocks.

Ellie came out from behind her hat. 'What's going on?' Ben shrugged his shoulders, avoiding her eye.

'Ben?' she said, slowly.

The others had now disappeared from sight and Ellie was struggling to push visions of Tyler dumping Kate from her mind. Obviously they would have to leave right away. Poor Kate! It was so unusual for her to find someone she was really happy with, and the two of them had hit it off right away. From what Ellie had seen, Tyler was as smitten as Kate so what was the sudden problem? She glanced over at Ben who was now lying on his side, facing her, propped up on one elbow reading his paper, still studiously avoiding her questioning.

'Oh my God!' Ellie shot up from her seat as Ben looked round from the sports section at her sudden exclamation. 'He's married, isn't he?'

Ellie was furious at Tyler for leading Kate on like that. And she was even more furious at Ben for letting him. How could he?

They were supposed to be friends. Ellie jumped up from the lounger, grabbing her sarong and hunting under the chair for her Kickers. She had to go and find the other two. Kate was going to be devastated.

Ben caught her wrist loosely. She spun around, glaring down to where he still sat, his body relaxed, his face laughing.

'Whoa there, firecracker!' His calm manner only infuriated her more and she snatched her hand away.

'Don't you dare "whoa there" me! I'm not one of your horses! How could you? I thought you had more morals than that. How could you, of all people, do that to her? To me?'

Ben watched, incredulous at Ellie's outburst. She was red in the face as she sat down again, struggling viciously with her laces. The more she struggled, the more knots she put in them. Ben reached over, took the shoe from her, and patiently set about the knots. Ellie made to take it back but he stopped her with a look. They sat in silence, Ben working methodically away whilst Ellie fumed in impatience.

'Tyler's not married,' he said, finally, handing back the first shoe.

'He's not?'

'Nope.'

Ben began work on the second set of laces.

'So – so what's going on? Why is he dumping Kate?'

'Who said he was dumping her?' He frowned, turning to look at Ellie.

'Well, no one. I guess I just assumed…' She trailed off under Ben's gaze. Finishing the task, he handed back the other shoe then looked away from her, studying the distant scenery.

'Ty's got to go out of town for a few days. Some meeting has come up that he has to be at. Bearing in mind he doesn't want to be away from Kate for a moment if he has to, he's asking her to go with him.'

Silence descended on them. Uncomfortable, oppressive. Ellie

pulled on her shoes, suddenly feeling awkward and ashamed.

'Where is the meeting?' she asked quietly.

Ben shrugged, his focus apparently now back on the paper in front of him. 'Dallas, I think. I'm not sure.'

In truth, he wasn't taking in a single printed word. All he could think of was the accusation Ellie had levelled at him – that he had lied. Not only did it make him mad, more than that, it hurt like hell. He turned the page and the paper crackled in the silence.

'Of course she won't go,' he stated.

'She won't?'

'Unlikely.'

'Why not?'

'Because if she did, that would mean you were left here alone with me and, if Kate is of the same opinion of my character as you appear to be, who could blame her?' Standing quickly, he began to stride back to the house, the paper gripped in his fist.

'Ben!'

He didn't stop.

'Ben!' Ellie called again, hurrying after him and grabbing his arm as she caught up. 'I'm really sorry.' His blue eyes focused out across the fields, over the top of her head, pointedly avoiding looking down into her pained face. 'Apology accepted,' he replied perfunctorily before turning back towards the house. Right now, he just needed to get away, accepting that he wasn't necessarily being his most reasonable self. He knew Ellie was desperately trying to apologise and he wasn't making that easy for her, but he couldn't help it.

Knowing the circumstances of his own failed marriage, how could she ever have thought that of him? Maybe the fact that it was possible for her to even think that he would condone a married man to take advantage of her friend meant that she didn't know him as well as he'd thought she did – or maybe as well as he'd hoped she did. Of course he knew, and accepted, her own experience would always help shade her opinions, but stupidly, he'd thought that when it came to him—

'Ben. Please wait!' Ellie's soft voice interrupted his thoughts. He stopped. This certainly wasn't how he'd hoped the vacation would end but he had a feeling it was going to anyway. Ellie came around and stood in front of him, looking up into his tense, handsome face. His blue eyes, normally so warm, were like ice, and Ellie shivered involuntarily. Ben gripped the paper in his hand tighter to prevent himself from stepping closer and wrapping her in his warmth. He knew it was pointless to try and deny it to himself any longer – he was in love with Ellie Laing. In fact, Tyler had finally got him to admit it that afternoon as they'd loaded the truck up with groceries, although he'd been sworn to secrecy, even from Kate. Not that any of that mattered now. For a few wonderful hours, Ben had looked forward to the hope of being alone with Ellie for a few days, just enjoying her company and the time together. He'd even entertained the possibility of finally telling her how he felt, this time without backing out, having been spurred on by the revelation from Tyler that, according to Kate, Ellie had feelings for him too. He almost laughed to himself. Man! Had they read that wrong. Sure, she had feelings for him but apparently those included the fact that he was a liar who thought nothing of stamping over friendships and condoned adultery in his own house. His mouth set in an angry line as he turned it all over in his mind.

It killed Ben to think that she'd thought that. A sharp tone wrapped around his heartache and he saw the words hit home and sting. He returned his gaze to the distance, unable to bear the hurt in Ellie's eyes.

'Ben, please don't be like this. I'm so sorry! I jumped to conclusions and got defensive, and I shouldn't have. I never meant to insult you…or hurt you.' Big green eyes searched his icy blue ones for a flicker of forgiveness.

'Tyler's my oldest friend, Ellie. It's not very pleasant to hear someone, least of all you, attacking his character.'

Ellie noticed Ben's accent had thickened, and recognised the trait from Sandy as a bad sign. 'I know,' she said, her heart heavy, and painful in her chest. 'I truly am sorry. I just didn't want Kate to get hurt.'

'Well, that's admirable, Ellie, but you shouldn't assume that every man you meet has as bad a character as some you've known.'

Ellie swallowed hard, knowing he was right. That was exactly what she'd done. Despite having known Ben for years, she'd lumped him and Tyler in the same pile as Carl, and God knew neither of them deserved it.

'I know,' Ellie said simply, her voice thick with restrained tears, knowing that her wonderful holiday, as well as any fanciful dream she might have entertained in the safety of her own mind was well and truly over. Kate would go to Texas with Tyler and she would go home. She'd had the opportunity of spending the next few days alone with this man, this man she was so desperately trying not to fall completely in love with, and she'd blown it by overreacting before she knew any facts, and basically calling him a liar. It was no wonder he didn't even want to look at her. She looked back up, attempting a smile.

'It's a bad habit I have.'

Ben pulled his eyes away from the vista. Tyler and Kate were walking back up the garden to meet them, but Ellie hadn't yet noticed. Her eyes were on him, searching his face, looking for the smallest sign of relent. Had she looked like that at that Carl guy, desperately tried to placate him so that he wouldn't beat her again? He thought back to the state she'd been in when he and Cyndi had walked into the kitchen that fateful day – her body, heart and confidence all beaten. As much as he tried, there was no way he could ever understand entirely what she'd been through. He knew she'd had therapy, and still went from time to time. Ellie was doing her best to put her past behind her but, he

154

knew there was always going to be something in there that might cause her to think, to stammer in some situations. He had to accept that. And help when he could. Ben nodded at her remark, his heart breaking at the relief her face showed when he returned her a small, wry smile.

'Hey!' Tyler's cheery greeting alerted Ellie to their presence, and Ben watched from the corner of his eye as she composed herself for the return of their friends, both of them noticing how uncharacteristically nervous Kate looked. Ellie realised Ben was right. Kate would see the trip as abandoning Ellie, despite the tease about the resulting opportunity of her and Ben having the house to themselves.

If only she knew. Ellie groaned inwardly. If ever there had been a flicker of attraction on his part, she had well and truly doused the flame now.

'I expect a souvenir,' she stated before either of them could say anything. Kate opened her mouth and looked at Tyler, who looked at Ben.

Ben shrugged. 'It came up.'

Leaving the men to chat, Kate linked arms with Ellie and they walked together towards the house.

'I'm not sure this is right,' she said, concern on her face.

'Don't you want to go?'

'Yes. No. Yes, I want to go, but no, I feel awful leaving you here.'

'Hey! I keep telling you, I'm a big girl now.'

'You know what I mean. It's the worst kind of person that goes on holiday with a friend and then abandons her because she's met a man.'

'Yes, it can be. But that's not the case here.'

'It's not?'

'No. Don't be silly. I think you should go.'

'Really?'

'Definitely.'

They headed into the kitchen and began making a fresh pot of coffee.

'Ellie?'

'Mm?'

'I'm sort of thinking of staying on out here for a while.' Ellie gave her friend a quizzical look before reaching up for another mug. 'Tyler's asked me to move in with him.'

Ellie dropped the mug, jumping as it smashed into pieces on the quarry tiled floor, the sound resonating somewhere in her memory, her muscles tightening in response. She snapped her thoughts back to the present.

'Great. I hope that wasn't a favourite mug.'

Kate bent down and swept up the smaller pieces as Ellie threw the larger remnants in the bin.

'Somehow, I think Ben will forgive you,' Kate teased. Ellie pulled a face, and Kate stopped sweeping. 'What happened?'

'Nothing.

Kate didn't move. 'Well, that's clearly a lie.'

'Honestly. It was nothing, really.'

'What was nothing?'

'Can we get back to you, please?'

Kate wasn't convinced but pushing Ellie on this clearly wasn't going to get her anywhere.

'Are you really thinking of moving out here to live with Tyler?'

'I'm seriously considering it as a possibility.'

'After two weeks?'

Kate shrugged, but her smile gave her away.

'Are you feeling OK? You're normally the sensible one!' Ellie laughed, her questioning light-hearted. If Kate was considering this, she'd already thought it through. Kate had never made a move in her life that she wasn't totally sure of.

'I know. It just feels so…right. I feel like I've known him forever.'

Ellie smiled at her friend, almost glowing with contentment,

156

before glancing out to the porch to where Tyler and Ben sat, apparently deep in discussion.

'You know, I think Ben might need some TLC when we're away.'

Pouring the coffees, she considered telling her that it was a bad time for a tease about Ben but something in Kate's voice caught her attention, and she looked round, a question in her eyes. 'Apparently they ran into his ex-mother-in-law in town.'

'And?'

'Well, nothing really. I mean, all rather amicable I think. Except...' Kate paused, looking out the window to where the two men still sat.

'Except what?'

'His ex-wife is pregnant.'

'Cyndi? She can't be. She told Ben the doctors said she couldn't have children.'

'Yes, well, her mother rather put her foot in it about that, so I understand. It appears that Cyndi told her family the reason they weren't getting pregnant was because of a problem that lay in Ben's department. He was, she informed them, a little touchy about it so they were instructed never to mention families or children when they visited.'

'Her mother told them all this?'

'Not a subtle woman it would appear.'

'Apparently not.'

'Tyler said Ben barely said a word on the way home. When they got here, Tyler tried to talk to him, but he got out, said "Can't change the past" or something like that, and that was it.'

'And then I finished off his afternoon perfectly by completely pissing him off.'

'You did? How?'

Ellie let out a huge sigh and slid down the cabinet to sit on the floor. Kate joined her, coffee mugs to the side of each of them on the tile.

'What did you do?'

Ellie pulled a face, giving Kate a sheepish look. 'When Ty took you off, I thought he was going to dump you and…sort of… jumped to conclusions.'

'What conclusions?'

She let out a sigh. 'That he was married.'

'Oh, Ellie!' Kate exclaimed.

'I know, I know. It just came out and then I accused Ben of covering for him and lying to us both.'

'And he was less than impressed?'

'You could say that. Understandably.'

Kate reached out and took her friend's hand.

'Anyway, I said I was sorry, and he said he accepted my apology but I'm pretty sure it was more out of politeness than from any real desire of forgiveness. I messed up big time.' The girls sat in silence for a moment as the day faded around them.

'Do you want me to stay?'

'No, it's fine. It's a big enough place to avoid one another if needs be, and if it's not working, I can just change my flight to an earlier one.'

'Ben won't want you to do that.'

Ellie shrugged her brows. 'You didn't see his face.'

'I don't need to, to know that.' Kate's tone was definite. When do you go?'

'Tomorrow.'

'I'll miss you.'

'Me too.'

'Liar.'

'I'm not lying. Tyler may be gorgeous, kind, funny, generous—'

'Yeah, yeah.' Ellie made a 'wind it up' motion with her hand.

'OK, he may be wonderful, but that doesn't mean I won't miss you.'

'Good. I'm glad to hear it.'

They finished their drinks sitting on the kitchen floor, chatting aimlessly as the room darkened around them. They talked about Kate's upcoming trip to Texas with Tyler before moving on to trying to understand how Cyndi could lie about something so important as children to her husband – and what that knowledge now might do to Ben.

*

The four of them sat down to a late dinner and both women retired early, leaving Tyler and Ben to return to their well-worn discussion spot on the porch.

'So,' Tyler asked. 'What was going on between you and Ellie when we got back to the garden this afternoon. And don't say nothing because you know that's not going to fly with me.'

Ben leant back against the porch support. The air was clammy out here now, with a bank of dark storm clouds building to the west. The pale moonlight of earlier was now hidden and the wind creaked and whispered through the trees. On the porch, tiny whirlwinds appeared, catching the rising dust and odd leaf in their pull.

'We had a fight. Sort of. If that's what you can call it.'

Tyler raised an eyebrow in surprise. 'Why don't you tell me what happened and then we'll see what I call it.'

Ben let out a sigh, relaying the argument to him.

'She was doing her best to apologise and I just stood there, making it as damned hard as I could. I got on my moral high horse and accused her of judging every man by her ex, but I was doing the exact same thing. All I could think about was Cyndi and her lies.'

'Don't you think you're being a bit hard on yourself? What you found out today would throw anybody a curve.'

'It's no excuse, Ty. Ellie's not Cyndi and I treated her badly today.'

'I doubt that.'

Ben pulled a face and began peeling the label from an empty beer bottle. 'I tell you man, if there was ever any chance for me with Ellie, I totally blew it out of the water today.'

Chapter 12

Ellie listened to the rain as it hammered against the window-pane. Flinging an arm out, she grabbed the clock, pulling it to face her – 3 a.m. She gave a groan, turning over just as a brilliant flash illuminated the room. Pushing back the bed clothes, she got up and padded over to the window, waiting for the thunder that would soon follow. Pulling the curtains, she peered out into the darkness as the sound boomed, echoing around the land. Suddenly, the sky was speared through by a huge fork of lightning that seared the ground several miles away.

Grabbing a sweater and pulling it over her pyjama top, Ellie crept quietly down the stairs. Ever since she was a child, thunderstorms had fascinated her and the lure to be outside was too strong to ignore. Maybe it was something to do with the feeling of experiencing nature at first hand. Whatever it was, these huge Midwest storms had always drawn her like a magnet. Her mother had worried about her daughter's attraction to these untamable forces but her father understood and soon after they'd moved to the States, he'd sat Ellie down and had a big talk about safety in order to help pacify her mother's nerves – a little at least. After that, she and her dad would share the storm together. Sheltered in the porch, they would wrap up in a blanket and watch the

161

spectacle, feeling both at one with nature and in total awe of it.

Ellie pushed the screen door open, then turned, closing it gently behind her. She was sure the storm would probably have woken the others, but she didn't want anyone to feel the need to come and check on her if they heard her moving around. A movement on the dark porch made her jump, and a chill rushed through her.

'Ellie?' Lightning cracked across the sky, illuminating the porch momentarily. Ben sat on the swing in shorts and a T-shirt with a blanket draped around his shoulders. 'What are you doing down here?'

Ellie hovered where she was, suddenly uncomfortable. Ben had been polite to her at dinner but nothing more. In fact, he'd been quiet generally and she knew the news about Cyndi couldn't have washed over him as he'd tried to pretend with Ty. None of them were fooled.

It was no secret that having a family was Ben's dream. He'd also said he would take his time, not wanting to rush into anything, wanting his family when he had it, to be close and not just one he'd see every other weekend. His relationship with Cyndi had been quick, but they all knew he'd been so sure. She'd made him feel that she was the only one for him. And now this? Another betrayal, maybe even deeper than the first. Anyone who knew him had to know how deeply this new information would have cut into his heart. Ellie hovered by the door, hesitating in her answer as she realised that having houseguests at the moment probably wasn't his first choice after the encounter in town.

'Ellie? Are you sick?' Her eyes were adjusting to the darkness and she saw him move on the swing.

'No! No, I'm fine. I came out to watch the storm, but I didn't realise you were here. I'm sorry, I'll leave you in peace. See you in the morning.' She turned to re-enter the house.

'Wait!'

Ellie turned back at Ben's call. He was standing now and indicated the spare seat on the swing.

'There's plenty of room,' he said. 'I mean, if you wanted to stay, that is.' A huge clap of thunder prevented her from answering. Ben took the opportunity to consider his earlier behaviour. 'I'd be glad of the company,' he added.

OK, so it was kind of a sneaky trick. Having said that, he knew Ellie was too polite to leave now. Even if it meant she stayed here with him for just a little while, it might give him the opportunity to see if he could work on getting that easy feeling back between them. It had only been a few hours and he was already missing that – quite how much was something he was still trying to get his head around. Ben sat back down on the swing as she made her way cautiously towards it, carefully avoiding bumping into the other furniture. As she got closer, he reached out his hand to help guide her, but she let go as soon as she sat down.

'Thanks,' she replied.

He saw the brief smile in the darkness but her body language was tense. In silence, they sat and watched as the storm gathered nearer and nearer, the thunder becoming more deafening with every roll.

'I used to see you and your dad out on the porch watching the storms when you were a kid,' Ben said, eventually.

Ellie smiled, her body relaxing as her mind revisited the memory, all the while becoming more and more absorbed in the wonder of nature around them. 'I always loved those times. We'd sit and talk about anything and everything – books, art, what was in the news. My dad always treated me like a grown up.'

She could hear the smile in his voice when he replied. 'Ah, but you'll still always be his little girl.'

Ellie laughed at his accuracy. 'That's exactly what he says.' She paused. 'I never thanked you all for not telling them about…things. I mean, after Carl…I know how close your mum and dad are with mine, and I know it was a lot to ask of them. Of all of you.'

Ben spread his hands. 'You had your reasons.'

'I did. But it was still a lot to ask and I appreciate your confidences.'

'I take it they know now?'

'They do.'

'Can't have been an easy conversation.'

'No…no, it wasn't.'

Ben heard her voice thicken at the memory.

'But we got through it, and although they were hurt that they felt I couldn't come to them when I needed them, they understood my reasons.' She turned a little in the seat, facing him more in the darkness. 'I just couldn't take the risk. Of Dad seeing me like…like you saw me, when he was still recovering from all the surgery. I couldn't do that to them. As much as I wanted to be with them, I couldn't.'

'You don't have to justify anything to me, Ellie. Ever. You did what you did for your own good reasons. I'm just glad that you chose to come here. That our family was your next choice.'

'It always has been.'

This time it was his turn to hear the smile in her voice.

They lapsed back into silence as the storm crashed and flashed around them. The wind had really picked up now and was whipping around their legs. Ellie shifted position and tucked hers up beneath her chin.

'You warm enough?'

'Uh-huh,' she said, trying to control the shiver.

Ben chuckled. 'You sure are one terrible liar, you know that? Here.' He stood her up and wrapped the blanket around her.

'No. Really, Ben, I'm fine. You have it.'

'You're not fine.' He took a hand in his own. 'Your hands are like ice.'

'They always are. Really. I'm alright, honestly.'

'Look, just let me take care of you for a minute, will you?' In the shadows, he saw Ellie's head jerk up to look at him. He was glad it was too dark for her to see his expression. The words had come out without thinking. She didn't reply but let him fix the blanket around her without resistance, apart from insisting that, as it was huge, he share it. He smiled down at her in the darkness, agreeing and soon they sat huddled together, watching nature's fireworks as the storm centred over the house.

As it began to pass, conversation became a possibility once again, and they both started to speak at the same time.

'You go,' Ben invited.

'Thank you. I just wanted to say thanks again for letting us stay out here. It's been wonderful.' She paused for a moment. 'And for tonight. This. It was really nice. I haven't done this in a long time.'

'My pleasure.'

'Not everyone likes to sit out in a storm.'

'Nope.'

'I didn't realise you did.'

'Well, I couldn't go letting you know all my secrets on the first day now, could I?'

Ellie giggled and turned to face him as the first pale streaks of the dawn began to break across the sky. 'Anything else I should know?'

Ben glanced down at her, a cool smile on his face. *Apart from the fact that I'm completely in love with you and want you to stay out here with me forever? Nope, nothing at all.*

'No, not for the moment.'

Her gaze hovered on his face for a moment, searching, before the smile widened.

'OK.'

The two sat together watching the dawn break slowly over the silent land, freshly cleansed from the storm. Ellie's eyelids were heavy and it was so comfortable here, snuggled under this blanket in the chill of the early morning, the heat of Ben's body keeping her warm as she leant against his side under the soft fabric. If she wanted to, she could just—

'You should get back to bed.'

'Huh?' Ben's deep tones clutched her from the very edge of sleep. She'd slipped further down the swing in her doze and was now looking sleepily up at her host, completely unaware of the effect she was having on him – big, innocent eyes struggling to focus, hair pulled back into two schoolgirl plaits, mussed up where she'd been lying. But Ben knew the body leaning against his arm and thigh was no schoolgirl's.

'Come on,' he said, gently easing Ellie to her feet, wrapping the blanket around himself as he stood. 'Get back up and grab some rest. You'll only be grumpy in the morning.'

Ellie stopped walking nearly causing Ben to bump into her. He stepped back, as she tilted her head round and met his eyes.

'I'm not sure I like the fact that you know all my bad habits.'

Ben pulled a wry grin. 'Oh, I'm sure you've got some I don't know about yet.'

Ellie's gaze dropped to the floor as she remembered her earlier behaviour. 'You mean like verbally attacking decent people without due cause.'

'I've gotta admit, that was a new one on me.'

'I am really sorry about that,' she replied, looking up, her expression thoroughly miserable.

'I know you are. And just to let you know, I'm normally far more gracious at accepting apologies than I was this afternoon, so let's call it quits and forget about the whole thing, OK?'

'OK.'

'Come on, you. Upstairs.' Ben softly turned her by her shoulders, hustling her upstairs and back to her room.

'You won't let Kate and Tyler go without waking me, will you?' she checked, hesitating as they reached her bedroom door.

'No, I won't. Now will you go get some sleep?' Ben whispered, an exasperated expression on his face. Ellie stifled a giggle.

'What's so funny?'

'You.'

'Gee, thanks.'

'No.' She touched his arm in reassurance. 'What you just said about getting some sleep. You used to say it sometimes years ago when Sandy and I wouldn't stop talking.'

'Many times!' Ben corrected, raising an eyebrow. 'Lucky for you I'm a patient guy, huh?'

'See you in the morning.'

'It is the morning. Remember that dawn thing…'

Ellie smiled a sarcastic smile at him, stuck her tongue out and disappeared into the bedroom, the door closing softly behind her. Ben stared at the panelled door for what felt like an age. His whole being urged him to follow her and once again look down into those eyes, be moments away from those lips, and to well and truly muss up that hair. Quickly stepping back from the door, he took a deep breath and forced himself on into his own room. There he threw off the blanket that had been disguising his desire for her and stepped straight into a cold shower.

Chapter 13

'You look tired. Did you sleep OK?' Kate asked over a late breakfast.

'Not really. I watched the storm.' Ellie bit into a piece of soft, freshly baked bread.

Tyler looked up, crestfallen. 'There was a storm?' He turned to Kate. 'And there I was thinking it was me making the earth move for you.'

Kate patted his cheek affectionately. 'Never mind, darling. There's always next time.' She placed a kiss on his cheek to soften the tease. Ben and Ellie exchanged glances as she took another mouthful of the delicious bread. Kate turned back to her friend.

'Where did you watch the storm from?' she asked, suspicion now lacing her voice. Ellie indicated the window with her head as she chewed.

'Outside!' Kate's voice shot up an octave. 'Ellie! I promised your mum I wouldn't let you wander out into any storms. You know that whole thing still freaks her out.' She turned on Tyler. 'This is your fault!' Tyler looked suitably surprised at the accusation as Kate turned back to Ellie. 'You're going to get yourself struck by lightning one day!'

Ellie was manfully chewing on a piece of crust as Kate reeled

168

off other dangers of sitting out in a storm. Ben and Tyler looked on in bemusement as Ellie finished her bread and listened to her friend. Judging by her calm reaction, this was a speech she'd evidently heard before. Ben took a guess it had probably been from her mum, who had relayed it all to Kate. He reached for a slice of the bread.

'Ellie wasn't in any danger. She was only on the porch, and I was with her.' Tyler, who had leant back in his chair during the scene caught Ben's eye and raised his eyebrows in question. Ben shrugged.

Ellie finished another mouthful. 'See? I had a chaperone.'

Kate stopped and looked from one to the other as she cooled down. Ellie's mother still worried about her daughter's fascination for such weather and had specifically asked Kate to watch out for her. She was a grown woman but her parents were naturally protective of her and since they'd found out the truth about Ellie's final night with Carl, that had understandably only increased. But Kate had been too busy with Tyler to notice the storm, and thoughts of her friend wandering off to watch it had been the last thing on her mind once Tyler's warm hands had begun exploring her body. She'd been given a task and she'd failed, her guilt at why causing her to flush. Hopefully Ty would understand once she explained the situation later in private. She looked from Ben to Ellie, and back to Ben.

'You were there too?'

'Uh-huh.'

'The whole time?'

Ellie could see the slight curve of her friend's brows. *Please say no*, Ellie pleaded silently with Ben. *Just for now…*

'The whole time.'

'Well,' Kate said, that one word loaded with meaning. 'I guess that's alright then,' she declared, looking pointedly at Ellie.

Ellie returned a thin smile and knew that this conversation was far from over.

'We'd better make a move soon. I need to pick up some files from the office on the way to the airport.' The sound of a car coming down the drive interrupted them.

'Expecting anyone?' Ty asked.

'Not that I know of,' Ben replied, puzzled as he rose and crossed the room to look out of the window.

'I want details! Quick!' Kate whispered when Ty went over to join his friend.

'There aren't any.'

Kate snorted in disbelief. 'So you two sit in the dark together, romantically watching a storm crash all around you and nothing happened.'

'That's about the size of it.'

'Really?'

'Really.' Ellie didn't bother to hide the disappointment in her voice.

'We-ell. What's she doing here?' Tyler wondered aloud, a tease in his voice which Ben attempted to silence with a look. He merely grinned in reply. The two men stepped off the porch to greet the new arrival, the women hanging back, watching as an expensive car slowed to a halt beside them. Stepping out from a shiny new Mercedes was Bianca, Ben's hand assisting her elegant exit. Ellie felt herself deflate as she compared her tired, casual, make-up free appearance, with Bianca who looked like she had just stepped out of a salon. She left the others to their guest and headed back inside the house. Kate followed.

'Ellie?'

'Mm-hmm?'

'What's up?'

'Nothing.'

Kate cleared her throat. 'I'll put it another way. What's up and this time no fibbing.'

Ellie couldn't help the resigned smile. 'Fine. I was just wondering why every woman Ben knows looks like she's stepped off the pages of *Vogue*? Although I guess that's kind of a stupid question when you consider who he is. Of course those are the type of women he'd going to associate with. Beautiful people go to beautiful people.'

Kate's tone was stern when she replied. 'Ben is still the person you knew growing up. Just more people think they know him now. But you do know him. And you're just as beautiful. You look lovely! Natural.'

'Tired.'

Kate rolled her eyes.

Ellie looked down at the soft yellow, cotton sundress she was wearing. 'I look like something from *Little House on The Prairie*.'

Kate spurted with laughter. 'No, you don't!'

'I really do. I'm going to change.'

Just at that moment, Ben stuck his head in the door. 'You two coming out?' His eyes lingered a little on Ellie.

'Sure!' Kate grabbed Ellie's hand and led her out onto the porch to greet the new visitor, her hopes for her friend buoyed by how Ben's eyes had lingered on Ellie. Returning to the sunshine, Ben turned back to them.

'You remember Bianca from the wedding?'

'Hi!' Bianca smiled, holding out her hand. 'It's so lovely to see you again! Are you enjoying your stay?'

Ellie smiled, relaxing as Bianca asked her some more questions, and chatting with them about a recent trip to London she'd taken.

'I hope I haven't interrupted any of your plans. At the wedding, Ben invited me out to ride one of his beautiful horses but it seems he's forgotten he made the offer – although he's far too much of a gentleman to admit it.'

'Of course I didn't forget!' Ben protested, but the blush that coloured his tan for a moment confirmed that Bianca might have been on to something.

'It's alright, darling. Perhaps we could rearrange something?'

'No, it's my fault. I did forget. I'm really sorry. The wedding day was kind of a long day, I guess I just forgot what day we'd said.' He smiled at Binky, thereby assuring himself of total forgiveness. 'But there's no reason we can't take the horses out now. Ty and Kate are off to Dallas shortly but Ellie and I didn't have anything planned, did we?'

Ellie shook her head, smiling, trying not to notice what a perfect couple they made. 'Are you up for a ride, El?' Ben looked back from Bianca to where Ellie was leaning on the doorframe. She smiled outwardly and groaned inwardly at the thought she was about to feel like a very large gooseberry.

'Sure! Would you like a drink, Bianca?'

'Something cold would be lovely. Thank you.'

Tyler and Kate were sitting on the sofa, and Ellie watched briefly as Bianca sat opposite them and crossed long, toned legs encased in clinging jodhpurs. Ben moved towards Ellie to go into the kitchen. She straightened away from the doorframe.

'It's OK. I'll get it.'

Ellie stood staring at the contents of the refrigerator, not really seeing it, until she finally pulled herself together.

'Come on, Ellie. Focus. Cold drink. Just pick one!' She was talking to herself as she tried to decide what 'cold something' Ben's guest would prefer. Finally, she grabbed a diet coke and closed the door only to find Ben standing behind it.

'Oh my...!' Her hand went to her chest and she dropped the can in fright. Ben caught it before it hit the floor.

'Do you always talk to the refrigerator?'

'Sometimes. Do you always hide behind them?'

'Sometimes.' He was wearing a lazy smile that was doing things it really shouldn't to her body. She gave him a look, grabbed the coke from him and set it on the counter to open it.

'Wait! That might—'

The contents sprayed straight up into her face. Squealing, she shoved the can away, hanging over the sink as Coke dripped from her nose and chin, reaching out blindly for a cloth. Ben caught her hand and she could hear him chuckling as she tried to blink the liquid from her eyes.

'I'm glad you think it's funny!' Ellie said, trying to maintain a straight face as he placed a damp cloth in her hand. She wiped her face and looked up to see Ben pouring the remainder of the contents into a glass – still chuckling. Looking back down at the cloth, Ellie turned quickly and flung it at Ben, catching him on the ear.

'Ugh! Right! Come here, you!' Laughing, he grabbed the cloth, stopping briefly to dip it in the sink as he passed and followed Ellie who had run into the dining room. They stood either side of the long, pale wood dining table, each waiting for the other to make the first move, both of them giggling like school children. Ben caved first and as he moved one way, Ellie ran the other back into the kitchen. But his move had been a bluff and he caught up with his guest in two long strides, grabbing her around the waist and shoving the now sodden cloth into her face. She squealed in between her laughter as she squirmed and grabbed his hands.

The noise had attracted the others from the porch and they'd now made their way into the kitchen to investigate the commotion. By this point, Ben had wrapped his other arm around Ellie's upper arms in order to prevent her tickling him to gain escape.

'Nope. No tickling,' he said, laughing.

Ellie was just about to make another bid for freedom when she caught sight of three pairs of legs standing at the kitchen doorway. Stifling her laughter, she looked up.

'Please! Carry on!' Tyler urged, a huge grin on his face, matched by the one Kate was wearing. Ben also looked up at the sound of his friend's voice, but made no move to release Ellie, who, although able to stand up straight now, was still pinned loosely by Ben's encircling arms.

'Hey there!' Ben said, casually, 'I guess you're wondering what happened to your drink?' Ellie was almost afraid to look at Bianca, remembering the cold looks she'd received from Ben's wife in the past. 'Sorry about that,' continued Ben as he finally released his captive, including Bianca in his gaze. 'Had a bit of trouble with the staff.'

'Staff? Cheeky sod!' came the muffled retort as Ellie dried her face. Ben grinned as she reappeared from behind the towel he'd handed her.

'Don't think that charming smile is going to get you off this time.' Bianca raised an eyebrow at Ben as she walked up to Ellie and tucked her arm through her own. 'I think you deserve dinner tonight at least for that. Somewhere fabulous.' Bianca tapped a long, perfectly manicured nail against her chin as she thought. 'Marconi's. That should go some way to making amends, don't you think, Ben?' She turned to Ellie. 'You like Italian, don't you?'

Ellie nodded, pleasantly overwhelmed by Binky's reaction. Guiltily she realised that maybe Ben was right, and that perhaps she did expect the worst from everyone. But what a lovely surprise to be proven wrong.

'Go on Ben, make the call.' Bianca bossed him along.

'No, it's OK really,' Ellie spoke up. She didn't know the restaurant Bianca was referring to, but she got the distinct feeling it wasn't a cheap diner.

'Ben?'

'Fine. Fine.' Ben pulled his phone from his pocket, hit a few buttons and then strolled out into the hall. Shortly afterwards they heard him talking.

'Bianca, this feels a bit awkward,' Ellie confessed, once she was sure Ben couldn't overhear.

'Nonsense, honey!' Bianca patted her hand. 'Ben loves that restaurant. It's about time he went back with some decent company.' She exchanged a glance with Tyler.

'What's going on?' Kate asked, craning her neck to check that Ben was still busy on the telephone.

Tyler filled them in. 'Last time he went to that restaurant was with Cyndi. It's his favourite but she did nothing but complain and embarrass him in front of the owner and staff, many of whom had become friends. He just needs another memory of it – a good one,' he said pointedly, looking at Ellie. 'To help him get over the painful ones.'

Ellie ran a hand nervously over her hair. 'I think you're all expecting a bit much of me.'

'Oh, I don't think so!' Binky smiled knowingly at Tyler.

He leant over conspiratorially. 'I haven't seen him act like that in a very long time.'

Ellie flushed. 'Oh, I don't think…'

'Right. Booked for seven-thirty. Happy now?' Ben asked his old flame as he returned to the kitchen, looking perfectly happy himself.

'Yes thank you, darling! Now you two have a good time. We've decided to ride all together when Kate and Tyler get back from Dallas so I'm going to head back into town now.'

'Are you sure?'

'Absolutely. It was lovely to meet you both again.' Bianca kissed the women first, before Ben saw her out to her car whilst Kate and Tyler went upstairs to collect their luggage. Stood together on the porch, Ben and Ellie watched their visitor drive off and disappear into the dust.

Half an hour later they were back, this time waving goodbye to Tyler and Kate as they too disappeared into the dust trails of their wheels.

'Well, I guess that just leaves you and me.'

'I guess so.' Ellie flashed a shy smile as they walked back into the house and began clearing away the brunch things.

'I thought I already told you I didn't invite you here to do this?' Ben took a plate from her and placed it on the counter. 'I was only joking about the staff thing.'

'I know, silly!' she giggled, taking the dishes from behind him and loading them into the dishwasher. 'So what exactly did you invite me here for?' she teased, as he handed her another place setting to load.

'Sex?'

Ellie laughed without looking up.

'Worth a try,' Ben replied, handing her the next batch of crockery. She loaded it in and closed the door, taking the hand he offered as she got up.

'Thanks. Look, Ben, this thing tonight? It was rather sprung on you and I don't mind not going. I won't tell, honest. I'll just say I had a lovely time!'

'Don't you want to go?'

'It's not that.'

'What is it then?'

'I rather think you were bullied into it.'

Ben's eyes twinkled as he smiled. 'That's OK. I need a bit of a kick up the pants sometimes. I've been meaning to go back for a while. I guess I just never had the inclination before.'

'Or instigation.'

'That too.'

'As long as you're sure.'

'I'm sure. Now why don't you go and make yourself beautiful? We only have a few hours before we have to leave.'

Ellie turned back to face him with a false smile. 'You are such a charmer.'

'I know. Comes naturally.'

'Yeah, I bet. If you're not careful, I'll tell Bianca.'

'Man. Then I'll really be in trouble.'

'That's what I thought.'

'So, I must then beg a thousand apologies from you, my lady.' He made a rolling action with his arm and bent low.

'Silly arse.'

Ben grinned 'God, I love how you say that.'

Ellie smiled, the faintest of flushes touching her cheeks. 'Right.

I'm going to have a long soak and read my book. What time do I have to be ready?'

Ben thought for a moment. 'About six-thirty. That alright with you?'

'Right. Well, hopefully that will give me *just* enough time to perform a miracle and make myself beautiful.' She pulled a face, turned on her heel and sashayed up the stairs in mock indignance.

'Nice tush!' he called out as she disappeared from view.

'There's no point trying to suck up to me now,' a disembodied voice called, and Ben could hear the smile in her voice. Chuckling, he strolled back out onto the porch, picking up his guitar as he passed. Finding a comfortable position on the swing, his fingers started to gently strum chords. He was in a good mood and felt more relaxed than he had in years. OK, so she'd laughed at the thought of sex with him – not necessarily a good sign – but they were having fun and that was something that had been sorely missing in his life for far too long. Plus, he had her all to himself for the next few days and right now, he couldn't think of anywhere else he'd rather be, or anyone else he'd rather be with. With dinner for two at his favourite restaurant tonight to look forward to, the day was shaping up to be a great one.

His mind floated between thoughts as his fingers moved easily, almost unconsciously, over the strings and fret board as he hummed quietly to himself. It seemed way too long since he'd taken anyone to dinner.

There had been a few drinks here and there, but that was about it. The fact that his 'date' tonight was intelligent, witty and beautiful, someone he could be himself with and that he enjoyed spending time with was more than a bonus to Ben. He chuckled again as he remembered their playfulness earlier. Geez, he certainly couldn't imagine ever having shoved a wet cloth in Cyndi's face – and there was certainly no way she would have laughed. In fact, he'd have put money on it meaning divorce sooner if he had! But then Ellie couldn't be more different from his ex-wife. Maybe that said something else about his marriage.

There were no airs and graces with Ellie. No tip toeing around or wondering how to phrase things so she wouldn't take them the wrong way. She'd accepted the jokes, given them right back to him and shared the laughter. As he replayed their water fight, his mind kept focusing on how it had felt to hold Ellie against him, how warm she was, the way her hair, soft to the touch, smelled of meadow flowers. The sound of running water brought him back to the present, and he looked up. The window to Ellie's en-suite was open. Ben gave himself a mental shake and returned his concentration to his guitar, doing his best to keep his mind off the images his brain was trying to associate with the sounds drifting from the window.

Chapter 14

Ellie finished running the bath and eased into the bubbles. From the porch, the soft lilt of a guitar floated up, occasionally accompanied by Ben's deep, harmonious voice. Relaxing into the warm water, she rested her head back against the edge of the tub and closed her eyes.

A little over an hour later, Ellie awoke with a start. The water was cold and her skin had taken a definite turn to the shrivelled side.

'Oops!'

Quickly, she washed and then drained the bath out. The rail holding the linen was positioned in the stream of sunlight by the window and the fluffy towel she enveloped herself in was deliciously warm. Leaning over the bathtub, Ellie washed her hair before wrapping it in another naturally heated towel. Peering out of the window, she saw Ben, feet resting on the low wicker table, still contentedly playing his guitar. As if sensing something, he looked up.

'Hello.'

'Hello.'

'How was your book?'

'I don't know, I fell asleep.' She pulled a face.

'Well, why don't you grab a robe and come sit down here for a while. I just got some of Sandy's famous lemonade out.'

'Ooh!' Ellie's mouth was already watering. This was her best friend's speciality and she'd still never tasted anything better. 'OK.' She paused, thinking back to their first day here. 'Do you have a spare bathrobe. I'm not sure mine is quite right for drinking afternoon lemonade in.'

'Oh, I don't know. I think it's perfect.' Ben grinned up at her. She held his gaze, before raising one eyebrow.

His smile widened. 'Spoilsport. Check in the closet in the bathroom there. There should be some guest robes hanging up.'

'Thanks,' Ellie called as she disappeared back inside. Ben poured another glass of his sister's lemonade and waited for her to appear.

'It might be a tad big.'

Ben turned as Ellie padded out onto the porch. The robe covered her from head to foot, and she probably could have got into it at least twice over.

'You think?' Ben said, laughing and thinking how damn cute she looked wrapped up in that robe, her cheeks all pink and fresh.

He made a space on the sofa and Ellie sat down, tucking her legs underneath her. In front of them on the table was a glass jug filled with fresh lemonade, and two tall glasses ready poured. Ben handed her one of them, feeling ridiculous at the warmth her smile of thanks brought to his body – and his heart. There was no chance of seeing any of her figure underneath that robe but hiding it did nothing to quell Ben's feelings for her. In fact, it only intensified them. She was sucking at the paper straw, gazing out into the distance and he took the opportunity to look upon her. Turning suddenly, she caught him.

'What?'

'What?'

'You look funny.'

'Thanks.' He smiled but offered no more information. Ellie frowned for a moment then snuggled down into the robe.

'There's something rather indulgent about a long bath in the afternoon,' she mused aloud, closing her eyes as she clasped the straw between her lips and took a long, refreshing draw.

Ben studied the serene face as she turned it towards the lowering sun, its fading rays gently warming her. The tension he'd seen in her at the start of the visit was gone. Right now, she looked as relaxed and contented as he felt. As if sensing she was being watched, Ellie's eyes suddenly opened and she found herself looking directly into Ben's. He knew he was caught and a sheepish grin crept onto his face. Ellie rubbed her face sub-consciously. 'What is it?'

'Nothing. Just that you look…'

'What?'

'Happy. You look happy.'

Ellie stopped rubbing her face. 'Oh.' She dropped her gaze for a moment and the faint pinkness left on her cheeks from her bath deepened a little. Looking back up, she gazed around, her eyes taking in the surroundings, the beautiful house, before eventually coming back to rest on her host.

'Who wouldn't be?' She shrugged. But the moment she'd said it, Ellie realised her mistake. 'Oh, Ben!

I'm sorry. I didn't mean to…'

Ben shook his head, eager to dissipate her discomfiture. 'Don't even worry about it. I should have known Cyndi would never love this place, let alone like it. I brought her here before I bought it, looked around, introduced her to the hands, that kind of thing. I told her I was looking into it for a friend and she didn't exactly enthuse over it then.' He glanced back at Ellie and she saw the sad, resigned smile on his face. 'I thought it would grow on her.' He shrugged before returning his gaze to the wheat. 'Marrying Cyndi was a mistake. People tried to warn me but I wouldn't listen. Or at least I was only listening with my heart. I was so in love with her, and I thought she loved me too. I thought that as long as we had that, then nothing else mattered. I knew that, in time, people would see what we had and change their minds, see that they'd been wrong.' Ben paused for a moment as he reflected on his marriage. 'But it was me that had it all wrong. I guess I realised pretty quickly that things weren't right. We were just too different in everything – our views, our humour, the kind of lifestyle we wanted to lead, even stupid things like our clothes. But it all added up.'

Pushing himself up from the sofa, he stood and went over to lean on the porch rail, looking out but seeing none of the view in front of him.

'At first I tried to adapt, be more what she wanted me to be, who she wanted me to be. We went to the right restaurants, the clubs, the parties, and the more we did it, the more miserable I became. That's not why I got into music – for the fame and the parties. I got into it because I love it. I do it because I can't live without it. I wanted to try and make a living out of doing something I loved, you know, write songs, play and just be happy. The fact that things have gone the way they have is something I'm thankful for every day of my life. I know how difficult it is, and how many don't make it. I am, and always will be eternally grateful for our success, but that's not why I do it.'

Ben turned back to face the figure huddled in the enormous bathrobe. She sat looking up at him, listening patiently, and silently to him. How was it that she knew exactly what he needed, just when he needed it? And how was it that he'd not seen it until it was too late?

He let out a sigh as he smiled and raised his eyebrows at her. 'I don't know why I'm telling you all this. I guess you know most of this stuff already from Sandy.'

'Go on,' she replied softly.

Much to his surprise, his usual disinclination to talk about his relationship had disappeared. Moving back to the sofa, he lowered himself down next to her and rested a booted foot on the edge of the table.

'There's not really much else to say. I guess we just drifted so far apart that eventually the gap between us got too wide to bridge. Changing someone from who they're meant to be is a road to disaster and I don't think either of us were the person the other thought they were – or could be. So in the end, there was nothing. I thought that buying this house would give us a chance. Bring us back together, put the focus back on us and away from other people and clubs and parties but living out here even part time would have made Cyndi as miserable as living in the city made me. I should have realised that. Cyndi needs to be seen, flattered and admired. That's not a hard thing – I mean, you've met her, she's beautiful.'

'She is.' Ellie managed to keep her voice even. *Of course she is. As is Bianca.* She delved further into her memory, realising something. All of the women she could remember Ben dating over the years were two things: blonde and beautiful. She yanked her attention back to what he was saying.

'At least she hated it as soon as I told her I'd actually bought it. That way, as things turned out, I got to keep it with no bad memories of my ex in it.'

'Have you seen her?'

'Since we split up? Once. She moved out to California with *that* guy. He's a photographer, I think. She always did hate the winters here.' He looked back at his guest with a wry smile. 'We met to discuss the terms of the divorce.'

'I'm guessing she did pretty well.' Ellie voiced her thought accidentally and immediately coloured. 'Sorry! I didn't mean—'

'That's OK.' Ben smiled at her honesty. 'Yeah, she did alright, but not as well as people might think. She got the apartment, car, more money than she'll ever need – which, being Cyndi, is saying something – but she didn't get half of everything.'

'Ben, you don't have to tell—'

'I want to.' For some reason, he did. He wanted to tell this woman everything.

He scooched round so that he was facing Ellie, one knee resting out to the side.

'Tyler's my lawyer and he absolutely insisted on this pre-nuptial thing. He'd drafted a very generous one but we still had a fight about it. Tyler and I don't fight so it was kind of intense but as it turned out, Cyndi was pretty happy to sign it. I don't think she ever really expected us to split either.' He rested his chin on his palm. 'But we were never right for each other.'

He shifted position again, turning his eyes to the distance. 'I'm not sure I'll ever be able to forgive her for lying to me about not being able to have children though. I can deal with the fact she was unfaithful now. It took a while and it hurt like hell but I guess, when it came down to it, she was lonely and bored, but the other thing…' He shook his head.

Ellie was about to respond when they were interrupted by a car approaching. Ben squinted up the drive, trying to discover the identity of the unexpected visitor.

'I'll go and change.' Ellie made a move to get up but Ben stopped her, checking his watch.

'Plenty of time yet.'

Ellie noted the car slowing in front of the house. 'I have to try and look beautiful!' she teased. 'That could take some time.'

Ben's eyes danced as he looked down at Ellie. 'I think you're already there,' he said, softly, placing a gentle kiss on her forehead.

Ellie stood for moment, her mind spinning, before she collected herself, berating her imagination for the temptation to read more into his action. *He's just being nice. Like he's always been.*

She glanced back at the car. 'I'm going to change. I don't think it looks very good me sitting here in a bathrobe in the middle of the afternoon.'

Oh, I don't know,' he replied with a mischievous half-smile. 'It certainly didn't do me any favours being known as a nice guy.

Maybe it's time I got a bad boy reputation.' He pulled a bad-boy face. Ellie giggled.

'You know, that wasn't quite the reaction I was going for.'

'Sorry. You looked funny!'

'It's not supposed to be funny. It's supposed to be mean and moody.'

'Then it needs work.'

'Well, thanks for your support, ma'am.'

'Pleasure. Anytime!' she said, smiling as Ben stood aside to let her shuffle back upstairs.

He waited until the screen door had closed before turning his attention back to the car that had now come to a stop in front of the house. He didn't recognise the model or plate and the tinted windows prevented him from seeing the occupants. It pulled to a stop in front of the house, the engine cutting, leaving nothing but the soft sounds of a country afternoon. The vehicle door opened and he started down the steps, halting as his ex-wife emerged from the air-conditioned cool of the luxury car's interior into the warmth of the late afternoon. She looked immaculate, as always, the emerging bump almost disguised under a designer tunic over a short suede skirt that showed legs still toned and tanned. Pushing her sunglasses to the top of her head, her long straight hair, now worn loose, rippled and the highlights in it shone gold as they caught the sun.

'Hello, Ben.'

'Cyndi.' Ben greeted her coolly. He glanced over the car. 'New model, huh?'

'It doesn't look like I'm the only one.' She raised an eyebrow as she peered around her ex-husband, trying to see into the house. Ben gave a non-committal shrug, secretly pleased she had seen Ellie in her bathrobe disappearing back inside.

Pathetic, he thought. But he was still pleased.

'May I sit down?'

'If you want. We're going out shortly.'

'Anywhere nice?'

'Yes.'

Cyndi waited for a moment, then realising Ben was offering no further details she climbed the steps and took a seat. Ben remained standing.

'So, who is she?'

'A friend.'

'She looked a bit like that girl, Sandy's friend. The one that got beaten up that time and looked so awful.'

Involuntarily, Ben winced at the memory and Cyndi looked satisfied at finally getting a reaction from him.

When he spoke though, his tone was even. 'That would be because it is her. She and a friend have been staying here, along with Ty, since my sister's wedding.'

'Cosy.' Cyndi gave him a thin smile. 'So where are Tyler and her friend? It would be nice to see him again.' She looked around innocently. The fact that both of them knew she and Tyler had rubbed each other the wrong way from the moment they'd met made this statement a little hard to believe.

Ben looked evenly at his ex-wife. 'I hate to point out the obvious, but we're not married anymore, Cyndi. That means I don't have to explain anything, or anyone, to you.'

Cyndi gave him what she imagined to be a friendly smile. 'I was just asking.'

Sure you were. But, just as his ex knew it would, his honesty kept jabbing him in the back. 'Kate and Tyler have gone to Texas for a few days on business.'

'Really?' Her eyes widened. 'So, you two are all alone?' She raised one perfectly shaped, expectant eyebrow.

'Gee! I guess they figured we were old enough to look after ourselves.' Cyndi's mouth drew into a thin line of distaste.

'Are you dating her?'

Ben studied the perfect face. She had gained a little weight with the pregnancy. Something he knew she wouldn't be happy about but to him she'd never looked more beautiful. But it was a cold beauty. Untouchable in more ways than one – he saw that now. It wasn't warm and inviting, like Ellie's. It was like a marble sculpture, perfect and stunning but cold. Realisation dawned within him, and a slow smile slid onto his face. He was truly over her.

'What are you doing here, Cyndi?'* Cyndi suddenly felt uncomfortable, her ex-husband's expression unsettling her. He seemed totally detached. She'd had a hold on him from the moment she'd caught his eye at that party and that was exactly how she liked things. She didn't want Ben back but she did want him to want her back. But he didn't seem even remotely interested. He just stood there, impassive, waiting for her to explain her visit. When she didn't say anything, he checked his watch.

'Cyndi, we have reservations—'

'Brandon is on a shoot here. God knows why they needed to come here, but still.' She gave a flick of her hand. 'I came with him.'

Ben frowned, shaking his head. 'I mean here here, not Kansas here.'

She paused. 'I spoke to my mother.'

'Well, that's a coincidence. So did I.' Behind him, his hand tightened a little on the rail.

Cyndi shot Ben a look. 'I know. That's why I'm here.' She got up and walked along the porch, running a manicured hand along the smooth wood of the rail, turning her head casually in an effort to hide the fact she was still trying desperately to see the woman inside. Ben watched and shook his head. Had she always been that transparent?

'I guess love is blind,' he mumbled to himself.

'What?' Cyndi returned along the porch.

'Nothing. You were saying?'

Cyndi took a deep breath and sat back down on the sofa. 'I didn't intend for you to find out like that. Despite what you think, I'm not without feeling.'

187

'I guess better that than through a glossy magazine spread, something I assume is already set up for when the baby arrives.'

Cyndi was now a famous name in her own right, playing off the back of once being married to a member of one of the most successful country music bands ever. Divorce didn't seem to sever that tie with celebrity. It wasn't something Ben even tried to understand. He had little interest in his own fame, let alone his ex-wife's. But he knew her, and he knew she'd be using the baby to her own advantage. Just as she had him.

Cyndi turned at his comment but his expression was impassive. 'I never meant to hurt you like that, Ben. I thought this was going to be forever. If I'd just wanted your money then I never would have agreed to sign the pre-nuptial agreement, would I?'

Ben remained silent, but Cyndi appeared to be awaiting an answer. He sighed and shrugged.

'I don't know, Cyndi, if you want the honest truth. I think you loved who you thought I was.' She began to speak but Ben cut her off. 'Look. We're divorced and everything was settled ages ago, so all of this talk is pretty academic. We've both moved on and going over past mistakes isn't going to help either of us.' He glanced down at her bump. 'Besides, I don't think you should be exposing yourself to extra stress at the moment. It's not good for either of you.'

Cyndi stood up and gently kissed Ben on the cheek. The surprise on his face sent a flush of guilt through her. It was an unfamiliar feeling, and not one she cared for.

'You were too good to me,' she stated as she eased herself back into the chair. 'That was the problem. I've been spoilt my whole life, and I love it. I need it. My parents spoilt me at home and being pretty got me attention everywhere else. Whatever I wanted, I got. Including you.'

Ben tilted his head, studying her for a moment. There was no shame in her expression. Cyndi expected to be treated like a queen – to her that was how it should be. Her God-given right.

'And then you carried on spoiling me. From day one, we did

what I wanted, lived where I wanted. It was wonderful and I didn't want to share that love, or attention, with a child.' Her statement was simple. She didn't blame herself for her actions. She was just stating them.

'So what's different?' Ben couldn't help himself. His curiosity was piqued, and he nodded at her stomach. 'How come you're prepared to share now?'

Cyndi looked down, laying a hand on the neat bump. 'Do you think I could have some of that lemonade?'

Ben looked at her blankly for a moment, trying to process what she was saying, and work out why she'd come all the way out here to say it in the first place.

He let out a sigh. 'Sure. I'll get you a glass.'

Pushing through the screen door, Ben strolled into the kitchen and took a glass from the cupboard.

'Unbelievable,' he mumbled to himself. His ex-wife was sitting out there telling him that she'd taken lovers and eventually left him because he was too good to her? Then again, he should have known that Cyndi was never going to shoulder any of the blame. That just wasn't her style.

The sound of movement upstairs jogged his memory, and he flicked his eyes to the ceiling, his mind casting back. He was pretty sure Ellie would have preferred a little generosity to what she'd been given. Taking the glass of lemonade he'd now poured, he detoured to the bottom of the stairs. 'El? You OK?'

'Yes thanks,' she called back.

He smiled to himself, happiness and calm spreading though him just at the sound of her voice. He'd just started to step away when he heard the bedroom door open and Ellie appeared on the balcony of the landing.

'Did you want to cancel tonight?' Her eyes slid to the front of the house.

'No. I'm afraid you're stuck with me. You've got forty-five minutes before we have to leave.'

189

'I'm going to need more than that if I'm going to look as good as Cyndi does.'

Ben's smile faded. 'We can talk about this later.' He turned and left to rejoin his ex on the porch.

'I have to go get ready, Cyndi,' he said, handing her the glass.

'Yes, of course.' She took a deep breath and looked back into the pale blue eyes that had intrigued her from the moment she'd met him. 'I just wanted you to know that I didn't mean to lie to you about not being able to have children. I was going to tell you everything when I got pregnant with your baby.'

Ben dug his nails into his palms and kept his face impassive. *Your baby.* It seemed unlikely that phrase would ever be used in association with him now. He pulled himself back to concentrate on what Cyndi was saying.

'I know you wanted children but I couldn't be bothered with fending people's questions off all the time, including yours. I just wasn't ready to give up my freedom, or my body. It was the easiest way to stop people going on about it.'

Ben was looking at her incredulously. 'You're some piece of work, you know that?' There was no malice in his voice, just resignation.

Cyndi shrugged.

'You didn't answer my question. Why now?' Ben asked, nodding at the bump as she stood to leave.

Cyndi placed a hand on her stomach and for a brief moment, her face softened. 'I guess I felt it was time. Plus Brandon's promised me a personal trainer to get back in shape and two nannies.'

'Lucky you.'

She turned at his reply. There was an edge to his voice but she couldn't make out his expression. He followed her silently to the car and opened the door, ever the gentleman. Cyndi got in gracefully and buzzed down the electric window.

'I just wanted to explain.'

190

Ben looked down at her, incredulous that she truly thought that was what she'd done. 'Drive safely.'

'I will. Have a nice evening with your *friend*.' She emphasised the last word and Ben gave a small head shake.

'I intend to,' he replied calmly, before stepping back.

Cyndi turned the car around and drove off back up the drive, leaving Ben stood back in the quiet. He let out a sigh at it all then jogged back into the house and took the stairs two at a time heading for the shower.

Chapter 15

Ellie heard the water running and her stomach squirmed again. The remark about Cyndi had sort of slipped out. Ben had looked less than pleased and she certainly wasn't looking forward to 'talking about it later'. 'With a bit of luck, he'll forget,' she told herself as she looked in the mirror and put her hair up for the third time. She'd actually been ready some time before Cyndi left but when she'd sneaked a look at who had stepped from the gleaming car, she'd made a very quick and easy decision to remain upstairs until Ben's visitor had gone.

Picking up her clutch, she left her room and went downstairs to wait for Ben.

A short while later, she heard a knock on one of the doors upstairs.

'Ellie?'

'Down here,' she called from the kitchen.

Ben jogged down the stairs, scooping up his keys from the side table as he passed.

'Ready?' he asked, looking around for his guest.

'Yes,' Ellie emerged from the kitchen. Ben was staring and she suddenly had a fashion panic. 'Is this alright?' She waved a nervous hand over her dress. 'I wasn't sure exactly what sort of place it was.'

Ben's eyes took in the silky dress, its bias cut skimming the curves of Ellie's body, finishing just below her knees. He let his eyes travel down to where high-heeled strappy sandals tied around her ankles, their height bringing her up to his chin. Her make-up was light and the wild auburn curls had been tamed into a French pleat, except for a few stray ones that had made a successful bid for freedom, and now hung softly, framing the sides of her face. Ellie shifted her weight to the other foot. Her movement nudged Ben from his silent admiration and he realised she was still awaiting an answer.

'You look lovely,' he said, groaning inwardly at his lame words. 'Do you have a jacket or something?' His gaze wandered back to her shoulders, bare save for two thin ribbon straps of fabric holding up the dress. *Straps that could so easily be nudged off those slim, lightly tanned shoulders.* Ben gripped his keys a little tighter as he pulled his mind back on track and concentrated on what Ellie was saying.

Ellie held up a wrap. 'Way ahead of you.'

He nodded, indicating that they should go, then followed his date to the door, enjoying the view from behind as much as he had from the front. She reached out to the door handle but her host was already there, reaching around and pulling it open for her. She waited for Ben to lock up so that they could walk to the truck together. The key twisted and Ben turned, catching her eye. Apart from the wedding, Ellie had never really seen him dressed so formally. He wore a charcoal-grey, handmade suit with a crisp white shirt beneath it, open at the neck, and the combination deepened his tan and made his eyes look even more blue.

'You look very nice.'

It had been such a long time since anyone had said that, and really meant it, Ben looked genuinely taken aback. To be complimented and then not have it followed up with 'but if you did this or that or wore this or that too'. He'd got so used to it that a simple compliment now had him tongue-tied. Of course, he knew a lot of that was because those words he had missed had now come so softly from Ellie, and that made them mean so much more.

He nodded a brief thanks while he regained control of his voice and walked up to the truck. Pressing the key fob, Ben opened the door for Ellie, but his body blocked her from actually entering. She looked up, frowning at his serious expression.

'I never want to hear you compare yourself unfavourably with my ex-wife again. OK?'

Ellie nodded, looking away from him, embarrassed. Hooking a finger under her chin, he very gently tilted it up towards him. Ellie's eyes remained lowered.

'OK?' he asked again. She nodded against his hand. 'Look at me.' His voice, though commanding was so soft, so tender, Ellie had no choice. Her gaze slid up to meet his. 'Promise?' Ellie smiled an embarrassed smile.

'I promise.'

Ben hadn't removed his hand and she was so close now. It wouldn't take much just to lean in and— 'Shall we?' Ben dropped his hand and stood aside. Ellie swallowed, hoping the flush she felt on her chest and neck weren't as obvious as they felt, and she did her best to both retain her smile and hide her disappointment as Ben helped her into the truck. Shutting the door, he walked around to the other side, quickly climbed in behind the wheel and started the engine. Bumping off down the drive, dust kicking out from the tyres, Ellie made a point of concentrating on something else, other than the overpowering feeling she'd had that Ben had been about to kiss her – and wishing that he had. Settling herself into the seat, she looked around.

'I like this truck.'

Ben took his eyes from the road for a second.

'What?'

'This truck. I like it.'

'You do?' Ben asked in surprise, remembering how Cyndi

would whinge like hell when he took a truck over a sportscar, even though it was always the latest model with all the bells and whistles. But she'd not been swayed, insisting instead on him buying the Porsche and using that whenever possible. He'd never particularly liked that car and was more than happy to give her the damn thing as part of the settlement. He'd changed his truck since the split, another separation from his previous life – a newer model, different colour but that was enough for him. He loved it. And so it appeared, did Ellie.

'I do.'

Ben grinned. 'Me too.'

'It's very "you".'

'I'm going to take that as a good thing.'

'You should.'

They chatted easily over the background music of the local country station, with Ellie nudging Ben excitedly and turning up the volume when they played one of his band's songs. He'd laughed, a little embarrassed but mostly thrilled at the expression of genuine pride on his friend's face. It was the same expression he'd seen on it when he'd got his first break, barely a foot in the door at the time but his family, and Ellie and hers, had all been there for him. Supporting him. Being proud of him for every achievement, big or small. He'd loved them all for it back then. And he loved her for it now.

They pulled into town and Ben parked the truck, jumped out and walked around to open Ellie's door. When he got there, she was already standing outside, gazing over at the expensive-looking frontage of the restaurant.

'Hey. I was just coming to get the door for you.'

'Oh, I worked it out.' She winked at him with a tease on her lips.

'Humour me,' he replied, tilting his head in a plea. 'I'm trying to be a gentleman here.'

Ellie smiled and nodded, then stood back as he reached into

the back seat for his jacket, having slipped it off before they left, his body close to hers as he moved. She breathed him in – all clean laundry, soap and sun. Ben pulled back and glanced down at her as he did. Her head was turned slightly, her eyes averted. Ellie felt the heat of him move away and she too stepped away from the door. The remote central locking whirred then chirruped its goodbye to them.

'Ready?'

She nodded and they walked towards the restaurant as Ben turned over the differences between Ellie and some other women he'd dated. Even the simple things. For many, it would never occur to them to exit a car on their own. Ben didn't mind. He'd been brought up to be chivalrous and he wasn't ashamed of it. It was just a pleasant surprise when people didn't assume they were due things. Petty though it was, he'd been initially hesitant to help Cyndi exit the car this afternoon, for once tempted to just let her get out on her own. Guilt had soon overtaken him though. He'd been so put out that her intrusion took away precious time he could have been spending with Ellie, he'd temporarily forgotten she was pregnant.

'Hello?' Ellie touched him gently on the arm.

He turned his head and looked down into the half smiling, half concerned green eyes.

'Hello,' he replied simply.

'You were miles away.'

'No. Not that far.'

Ellie dipped her eyebrows in question at him but he merely smiled and placed his hand on the small of her back as they approached the entrance to the restaurant. Suddenly a piercing scream rang out, making them both jump. Automatically, Ben slipped his hand further around Ellie's waist, pulling her close. Two women were hurrying towards them from across the street.

'Oh my goodness! It is you! See!' The first woman turned to the second. 'I told you it was him! Ooh! You're even more gorgeous in real life, if that's possible! And so tall too! Oh my!' The woman had a good fifteen years on Ben, bright orange hair piled on top of her head and a camera slung around her neck.

'We're just visiting here, but I said to Virginia, wouldn't it be just wonderful if we saw Ben Danvers! Didn't I say that?' She turned back to her friend whose head bobbed up and down in agreement, her eyes remaining glued to Ben's face. 'Because we knew you lived around here someplace, and now here you are! I can't believe it! Can you believe it, Virginia?'

Virginia apparently couldn't believe it as she shook her head, her entire focus still set on her idol's face.

'Could we have your autograph?' the first woman asked, thrusting a piece of paper and pen at him. 'And a photograph?'

'Sure!' Ben replied easily, 'Who's it to?'

The two women giggled like schoolgirls and told him, requesting that he sign it 'Love, Ben.' 'Are you going in there?' The woman noticed the restaurant they'd been just about to enter as Ben began signing the second autograph.

'Uh-huh,' Ben nodded, concentrating on trying not to pierce the paper with the pen.

'Together?' she asked, with more than a hint of interest in her voice as she finally noticed Ellie, who had slipped away from Ben's arm. Ben handed the paper back to the women and rewarded them with a trademark smile.

'Yes ma'am,' he replied, reaching out to take Ellie's hand. She let him – a little reluctantly but not enough for the women to notice.

'I didn't realise you were dating.' The second woman spoke for the first time, disappointment clear in her voice.

'Oh, honey! Of course he's dating! Just look at him! To. Die. For!' Ben blushed and Ellie tried to release her hand, waiting for Ben to deny that they were dating. He didn't.

'Could we get a picture too? That's the thing now, isn't it?' Ben's fan said, ignoring her camera and instead concentrating on the screen of the smartphone she'd just taken out from the enormous shoulder bag she had slung over one shoulder.

Ben stood patiently as they took a bunch of selfies with him.

'Oh dear. I'm not good at these things. You're kind of in it, Virginia. That'll have to do.'

'Would you like me to take one of all three of you with your camera?' Ellie spoke for the first time. The two women stared at her for a moment.

'Oh my! Now, what a darlin' accent!' The one with the orange hair beamed. 'I bet that's what hooked you, huh?' She laughed, turning back to Ben. Ellie looked at him awkwardly, but he was still just stood there, relaxed and smiling.

'Well, and the fact she looks like…that!' The woman finished, nodding up and down at Ellie. Ben's smile was the only answer she got.

'Which button do I press?' Ellie asked the woman, desperate to distract her.

All of them, Ben thought to himself as he watched Ellie concentrating on the camera's screen. *Every single one.* Ellie clicked the shutter and checked the screen, then peeped out from behind it.

'It looks OK, but shall I take another one, just in case?'

'Good idea, honey!' The women clung to Ben again as Ellie snapped another couple.

'Well, I guess we should let you get on and enjoy your evening.'

'Thank you. It was nice to meet you.'

'Oh, believe me—' the woman widened her eyes '—the pleasure was all ours!' With that, she tucked her arm in her friend's and bustled off, Virginia throwing one last longing look at Ben before they turned the corner.

'Sorry about all that. You ready?'

'Don't apologise. They seemed nice. But yes, I'm definitely ready for some food now.'

Ben and Ellie finally entered the restaurant where he and the owner greeted each other warmly. Ellie was introduced and they were shown to their table, the best in the house. When they were alone, Ellie looked across the spotless white linen at Ben. He could see her mind working.

'What?'

'It's just all a bit weird.'

'What's weird?'

'You.' Ben opened his mouth to protest but Ellie was already correcting herself, 'I mean, not you as such. I just really have trouble seeing you as a superstar.'

Ben shook his head and bit into a breadstick. 'I'm not a superstar.'

'You kind of are. And you definitely are to those women.'

Ben shrugged. 'It's Ben from Cheyenne they want, not me. It's flattering but it's not real. That's why it's good to have people who know us for being the people we really are, not just for being in the band.' He took a sip from the glass of wine that had now appeared, 'People we can really be ourselves with.'

'Well! That's good,' Ellie said as she too sipped the excellent wine, 'Because I'm afraid, famous as you are – which I always forget until something like that happens – you'll always be Sandy's big brother to me.'

There was a flicker on Ben's face before he smiled. 'Right. Good. So, what do you want to eat?'

*

'It should be warm soon,' Ben said as Ellie snuggled down a little in her seat, pulling her wrap closer around her.

'I'm alright,' she said brightly. 'Thank you for tonight. It was lovely.'

'My pleasure.'

Checking the vicinity, Ben looked across at his passenger as he set to pull out of the parking space. Her eyes were heavy lidded and sleepy, as was her smile. Hardly surprising since she'd pretty much had the bottle of wine to herself. He'd laughed when she picked up the bottle, and then realising it was empty, said nothing but 'Oops' and hit him with a smile that was still having repercussions around his body and his brain even now. She was relaxed, not obnoxiously drunk, but still way too drunk for anything to happen between them tonight. Not that anything was likely to, he thought, pulling out from the parking lot. A frown creased his forehead as he replayed her words from earlier in his head.

You'll always be Sandy's big brother to me. Was there any chance he could ever be anything more to this woman?

'I guess you'll have to get your PR people on that,' Ellie stated in the low-lit interior of the truck.

Ben glanced across. 'On what.'

'Those women tonight.'

'I'm sorry but you've completely lost me.'

'Those women. They think we're dating!' She flapped a hand between the two of them to emphasise the point. 'You and me.'

'So?'

'So, we're not.' He didn't answer, so she filled the silence. 'So you'll have to get your PR people on to it. That's very hard to say, you know. PR people.' She said it again, and Ben couldn't help but laugh. She turned, pleased she had made him laugh. He looked into her beautiful smile as they waited at a red light.

'Does it bother you that they thought that?' he asked.

'No, of course not. But don't you have to be careful about being seen out with women?' Her voice had dropped to a whisper, though Ben was unsure whom she thought might overhear them in the truck.

'Not if they're beautiful,' he whispered back.

It took her a minute to realise what he'd said and he watched as realisation dawned. She sat up abruptly and opened her mouth to say something. Apparently changing her mind, she absentmindedly wet her lips with her tongue instead and Ben did his best not to swerve off the road.

The country station was still playing quietly and Elle drifted off until a pot hole bumped her awake sharply. Ben looked over apologetically.

'Sorry. I didn't see the dip.'

Ellie shook her head, dismissing his apology as she pulled an errant curl away from her mouth. 'Are we nearly home?' She peered out of the window, trying to see a landmark, but it was an overcast night and clouds had hidden the moon.

'Just a few minutes.' He felt her shift in the seat beside him. She'd turned slightly and was looking back into the rear of the truck.

'It's very spacious, isn't it?' Ben looked back at her as he took the turn that led to the house. She was so serious he couldn't help but laugh.

'Yeah, I guess it is.'

Ellie joined his laughter but he was pretty sure she didn't know what they were actually laughing about. His suspicions were confirmed when she stifled a hiccup and asked, 'What are we laughing at?'

'Nothing.' But his smile remained in place as they turned down the driveway. Yep, it was definitely spacious. Unfortunately, that space hadn't been put much good use since he'd bought it. He rolled his eyes to himself. Shouldn't he have grown out of thinking having sex in the back of his truck was kind of hot? He pulled up in front of the house.

'Wait there,' he cautioned Ellie as he got out and hurried round to the other side. She had already opened the door and was leaning dangerously out of it as he came around.

'Hey, what did I say?' he chided her gently, taking her hand with his.

'I can do this on my own you know. I proved that earlier and I don't normally have someone running around opening doors for me.' Ellie grinned, pleased with her riposte.

More's the pity, Ben thought, *so long as it's me.*

'Yes, but you weren't quite so likely to end up on your butt earlier,' Ben parried, his gaze flicking over to the back seat she'd been eyeing earlier. Ellie jerked her head up to say something and stopped as she saw the look on his face.

'Why are you smiling like that?'

Ben looked back at her. The moonlight was bright through a break in the clouds, and she was studying him.

'I'm not allowed to smile?' he asked, his voice soft and low.

Ellie felt a shiver run through her, and a distant part of her brain that wasn't swimming in red wine wondered if Ben had felt it too.

'Ye-es,' she answered. 'But it isn't your usual smile. It's different. It's like a…a…' She waved her free hand around as if trying to catch the word that was eluding her. 'A naughty boy's smile!'

Ben's eyebrows shot up and he burst out laughing. 'A naughty boy's smile? Wow! I didn't even know I had one of them!'

'Well, now you do.' Ellie confirmed and started walking purposefully towards the house, no mean feat in four-inch heels on a dirt driveway. Ben bleeped the alarm on the truck and walked quickly to catch up with her. He was just behind her when a thought struck her and she stopped in her tracks, causing him to bounce into her and knock her off balance. His arm shot out, and caught around her waist, steadying her. She turned around in his arm and looked up at him, her eyes half closed though fatigue and wine.

'You said I was beautiful,' she said softly.

'You are,' he replied, looking down into her upturned face, lips so close he could almost taste them.

'Very beautiful.'

'That's a very nice thing to say.'

'I'm a very nice person.'

Just one kiss. That wouldn't hurt, would it?

But Ben knew it could never just be one kiss with Ellie. Not for him. And not tonight. If anything happened between them, he had to be sure it was because she wanted it to, and not because a bottle of red wine thought she did.

Pulling back, Ben steered Ellie towards the door, unlocked it and stood aside for her to enter. A table lamp lit their way and Ellie headed straight for the stairs as Ben threw the bolts on the door.

"Night,' she called. Ben turned and saw she was halfway up. His eyes took in the heels, his mind took in the bottle of wine, and his body took in the delightfully tempting sway of her hips as she moved.

'Hold on to the rail please, El.' Her hand reached out and she held on to it obediently without looking round.

Ben sat in the dim room for a while collecting his thoughts before making his own way up. This was getting more difficult than he'd ever thought possible. Part of him wanted to just tell her, but most of him didn't. He wanted Ellie. Needed her even. But if she didn't feel the same, the possibility of losing her from his life entirely…that would be worse than anything. The clouds had cleared now and he sat in the glow of the moon for a while after the timer had switched off the lamp, his mind turning things over and over until it all got too complicated and he gave up and started making his way up the stairs.

As he approached the top, his eyes drifted to Ellie's door. The thoughts that suddenly pinged into his head caused him to miss his step and he fell with a loud thud onto the landing.

'Ben?' Her voice was unsteady, an edge to it.

Hurriedly, he picked himself up and went to her door, tapping once before opening it. Ellie was sitting up in the bed, a sheet pressed up against her and a worried look on her face. 'I heard a noise.'

Ben thought how small she looked sitting there, pale in the moonlight, gentle and unsure. All he wanted to do was wrap her in his arms and comfort her. But he knew he couldn't set foot in that room tonight.

'It's OK, it was just me. I tripped on the stairs.'

'Are you alright?' Her expression changed immediately from fear to concern.

'Fine.'

'What was that you were saying about me ending up on my butt?' Ellie teased him with his own warning.

'Actually I fell on my face, not my butt.'

'That was lucky.'

He smiled. 'Yes, it was. Now go back to sleep.'

'Mm-hmm,' she agreed, flopping down onto the pillows. He closed the door gently, sure that she was asleep before it had even clicked shut.

Chapter 16

The next morning, Ben found his guest out on the porch, a small watercolour set at her side. She looked round, her eyes bright and cheerful.

'Morning. There's fresh coffee in the...' She stopped as Ben held up the mug to show that he'd already found it. 'Oh.'

'How long have you been up?'

'Couple of hours,' she replied, focusing back on her painting. Ben watched her, perched up on his swing, one leg tucked underneath her, art pad resting on her lap. How at home and perfect she looked sat there, as though it was exactly where she was meant to be. Ellie looked up at him.

'What's wrong?'

He shook his head, taking a sip of the strong black coffee and sat down opposite, still watching.

'Stop it,' she said, not looking at him.

'What?' he laughed, forcing an innocent inflection into his voice.

Ellie looked up from the paper, directly into his ice-blue eyes. 'Do I have paint on my nose or something?'

'No.'

'Then why do you keep staring? Don't you know it's rude?'

She looked away from him with an embarrassed smile. Ben was trying to work out whether the fact that she was driving him crazy with desire had never actually occurred to her was a good or a bad thing. He shifted in his seat.

'I just can't believe that you finished almost an entire bottle of red wine on your own last night and can sit here bright as a button the next morning.'

'It's champagne that gives me a hangover.'

'Great! Cheap date,' Ben said as he swallowed some more coffee.

'I beg your pardon?'

Ben looked over the top of his mug. Ellie was facing him, trying to look indignant.

He grinned back. 'That didn't come out exactly how I meant it to.'

'I should hope not. Also, I saw the price of that wine. That was not a cheap date. I'm still upset you wouldn't let me pay anything.' She returned to her painting and continued in silence for a few minutes before looking up again. 'Was I that bad?'

'No! Not at all. You were funny.'

'Oh,' she replied uncertainly. Ben got up and walked round to stand behind her.

'How's it going?' he asked, indicating the painting, amazed at her talent as she transferred the scene in front of them into a watercolour copy. He was leaning on the back of the swing, his words deep and soft near her.

'OK, I think.'

'It's beautiful.'

'Thanks.' She flashed a smile back around at him.

'Did you have plans for it?'

'Plans? No, not really,' she replied, taking the pencil from her hair, setting the auburn curls free. Ben watched them as they bounced down the back of the swing. She'd always had such beautiful hair, although he knew she had spent hours as a teenager trying to straighten it, just as his sister had spent hours putting curls in her own. But straight or curly, it was where she'd always kept her pencil when she was sketching. It was quirky, and yet another of the many reasons he loved her.

'Can I have it?' he asked, fighting the urge to bury his face in her meadow-scented hair. Straightening, he moved back around to sit on the swing beside her in order to ensure he didn't give in to the temptation.

'Oh Ben, I don't think it's—'

'I'd really like to have it.'

She turned at the gentleness in his voice, unintentionally whipping him in the eye with her hair.

'Ouch!'

'Oh! I'm so sorry! Here.' She leant closer and held a tissue to his now watering eye. 'Better?'

'Much.' They were silent for a moment, both secretly enjoying the closeness.

'Now I see why you cut it,' he smiled, breaking the silence.

Ellie pulled her hand away, her whole body suddenly growing very still.

'What?' Her voice was small and cold in the warmth of the morning.

'Your hair,' Ben began, a little uncertainly, shocked at the sudden change in Ellie's demeanour. 'When you came – before – it was short.'

She was haphazardly gathering up her paints, and materials, her hands shaking as she did so.

'El? What's wrong?' Ben grew more concerned as she ignored him, grabbing her brushes from the water jar on the table beside her. In her haste, it over balanced, clattering to the floor of the porch and smashing into pieces. Ellie's eyes widened as she looked at the mess. Everything came rushing back at her, the broken glass, the spilt liquid, Carl's vicious tone as he advanced on her. *'You clumsy cow!'*

Ellie ran from the swing, causing Ben to grab at the chain with one hand to steady himself as he reached out with the other to stop her. Catching her arm as he stood up, he immediately let go as she looked up at him, absolute terror in her eyes. He had never seen that look on anyone and prayed to God he would never see it again.

'Ellie! I'm not going to hurt you.' Ben was shocked, his voice breaking on the words. 'I would never, ever hurt you!'

She focused on him then, looked properly and saw who was really standing there. Saw that it was Ben, and not the spectre of Carl that, despite everything, still loomed in and out of her life when she least expected it.

'I know,' she said softly, her eyes suddenly full of unshed tears. 'I'm sorry.'

'It's OK.'

'No,' she said firmly, 'It's not.'

Ben was taken aback at the strength in her tone. Her voice, so gentle normally, now had a sheet of steel lying just hidden beneath the smooth silk. He looked down and saw that her hands were balled into fists, the knuckles showing white. Ellie followed his eyes and forced herself to relax them. She then turned her gaze across to where the water jar had smashed.

'Oh no!' she said, starting towards it, but Ben stopped her.

'It can wait.'

'But there's broken glass!' she said, looking past him, trying to blank out the image that the shards she saw kept forcing back into her mind.

'It can wait,' Ben repeated, before leading her very gently back to the swing.

They sat together in silence for a while, and when eventually they spoke it was at the same time. Ellie insisted Ben go. He shifted in his seat, looking uncomfortable as he prepared to speak again.

'Can I ask you something?'

'Yes.'

'Do you really think I would ever hurt you?' His voice caught on the last word and her hands wrapped around his arm as she answered him.

'No, Ben. No! Of course I know you wouldn't.'

He turned and met her eyes. 'The look on your face...it sure as hell didn't look like you knew that.'

'That's because...it wasn't you I was seeing.'

Ben's face creased in puzzlement and Ellie let out a huge sigh and leant back heavily on the swing. 'You wouldn't believe I've had counselling for all this, would you?' she asked, only half joking.

'If you want more, you know all you have to do is ask.'

Ellie looked up sharply at him. 'I don't want your money, Ben.' The surprise on his face filled her with immediate remorse. 'Oh, bloody hell.' She ran her hands up over her face. 'I'm sorry. Thank you for the offer. That's very kind of you.'

Ben shrugged, not looking at her, hurt and confusion etched into his handsome features.

Ellie leant closer. 'I really am sorry.'

He could feel her pressed against his arm, her velvet smooth voice close to his ear sent a shiver of heat through his body. She moved a little and as Ben turned his head to check on her, the kiss that she'd been aiming for his cheek landed softly on his grateful lips. The smile it brought was involuntary.

'Oh!' she stammered. 'That, er, that, wasn't...erm...' She trailed off.

'No problem,' Ben replied, still smiling.

Ellie blushed. 'I was aiming for your cheek.'

'You missed.'

'You moved.'

Ben shrugged, amusement dancing in his eyes, and Ellie gave a soft laugh. His attention caught sight of something glinting in the sun. Disappearing for a moment, he returned with a dustpan and brush. Ellie moved to take it from him.

'I'll do it,' he said, easily.

She bent down to pick up a larger piece of glass but Ben gently stopped her hand. 'Don't. You could cut yourself.'

He released her hand and quickly swept up the mess. The glass tinkled under the bristles. Ellie stared at it, her face blank but her mind racing.

'I smashed the drinks cabinet.'

Ben looked up at her, and then into the house, confused. 'What?'

She was still staring at the glass on the floor. 'I smashed the cabinet. Carl hit me and I fell against the cabinet, and it knocked over all the bottles and this tray of really expensive crystal glasses.' Ben laid down the brush and sat cross-legged on the floor in front of her. She was twisting her hands as the memories ran through her mind. Gently, he laid his own around hers to calm them.

'I think they were his grandmother's,' she said, frowning as she tried to remember.

'What were?'

'The glasses. I think they were his grandmother's.'

Ben wasn't quite sure where all this was going but it was clear she had something that she needed to say, and he would stay there as long as it took for her to do so. Suddenly Ellie looked down at her lap and seemed surprised to see his hands cradling hers. Turning her head, she looked out past the porch then back at Ben.

'Do you think we could go for a walk?'

'Sure.'

She stood and helped him to his feet and they sat next to each other on the porch steps as they pulled on their shoes.

'Ready?'

Ellie nodded and took the hand Ben offered, pushing herself off the step with the other. They walked down through the garden and out towards one of the paddocks.

'I'm sorry I freaked on you. I got some news about Carl in an email earlier and then you said about my hair being short and it all kind of blew up in my head.'

At her words, and despite the warmth of the morning, Ben felt a chill throughout his body, his steps faltering. Surely they wouldn't be releasing him this early. 'What news?'

'He's had his sentence extended. Apparently, he got into a fight with another prisoner. Put him in hospital.'

'Yeah, well. He seems to be pretty good at putting people in the hospital.' Ben's jaw clenched, the blood now searing hot through his veins. Although he didn't usually condone violence, having Carl's stay in prison extended meant he was securely away from Ellie for longer. That could only be a good thing. He couldn't pretend that he didn't worry what might happen when the loser was finally released, but he'd speak to her about that nearer the time.

'Ben?' Ellie touched his arm. He was so relaxed normally, such a calm soul, that she felt guilty at putting him through this, but it was something she needed to do. Something he deserved to know. She slid her hand around his arm and began to walk again. He felt so warm, so solid.

'When I came…before, and my hair was short? I didn't choose to cut it,' Ellie stated as they walked along. 'Carl did. I said something to upset him and he picked up the kitchen scissors and came after me.' She swallowed and took a deeper breath. 'I actually thought he was going to kill me. He looked…' Her throat caught as she pictured the venom in Carl's eyes that night. She felt Ben's arm tense under her fingers, and looked up, meeting his cool blue eyes. She couldn't do this looking at him.

Ellie stopped, turning around to take in the peaceful scene in front of her as a traumatic one ran through her own head. 'I ran for the bathroom because it was the one door with a lock on it but Carl caught me by my hair and slammed me into the wall. Then he went kind of calm. I don't know if that was more terrifying than his temper. I could see him in the mirror holding this big bunch of my hair in his fist. Then he just hacked it off. And he was laughing.' She paused, her voice raw. 'He just laughed.'

'When was this?' Ben asked, trying to calm the thoughts rushing through his own mind.

'The day before he was arrested.'

'So that was when you decided to leave? For good?'

Ellie nodded, flicking her gaze to his briefly before she looked away again. Something in her eyes turned Ben's heart to ice.

'Something else happened, didn't it?'

After a moment she nodded. Gently he took her hand.

'Will you tell me?'

Ben felt sick as Ellie's hand gripped his, and he listened to the woman he loved tell him that her ex-boyfriend had tried to rape her. The only reason he hadn't succeeded was because Zak had called round. Having seen Carl leave the pub, and the state he'd been in, he'd decided to make an excuse to drop in, arriving at the apartment a few minutes after Carl. He'd immediately heard Ellie screaming and begun banging incessantly on the door. Carl had stormed to the door, hurling abuse at both of them but as he opened it, Zak had shoved it hard, knocking Carl off balance. Racing into the flat, Zak found Ellie in the spare room, huddled into a corner, her dress ripped and her beautiful hair hacked short.

'He'd been drinking heavily. At the trial he said he couldn't even remember coming home after the pub that day.' Her voice was oddly flat. 'I don't know why I went back. Zak took me home that night but I should have just left then and there forever. But I didn't want to leave all my stuff behind.' She looked up at Ben, her eyes shining. 'How stupid was that? It was just stuff!'

Ben wrapped her up in his arms. 'It's OK baby, it's all over now.'

'I just wish I'd gone straight away. But he wasn't supposed to be there. I'd planned it so that I'd be gone long before he came home that day.'

'I know, honey.'

'I can't believe I—'

'Hey,' he said, softly as he stood back to look at her, but not letting go. 'None of this was your fault. None of it.'

Ellie let out a sigh. 'I know.' She started walking again but held onto his arm, this time with both hands.

'The counsellors I had were really good. Kate was the one that arranged the first meeting. She took me there, stayed in the waiting room so I couldn't bolt, then drove me home. It took a while but it really did begin to help. I didn't see them straight away after it all happened. I guess I should have done but I went through a period of denial, I guess. You know, if I don't think about it, maybe it didn't happen.' She glanced up at him with a sad look. 'It didn't work. Obviously.'

'Hey?' Ben softly tucked a curl behind her ear. It was a small, gentle gesture but Ellie felt it in every part of her body. 'I think you're allowed some slightly off decisions after what you've been through.'

'The thing is, I thought I was fine. That maybe relationships weren't really my thing. The odd dates I had when I felt ready didn't do anything for me and when I think back now, I don't know if I ever was ever truly in love with Carl. I know I thought I was. But he was very charming when we met, and I wonder now if I just didn't get swept along with it all.' She looked out to the horizon, her voice soft. 'I'm not sure I even realised that I hadn't felt the way I should about him until I met you again. I don't know if that makes it all so much worse somehow.'

Ben stopped walking, and Ellie pinged back on his arm.

'What did you just say?'

'About it being worse?'

'Before that.'

'Oh…I don't know. I was just rambling.' Ellie turned and began walking back towards the house.

'Hey!' Ben caught up and came around to stand in front of

her. 'OK, first. You can't think about it being worse or better. We can't change the past. It is what it is. But it is the past. Thinking about it too much only serves to drive us crazy. '

Ellie gave a head tilt of agreement.

'Good. And secondly, what did you mean when you said "until you met me again"?'

Ellie looked shyly at him now as he stood close to her. She'd tried not to think about Ben since she'd left after Todd's recovery, putting the attraction she'd felt down to the intensity of their situation but even just innocently spending time with him had woken her in ways she'd never known. But she'd thought she'd loved someone before, and look how that had turned out?

Suddenly she felt a wash of panic. What if she'd been right and that attraction to Ben really had just been a reaction to an intense situation? He was the only man she trusted, aside from Zak and her dad. That, on top of what she'd felt previously, could easily explain why she was feeling the way she was now. Not to mention that, despite everything, she was still a woman and Ben Danvers was probably the most gorgeous, well-built man she'd ever known. But...oh God, she couldn't risk his, and possibly Sandy's friendship on some confused feelings and basic instincts! She couldn't do this. She must have been stupid to—

'El?'

'I'm sorry,' she explained. 'I shouldn't have said that.'

'Why not?'

Why not, she thought. Maybe because Ben would say thanks but no thanks and he'd be so damn nice about it, which would make it much, much worse.

He watched her twisting her hands. When he spoke, his voice was soft.

'Ellie, why did you tell me all this?'

'I don't really know,' she said, honestly. Then, to top off her embarrassment, she burst into tears. Whatever she tried to tell herself, she knew the truth. She was utterly in love with Ben

Danvers but the risk of being rejected, by him of all people, was too much. The secret would have to remain hers forever.

Ben let Ellie cry but led her to a boulder in the shade as she did so. Sitting, he pulled her ever so gently down beside him. The rock was ancient and smooth and warm from its exposure to the earlier sun. Ellie swallowed a final sob and sniffed. They both searched their pockets for a handkerchief in vain.

'OK,' Ellie said, trying to regain her composure. 'Can you look away for a minute?'

Ben raised an eyebrow but did what he was told, then turned back to catch Ellie wiping her nose on her shirt sleeve. She lowered her eyes to the rock, and Ben couldn't help but laugh.

Ellie looked up startled then rolled her eyes. 'Fine. Just don't tell my mum I did that.'

'Promise.'

She dropped her head in her hands 'This really isn't going to plan at all.'

'Ellie?' Ben's voice was close, soft and deep, his warmth breath brushing over her ear. She turned and his lips met hers with such tenderness that she reached out for him, forgetting that her arm had been holding her up from the boulder. Ben caught her without breaking the kiss. Finally he let her go, and Ellie released a shaking hand from his shirt to support herself. Ben smiled down at her – a lazy, sexy smile.

'I was aiming for your cheek.'

'You missed.'

'You moved,' he said as he leant in towards her again. Ellie placed a hand on the broad, strong chest, feeling the defined muscles beneath the fabric. Ben looked down at her hand, then back at her. She took a deep breath.

'Ben, I need to know if you're just doing this to make me feel better.' He opened his mouth to reply but she rushed on. 'Because, believe me, it's working, but, really, that's not fair to either of us and I need to know where we stand and…' Ben moved towards

215

her again and her train of thought derailed. 'And stuff...' she finished weakly as Ben moved in to kiss her again.

'Actually, I'm doing this to make me feel better,' he said, kissing his way down her neck.

'Oh,' was all Ellie could manage as heat blinded her and she went past caring why he was doing it so long as he carried on doing it. Ben laid her back gently on the warm rock and pulled away to look into her eyes.

'Don't stop,' she whispered. Ben grinned down at her.

'You like me.'

'You like me too.'

'That—' he whispered back '—is one hell of an understatement.' Ellie could hear the smile in his voice as he buried his dark head in her neck.

'Really?' she asked, turning her head to try and see his face.

Ben pulled back, studying the delicate face, the long red curls vivid against the grey rock, and the bright green eyes looking into his, wide in anticipation.

'Really,' he stated, moving to lay back against the rock next to her, letting out a breath between his teeth as he did so. Ben rolled his head to look across at her. 'OK. I'm just going to say it. It's way overdue anyway. I love you, Ellie. I've loved you ever since I saw you sitting on my folks' tree swing.' He turned to look up at the sky. 'Actually, I haven't been able to stop thinking about you since I talked to you on the phone that day.'

'When?' Ellie asked, trying to get her head around what Ben had just said.

'Sand was talking to you in the kitchen, I came in to get a drink and I took the phone off her to thank you for the painting.' He shifted himself and rested on one elbow as he looked down into her face. 'And this soft, sexy voice floated down the line to me and I thought "Oh boy!". And then I did everything I could to forget all about it.'

'Thanks.'

'I was married.'

Ellie winced. 'Oh. Yes, of course. Sorry. I...'

'But it was a hell of a lot harder than I thought it would be. And then I saw you on the swing and you looked so—'

'Dreadful?' Ellie filled in. 'Are you sure this isn't about feeling sorry for me?'

Ben gave her a look. 'Not the word I had in mind. But I truly did love Cyndi and I concentrated on my marriage, even though by then we both knew that it wasn't going how either of us had hoped. But I still had to try. So with that, and work. I did a pretty good job of putting you back in the friendship file.'

'Friends is good.'

'It is. But once I was free to think about whatever, and whoever, I liked, there was only one person in my mind. And she was there pretty much the whole time. When you came out here last time, I was so close to telling you then but I was worried...'

'That I might think it was more to do with the intensity of the situation rather than a real connection?'

He nodded, then ran his hand lightly across her stomach, making her shiver. Her reaction made him smile.

'Yes,' she agreed. 'That was a possibility. And also that I might feel you needed to show me people were different. That you might feel you needed to be the one to be nice to me.'

'Nice? Ellie, this about a whole lot more than being nice. Believe me.'

'Yes. I know that now. But...'

'But what?'

'I couldn't help thinking that. You've always been so kind to me. And nice,' she added, teasing. Ben stopped moving the hand that had been roving gently over Ellie's stomach and hips.

'Nice? Nice? Oh man, am I in trouble.'

'I do have other words if you don't like that one.' Ellie smiled up at him, as his hand began moving against the soft fabric of her shirt once more.

'And what might they be?'

'Oh, now…let me see. How about gorgeous, sexy, intelligent, funny, kind, understanding – need I go on?'

'Don't let me stop you.' Ben smiled, reaching over and pulling her gently over on top of him. She looked down into his face and then back at the rock.

'You are so much more comfy than that boulder.' She wriggled a little, and Ben quickly grabbed her hips, stilling them.

'Don't.'

'What?'

'Just…don't do that.'

'What? This?' she asked, her eyes wide with teasing innocence as she wriggled again.

Quickly Ben slid her off, back onto the rock, before pushing himself up on to his feet. He then held out a hand to help Ellie up. She took it and they began their way back to the house, Ben walking so fast that Ellie had to take two steps to his one as he gripped her hand, propelling her along.

Halfway back, Ellie tried to speak. 'What's wrong?' she puffed out as she half ran beside him. Ben's only reply was to stop momentarily and kiss her, one hand cupping her face, the other running slowly down her back, coming to rest on the curve of her rear as he held her close towards him. When he pulled away, there was fire in the ice-blue of his eyes and his normally calm demeanour looked more than a little shaken. He smiled down at her before heading off again.

When they got back to the house, Ben held the door for Ellie and she headed up the stairs before coming to a halt at the top. Ben was right behind her and she turned to face him, the stairs making them level.

'My place or yours?'

'Definitely mine. My bed's been empty of you for way too long already.' He turned her around, patting her behind to get her to move. She giggled, taking his hand as he stepped onto the landing, the whole thing feeling completely natural and holding none of the fear she'd worried about. As they got to his door, he reached across for the handle.

'El?'

She turned at the sudden change of tone, his voice now serious.

'You've changed your mind.'

'Oh God, no I haven't,' Ben replied quickly, his body responding as Ellie pressed against him, the wanting in his voice driving a hot flare through hers. He leant her back so that he could look into her eyes. 'I just need to be sure this is what you want.'

'This is what I want,' she said, her voice steady and sure. 'I know it now, and I knew it back in the middle of that field earlier.' Ellie looked up at him from under her lashes, teasing. 'But you didn't want to play outside.'

'Oh, how wrong can you be,' Ben replied, opening the door and nudging her in with his hip. Ellie moved a step and stopped again.

'So why—'

'Because unlike some guys, I don't go around prepared for anything all the time.' He bent and kissed her neck, his lips moving slowly down her collarbone. 'I didn't have anything with me out there. But, believe me, that's not a mistake I'll ever be making again.' Straightening, he pushed the door closed and placed his arms around Ellie.

'Now, any more questions?' he asked, as he kissed his way down her throat, his hands moving up at the same time, undoing the buttons on her shirt. They fell towards the bed, Ellie letting her shirt fall to the floor as she pulled at the buttons of Ben's. His kisses were gentle but strong, tender yet full of desire. Then his hand was on the waistband of her shorts, feeling for the fastening, finding it and pulling the zipper, freeing his hand to move lower.

Ellie gasped as he touched her. She had been so frightened after Carl that she wondered whether she'd ever want to be with a man again. Even once she began to rebuild her confidence, sex had been incredibly low on her priorities. But then she'd met Ben again. And now, she wanted him so much she was losing her mind. His hand moved and teased, sending a fresh wave of heat and blood through her body. She moaned, and blushed a little as Ben smiled.

'You are so beautiful.'

'Thank you,' she forced out, her voice low and hoarse with lust. 'So are you, which is kind of why I'm here so could we—'

'Shh.' Ben silenced her with a kiss as his other hand moved to push her shorts further down. Ellie kicked her legs to free them of the denim. Ben looked down at the scrap of satin now left.

'You look good in blue.' He grinned as Ellie twisted her head and gasped as Ben slid his fingers back into her underwear.

'There's not much to look good in.' She struggled with the words as the speed of Ben's movements increased.

'That is true. In which case, there's not much point in having them on.' His voice was deep and rough and the sound of it sent fresh ripples of desire through her as he hooked his fingers each side of her hips and pulled. Ellie kicked once more to remove her underwear whilst Ben deftly undid her bra with one hand and tossed it on the floor.

'You're worryingly adept at that,' she breathed as she helped him fervently dispose of his own clothes.

'I had a lot of practice in my youth.'

'I see you kept up your skills.'

'It's good to keep your hand in with some things,' he said, his eyes roaming her body as his eyebrow raised in a tease. She brought her hand up to playfully slap him away but Ben caught it and laid them both back on the bed with his weight, holding her hands by her sides as his chest pressed against hers. It felt so good to have him there, solid, safe and sexy as hell. He moved and Ellie missed a breath as she felt how much he wanted her.

'Ben,' she whispered, her desire spiralling beyond her control as she grabbed at his hips, but he held her back.

'Wait,' he replied throatily as he moved down her neck again and onto her breasts, teasing and playing with his lips, tongue and teeth until Ellie moaned at their tenderness and the pleasure of his touch.

'Wait,' he said again as his fingers moved lower, hovering briefly, causing her to arch her back to keep him touching her. Ben moved across her, one hand driving her to distraction whilst the fingertips of the other drifted over her skin, soft and smooth beneath them. He could barely take his eyes off her, this woman he'd waited so long for. This woman he loved with everything that he was.

Ellie opened her eyes, looking up into his. Her mind was fuzzy and all she knew was that Ben loved her, and all she cared was that he was here, and she was with him. And then he smiled a slow, sexy smile as he slid down the bed, his hands never leaving her. Ellie closed her eyes as the wave built inside her, bubbling up, taking her over, until finally it broke and she screamed out, half in release and half in surprise.

Ben slid up Ellie's body slowly, kissing each part he passed on the way, before reaching her face and placing his elbows either side.

'Hello.'

'Hello.'

'Everything OK up here?'

'Oh, yes,' she breathed as he reached for the protection he'd been without earlier. His touch still gentle, but his desire obvious, he moved across her and Ellie reached up, kissing him deeply as he entered her.

Chapter 17

It was early evening when Ellie woke and felt Ben spooned against her back, one arm draped protectively around her. She snuggled back against him and felt him warm and solid against the length of her body.

'Fidget,' a sleepy, slightly muffled voice mumbled.

'I didn't think you were awake.'

'I wasn't.'

'Did I wake you?'

'Yes.'

Ellie fidgeted again and turned around to face him. His face was half buried in the soft, downy pillow.

'Are you hungry?'

'No, I ate earlier.' His eyes remained closed as a broad smile spread across that gorgeous mouth.

Ellie's eyes widened at the realisation of his comment. She shoved him over onto his back.

'You are a very rude man.'

'I didn't notice you complaining before,' Ben replied, sliding his hands around her waist and pulling her closer. She tried to think of a smart comment to come back at him with, but she couldn't. All she could think of was how wonderful she felt.

'I am hungry though.'

'OK.' Ben sighed as he drew his finger lazily up and down her spine. 'Do you want to eat in or out?'

'Out.'

Really?' Ben couldn't help the disappointment in his voice. He'd kind of been hoping for a repeat performance after a quick bite to eat.

'Yes.' Ellie tangled her fingers in his dark hair. 'I want you to take me to the place we went after we left the hospital the first day. Do you remember?'

'I do. That's where you want to go?'

'It is.' Ellie kissed his sleepy lips and pushed away from him, taking the sheet with her. Ben watched as she wrapped herself in the expensive cotton and padded across into the en-suite bathroom before letting his head drop back into the soft pillows. Splaying a hand out, he felt the warmth where she'd laid and smiled, satisfied and happy as he drifted back off to sleep.

*

They were resting on the front on the truck, having finished up the last of the pizza, looking up at the painted sky.

'I love it here.'

Ben took the beer they were sharing from her. 'Yep. It's one of those places.' It didn't even bother him that Cyndi hadn't felt that way about the place. Ellie did and that was all that mattered. She was all that mattered. Her head rested against his chest as he tenderly stroked her hair.

Ben had never been happier. This. This was what love was supposed to feel like. To sit in silence, but not have to fill it, watching the stars come out and wishing on them. Although he was pretty sure his wish had already been granted.

'Do you remember that time Sandy and I were having a sleep out and we thought we saw a UFO, but you told us it was a satellite?'

Ben finished the last of the beer and put it down beside them. 'Yep. Actually, I thought it was a UFO too but we'd never have heard the last of it if I'd agreed with you.'

Ellie sat up quickly, spinning around to look at him. 'Really?'

'No!' Ben replied, his voice dipping in the middle, before he burst out laughing at her expression.

She narrowed her eyes at him. 'You know you're going to pay for that.'

'I am, am I?' Ben asked, his voice low as he gathered her back against him, 'And just how am I going to pay?'

'I'll think of something.'

'I don't doubt it.'

Ellie grinned at him then leant forward, falling into his kiss. Ben moved his hands down her back, enjoying the feel of her, the taste of her. He had waited so long but it had been worth it. Ellie was his and he was hers. At last. Turning, she settled back and snuggled against him again. Looking up, she focused on a plane way, way up, its lights blinking bright in the dusky sky.

'I wonder where that's going?'

Ben followed her eyes upward. Ellie carried on as she watched the aircraft getting smaller in the distance. 'I can't believe three weeks is nearly up.'

Behind her, Ben's brow darkened. 'And I can't believe I wasted two of them not sleeping with you!' She laughed but he heard the sadness in it. '

Still,' she said, brightening and pushing herself up from the ground before holding out a hand to Ben. 'We have the rest of the week to make up for it. Do you have a Do Not Disturb sign for your door?'

'No,' Ben took her hand it but put the force on the truck as he got up. 'But I can get one on the way home.'

'Good.' Ellie tilted her head. Ben was looking at her funny. 'What is it?'

'How often do you go down to see your parents?'

Ellie straightened away from him. 'Well, I guess that cooled the mood,' she replied, half laughing but not quite able to hide the confusion on her face. She let out a sigh. 'I don't know, every two or three months I suppose. It's quite a drive down to Cornwall. We Skype every week though, and text and stuff, obviously.'

'If you could still do all that, would you consider moving out here?'

'Sorry?'

Ben took her hand. 'I wondered if you would consider living out here again?'

'Well, yes I would, but it's not as easy—'

'With me.'

'What?'

'With me. At the ranch.' Ellie was staring at him with her mouth slightly open. It closed then opened again slightly in that cute way of hers and he fell in love with her all over again. Stepping closer, he boosted her up onto the hood of the truck.

'You know that I love you?' Ellie nodded.

'And you love me?' She nodded again. 'So will you stay?' He'd never been one for stage fright, even in the biggest of arenas, but right now there was a distinct nervous timbre to his voice. He knew there was a good possibility that Ellie would say no. Her whole life was back in England – her job, friends, family. He knew it was a lot to ask.

'I think you just paid for that earlier comment,' Ellie finally answered, a mixture of shock and delight on her face.

Ben caught his breath. 'Is that a yes?'

'Yes,' she said, laughing as he scooped her up from the truck and spun her round before pulling her into a kiss. 'Definitely, yes.'

They were both a little breathless when they pulled apart.

'So I'm fully paid up then?' He grinned down at her, happiness flooding every fibre of his body and mind.

'I think so. In fact, I think you may even be in credit.'

'Oh yeah? So when do I get to collect that?'

She smiled a smile that hit him square in the chest as she looked him up and down, slowly, appreciatively. His body coursed with heat and he marvelled at how she could make him feel so wanted without even touching him. Eventually, her eyes came to rest on his face.

'What are you up to?' he asked, smiling but not caring. Whatever it was, he was up for it.

'It's time to collect your credit.' With that, she reached down and hooked two fingers in his belt buckle before walking slowly backwards towards the truck, pulling him with her. Her other hand was unbuttoning her shirt. When they got to the truck, she pulled open the back door. Her shirt, now open, flapped in the gentle breeze. Ben looked at the truck, then back at Ellie, standing there half undressed. His brain had trouble forming any words. Probably because there wasn't a whole lot of blood flow there right now. 'Here?' was all he could manage.

'Unless you don't want to, but I seem to remember it looked very spacious back there.'

Ben had already lifted her onto the seat but he pulled back, realisation dawning on his face. 'That's what you meant? The other night?'

Ellie yanked at his belt. 'Yes but you didn't seem to get the hint.'

'It did cross my mind but I didn't think you meant…I thought you were just, you know, yammering after the wine'

'I do not yammer! And I was quite in control, thank you.'

'OK. But if something happened, I wanted it to be right. Not something you might have regretted in the morning.'

'I wouldn't have regretted it. But the fact that you considered that is just one of the many reasons why I love you.'

'I look forward to hearing the others.' He smiled, inwardly swearing at the missed opportunity. 'And for future reference, I'm not real good with subtle hints.'

'So I noticed.'

'So next time, you just come right out and tell me, OK.'

'I thought that's what I was doing.'

'See? We're progressing already,' he murmured into her neck as he leant down and, under the stars, in the middle of nowhere, they christened his truck.

Chapter 18

'You can stop grinning now.'

Ben looked up from his cereal at Ellie and his grin widened. 'After yesterday? Are you kidding?'

Ellie smiled back, a faint blush touching her cheeks. Ben saw, adding it to his list of reasons of why he was so crazy about her.

'What did you want to do today?'

'How about going riding.'

'OK.'

'Is that alright with you?' Ellie checked, unsure of his expression.

'Of course. Your wish is my command.' He waved his hand and his smile was back, but Ellie wasn't laughing.

'Don't say that.'

'What? It was a joke. What's wrong?'

'I don't want you to do stuff just because I want to.'

'I know.'

Ellie didn't look convinced. Ben took a deep breath and covered her hand with his. 'I know what you're thinking.'

'I'm not thinking anything.'

'Yes, you are. You're thinking that I let Cyndi have her way all the time and look how that turned out.'

'I know it's early and I'm overreacting but I don't want that to happen. I'd rather stop it now than—'

'That's not an option.' He lifted her hand to his lips. 'Don't worry. We're going to be fine. I know it's a huge thing for you to move out here, but I would never have asked if I didn't think we could make it work.'

'I know.'

'Good. So, did you want to go ride now?'

'OK.'

'Damn.'

'What?'

'I was kind of hoping you were going to say no and drag me back to bed.'

'Later.'

'Right!' Suddenly, he began hustling Ellie out of the door.

'What are you doing?' She laughed, practically tripping onto the porch.

'Sooner we get out, sooner we get back!' he said, scooping her up and sprinting down to the stables.

*

Ellie kicked her heels, spurring Merlin into a gallop. It felt so good, the sound of the charging hooves thudding over the sunbaked ground, the wind in her face and her braid thudding against her back in rhythm with the horse. She could hear Ben gaining and she slowed as he came alongside.

'Can't even beat me when I give you a head start,' Ben teased as Ellie stopped beside him.

'You know, smug doesn't suit you.'

'Really? I thought it was a good look.'

'I should think again then,' she replied, looking down at her boot.

'Want to head back?'

'In a minute. I just need to adjust this,' she said, leaning down to her left stirrup. 'It's not feeling quite right.'

'Excuses.' Ben teased her again.

Ellie looked under her lashes at him. 'Make the most of it, sunshine. I just need a little more practice to get back into it, then you'll be the one trailing behind.'

'Is that right?'

'Yep.' Ellie went back to her stirrup.

Suddenly there was movement in the grass in front of them, and Merlin threw his head back. Ellie tried to calm him and regain her seat, but a second movement spooked him further and he reared violently, hurling her from his back and galloping free. Ben was off his own horse almost before Ellie had landed on the ground with a sickening thud.

'Ellie! Oh Jesus, Ellie?' Ben heard his own voice crying out to her as he ran, but it almost sounded like someone else's. *Please, please not this again!* Memories of Todd's accident flooded Ben's mind, centring on the absolute stillness with which he had lain in the arena after the fall. Just as Ellie – his Ellie – was doing now.

Ellie's eyelids fluttered and she opened her eyes to see Ben leaning over her.

'Ouch.'

'Don't move,' he instructed as she tried to sit up.

'I'm fine,' she protested. 'Don't fuss.'

Ben glanced back as he checked her for broken bones. 'I'm entitled to fuss, so just sit there and let me fuss for a minute, will you?'

She let out a huff but remained where she was until he was satisfied that there was nothing obvious wrong – the most he was going to get her to agree to right now as she resolutely refused to let him go fetch a doctor out here in the middle of nowhere. Quickly, he sent a message to Jed and then turned his attention back to his guest. Merlin was long gone, so he helped Ellie up into his saddle, before hoisting himself up behind her. Ellie leant back against the warm, broad chest and closed her eyes. Ben wrapped his arms around her to steady her in the saddle, and walked his mount on.

'You feel alright?' His voice was steady and normal as he did his best to cover the shock and concern filling his mind.

'Mm-hmm.' She snuggled back against him.

Ben sat straighter and looked down at her face. 'Honey, don't go to sleep.'

'I'm just resting my eyelids.'

'Well, don't. Not right now. You can rest all you like after the doctor's seen you, but I need you to stay awake for me now. Please.' Ben's concern was possible concussion. He looked across the distance, trying to estimate how far they had come. He didn't want to take it too fast and bounce Ellie around, but it battled with his wish to get the doctor to her as soon as possible. Ben stuck with the slow pace, and kept Ellie talking as they made their way back.

Jed came running out to the yard when he heard another horse. He looked from Ellie to Ben then back again. She was very pale. 'I sent for the doc as soon as you messaged. What happened? Merlin came back like he had the devil himself behind him.' Jed lifted his arms and helped Ellie down from the horse. Despite her protestations, she was actually feeling a bit on the grim side now, and in need of a nice, comfy bed.

'What'd you text him for?' Ellie frowned at Ben before turning back. 'I just fell off,' she said, giving Jed a lopsided, rather tired smile as she plopped down onto a handy hay bale.

'Stupid damn horse spooked at something and threw her. She hit her head. Thanks for getting on to the doc. Did he say how long he'd be?'

'Not long. He was already out on a call not too far away. She lose consciousness?' Jed asked, nodding at Ellie who was sliding slowly down the bale, and looking to get comfy.

'Less than a minute but I still want him to check her out. I'm going to get her back up to the house now. C'mon sweetheart, let's get you inside,' he said, bending to pick her up.

Ellie fought against the fatigue but her back and head were already aching and she just didn't have the energy. Giving up, she laid her head on Ben's chest and closed her eyes.

Ben looked down at the woman in his arms as his long strides took them both quickly back to the house. He'd waited so long to be with her. Fear cast an icy shadow over him, and he held Ellie even closer, reassuring himself that she was still there, still breathing in his arms. As he shifted his position, Ellie roused a little.

'You can put me down now. You've proved you're a hero.'

Ben looked down into her sleepy eyes and forced a smile. 'And don't you forget it.'

They reached the porch and Ellie leant out a little from Ben's arms to open the door. He stepped in, holding it open with his shoulder before letting it shut behind them.

'Where are we going?'

'Bed.'

'Both of us?' she asked, a weak smile teasing the full lips.

Ben glanced down briefly at her, as he concentrated on the stairs. His face was creased with worry. 'Just you for the moment,' he said, casting a glance as he pushed open the door of his bedroom with a knee. 'Unfortunately.'

Ben set Ellie down gently on the bed, releasing her as though she were a fragile piece of china, terrified she might shatter at any moment. He crossed to a large chest of drawers, opened one of them and took something out of it then handed it to Ellie.

'Here, put this on. I'm just going to see if I can find out how far away the doctor is. I'll be back in two minutes. You OK?'

'Yes. You're fussing again. I don't need a doctor anyway,' she said, standing to change into the T-shirt Ben had lent her and immediately wobbled.

He was across the room in two strides and caught her arm, carefully sitting her back on the bed.

'Too bad. You're seeing one.'

Ellie studied him for a moment, the sharp cheekbones, that striking combination of dark hair and light eyes. 'You're beautiful.'

Ben raised his eyebrows. 'You really did take a bump on the head, didn't you?'

'You know you are.'

'Actually, no, it's not a description I've had before.'

'Hello?' Jed's voice called from below.

'Stay there.' Ben instructed her before heading out, hoping that Jed might have an ETA on the doc.

Ellie slipped her shirt and underwear off and slid Ben's T-shirt over her head. Unzipping her jeans, she leant forward to pull them off. Suddenly the room span violently, and she flung her arm out, grabbing hastily at the bedstead, sitting still until the world slowed down a little before changing tack and lifting her legs up onto the bed to meet her hands and pull her jeans off that way. Ben re-entered the room to find Ellie sitting on the edge of the bed, still pale, and swamped in his T-shirt, tanned legs dangling above the floor.

'Doc's going to be here soon. Come on, into bed.' Ben eased her up for a second so that he could pull the sheet down, then helped her climb into the huge, elegant bed. Ellie closed her eyes as she sunk back against the soft downy pillow.

Ben stroked her hair and held her hand as he listened out for the doctor's car on the drive. Thank God he'd already been out on a local call. Jed had just caught him as he finished so he should be here in no time. Ben looked back at Ellie. She looked so tiny in the huge T-shirt in the huge bed. Suddenly her eyes flew open.

'Oh God!'

'It's OK, baby.' Ben soothed her but she pushed him out of her way with a force that belied her frame as she struggled to get out of the bed, tripping on the covers as she ran for the bathroom,

233

arriving just in time to throw up violently in the appropriate place. When it was over, Ellie rested her forehead against the cool porcelain.

'Can I come in?' Ben's voice came from the open doorway.

'No,' she replied, miserably.

He entered the room anyway.

'Feel better?'

She raised her head and gave him a look before dropping her head back.

'OK. Take that as a no then.' He crouched down until he was level with Ellie. 'Going to do that again anytime soon?'

An unintelligible sound was the only response so Ben helped her to her feet and guided her to the sink where he handed her her toothbrush and the paste. She looked into the mirror, and into the face of Ben who was still standing behind her.

'Are you going to stand there and watch me brush my teeth now?' Ellie was tired, sore, embarrassed and grumpy as she held her hair back with her free hand.

'No,' Ben answered, relaxed as ever. 'I'm going to stand here and make sure you don't crack your head open on the sink if you pass out.'

'I'm not going to pass out,' she grumped, around a mouthful of toothbrush. As she said it, the room spun again and Ellie grabbed the sink to steady herself. As her hair fell in her face, she felt Ben's arm around her, steadying her whilst his other hand gathered up her hair and held it back. Ellie finished brushing and placed the toothbrush on the side of the sink. Ben turned her around in his arms.

'How come women always look better in a guy's clothes than the guy?'

'Had a lot of women wearing your clothes then?' Ellie grouched at him, pushing her hand against his chest and wriggling to get free.

'No, not really,' he replied, unphased as he gently steered her back to the comforting mass of the bed. 'Are you always this crabby when you're sick?'

She kind of was but a crunch of car tyres on the drive alerted them to the arrival of the doctor and Ellie, thankfully, avoided having to apologise for her mood.

*

'Thanks again for getting here so quick,' Ben said as he walked Doctor King back to his car.

'No problem. It's always best to make sure in these circumstances. But, as I said, Eleanor should be fine. Just make sure she takes it easy for the next few days and call me if you're at all worried.' With that, he shook Ben's hand, got back into his sedan and set off back to town.

Chapter 19

Two days later they were sitting on the old porch swing, drinking hot chocolate in the twilight. Ben was stretched out across the seat and Ellie sat nestled in front of him, his body folded around hers like a blanket as they sipped their drinks and watched the stars slide out shyly into the deepening blue of the sky.

'What time did Kate say they would be back?'

'Just later tonight.' They fell back into peaceful silence until Ben voiced a thought.

'Have you spoken to anyone yet – about staying out here? I guess Zak'll want you to give notice.' Ben felt Ellie tense in his arms and the blood cooled in his veins.

'No, I haven't spoken to anyone. I don't really know about Zak. He'll be supportive, of course, but I don't want leave him in the lurch, especially after everything he's done for me.' So, she had changed her mind. She was going back after all.

Ellie pushed herself up, using Ben's broad chest to help. She swung her legs around so that she was sitting on the swing, both her legs hanging over Ben's right one, her expression serious. She opened her mouth to speak but Ben jumped in.

'If you're planning on breaking up with me, could you at least let me sit up first.'

She didn't move off his leg but turned to meet his eyes. Turning once again, she moved so that she was now sitting across his body facing him, one leg tucked alongside the back of the swing, the other hanging down in front of it. Ben shifted position, moving her up his body a little. She'd felt rough for a few days, so they hadn't made love since her fall, and already it felt like a lifetime. Considering the fact that he was about to get his heart smashed into pulp, he was going to make the most of what he could get. Ellie was still staring at him. Then she started to laugh.

'What?'

Ellie shook her head, then leant forward kissing him softly on the lips.

'And you say I expect the worst from people!'

Ben started to smile. 'Does this mean I still have the job?'

'If you still want it.'

'Oh. Believe me, I want it.'

'Good.' She pulled back to look at him properly. 'I can't believe you thought I was breaking up with you.'

Ben shrugged. 'You haven't told anyone you're planning to stay out here, and you went kind of funny when I mentioned it.' Ellie let out a sigh. 'I love you, Ben. More than anything. And I love it here, but it's still a big step. You have to realise that. My family and most of my friends are in England. I see Zak every day and if I don't, I speak to him at least five times. It's just going to take a bit of getting used to.' She took a deep breath. 'And I think it's going to be easier telling everyone in person that I'm leaving, which is why I still have to go back on Friday.'

Ben nodded. He'd known this was coming. It was ridiculous to think that Ellie could just stay out here and take care of things from abroad. The internet and instant communication had made the world smaller but there were still things that were easier to do in person. And that ought to be done in person. Of course she had to go back for a while. The summer break that the band had decided to take was nearly over anyway and he was due back in the studio to start recording for the new album. He knew all the sensible arguments for it all – but that didn't make it any easier. They had waited for so long to be together, any time apart now seemed unbearable.

'I'll miss you.'

'I hope so. I'll miss you too.'

'How long do you think you'll be gone?'

'I don't know. It depends on what I can work out with Zak, but I'm guessing at least a month. Maybe two.'

'A month?' Ben repeated.

'Maybe two.'

He nodded, accepting the fate, and cast a glance around the porch.

'What is it?'

'Nothing really.' He looked back at her beautiful, quizzical face. 'It's just that I can't imagine this place without you now.' Reaching up, he pushed the curls away from her eyes. 'I don't even want to.'

Ellie placed a gentle kiss on his lips and smiled down at him. 'I'll be back before you know it and besides,' she said, her voice becoming lower as she shifted on his hips and felt him react immediately, 'we still have until Friday.' Ben wanted her more than he thought possible but he was still concerned after her accident, especially now that she was planning to fly in a few days' time.

'As much as I want to, the doc did say you were supposed to take it easy.'

Ellie looked evenly at him, then stepped up off the swing. Ben sat up and awaited her reaction. Bearing in mind he'd just blown her off, he was expecting either a blasting or a sulk. But it was neither.

Ellie stepped back closer to the swing and stood in between Ben's legs, forcing his knees apart with her own. He looked up at her. The sun had said its last goodnight for the day, a full moon stepping in to fill its place, illuminating the porch with its soft, cool light. She bent and placed a kiss just below his ear, which also gave him the opportunity to take in the fact that she wasn't wearing any underwear beneath the cotton sundress. Her voice was low and soft in his ear. 'If I'm supposed to take it easy, I guess that means you have to do all the hard work.' Pulling him up, she reached around into the back pocket of his jeans, pulling out the condom she had put there earlier. He smiled in disbelief at her. And at his luck.

His reached out to her, voice low and throaty. 'Come here.'

His lips were on hers, hungry and wanting. He moved his hands up to her face, in her hair, up her body, caressing her back. Then they moved to the dress, working at the buttons with an urgency as he kissed down her neck. The fabric parted and Ben pushed it away, bending his head to kiss the body now exposed to him. The heat of his mouth on her skin almost burned as Ellie reached for his belt buckle and released it. Ellie heard him moan as her fingers moved to the buttons on his Levis. He moved her back before she could finish. His voice was raw and husky in her ear, causing the heat to surge again.

'You're not supposed to be doing anything, remember?' Then gently, he slid his hands up her arms and held both her wrists above her head with one hand as his other moved lower and sent her world spinning.

Pinned up against the support of the porch, Ellie was in full surrender as Ben's mouth and hands covered her body. He drew back up and pressed into her. The wooden post dug into her tender back, still healing from the fall. A mixture of pain, pleasure and longing made her cry out. Ben pulled away, his eyes searching her face. It took a second for him to realise his error.

'Oh El, I'm so sorry,' he breathed.

Ellie shook her head and tried to pull him back against her. Ben moved her away from the offending post and lifted her effortlessly onto the balustrade. Her mind went white as he moved closer and pushed her legs apart with his body, just as she had done to him on the swing. She pulled him towards her, closer, closer, and her nails dug into his back as she felt his hands on her.

'Oh Ellie,' he whispered as he felt how ready she was for him. His finger moved inside her, and was soon joined by another. His thumb gently played, teasing, moving faster and faster. She cried his name as she came, his hands on her, feeling her pulse beneath his fingers.

Ben paused as he reached for the condom and then he was there, securing her on the ledge with one strong arm as he entered. Ellie closed her eyes as he filled her and began to move, his rhythm gaining speed as the moment approached. Ellie's hands were locked behind his neck, legs around his waist, pulling him as close as he could be.

Ben felt her grip increasing, her hot breath on his neck. He thrust deeper and Ellie gripped his neck tighter, the sounds of pleasure she made turning him on even more. Suddenly, her back arched and her fingertips dug into his shoulder muscles as the spasms wracked her body, seconds before Ben's own release came hard with an animalistic growl of pleasure. His arms held her so tight that she could hardly breathe. But Ben's grip was passion, not control. That thought alone caused a shiver of pleasure to travel through Ellie as Ben moved and re-buttoned his jeans. He noticed the movement and smiled at her – that sweet, sexy smile, reserved especially for her – as he slipped his hands back around her hips. Ellie's legs were still crossed behind him, looser now but she tightened them to bring him back to her. His smile widened as he brushed a damp curl from her eye before leaning in to place a soft kiss on the full lips.

'You're amazing.'

'It takes two to tango, don't you know?' Ellie smiled back at him as she began to fasten her dress. Ben watched her for a second then gently brushed her hands away as he took over the task himself.

'Then I think we should tango again real soon.'

'Me too.'

*

'We probably ought to start heading back,' Ellie said, feeling no inclination to move from where she lay on the soft blanket, her head on Ben's chest, the rest of her body pressed against his side as his strong arms held her close and warm.

'Probably,' he agreed, not moving either.

'The time will go quickly. I'll be back before you know it.'

'Uh huh.'

Neither of them were able to put any real belief into their words.

'I'm going to miss you so, so much,' Ben said.

Ellie nodded against him, and he felt the slight shake in her shoulders. Pushing himself up, he brought her with him, tipping her chin up to meet him.

'El, please don't cry.'

'I'm not.'

He raised a brow, and she laughed through her tears. 'OK, I am. But I know it's silly.'

'It's not silly at all, my darlin'. I'm pretty much there myself.'

Ellie wiped her eyes and leant forward, wrapping her arms around his neck and feeling his comforting return embrace.

'It just feels like forever right now.'

He nodded against her. 'It sure does.' Letting out a sigh, he gently loosened her arms and set her back. 'And with that in mind, I wanted to give you something to remember me by, when you're over there.'

Ellie shook her head. 'You really think I'm going to change my mind?'

'No. I don't. But I've been wanting to give this to you anyway, and now seemed like a pretty good time.' Leaning over, he retrieved something from his jacket pocket and then placed it in front of her. Ellie looked down at the small, square box, then back up at Ben.

'Aren't you going to open it?'

She shook her head. 'Ben, you said...I mean...'

'Just open it, please.'

Inside sat the most beautiful ring Ellie had ever seen. On a shining band of platinum sat a stunning, flawless emerald. On either side, two diamonds protected it, the outside stones, slightly smaller than the first.

'Ben...' Her voice was barely a whisper. 'It's beautiful.'

'If you want something different, we can get whatever you like but I always think of emeralds when I look into your eyes.'

'No. It's perfect. It's...' She looked up at him. 'It's just that you said you'd never marry again. That it wasn't for you. I don't want you to feel that you need to do this. I never expected this and my coming back to live with you had no condition of marriage on it. I love you, Ben. I don't want you putting any pressure on yourself to do what people expect. I don't want any pressure on us. At all.'

'Ellie,' he said, taking her hands within his. 'I love you. More than I even knew it was possible to love a person. I want to be with you all the time, talk to you when I can't be, share everything with you, including my life. If I had any doubts about anything, I wouldn't be doing this. Any of this. But I don't. I love you, Eleanor Laing, and I really, really want to marry you.'

Ellie had given up trying not to cry now, and the tears streamed down her cheeks.

'I'm praying so hard that those are happy tears,' Ben said, as his hands cupped her face and his thumbs gently wiped them away.

Ellie nodded. 'They're very, very happy tears!'

'So I can take that as a yes?'

'Yes,' she said, placing her hands over his. 'Yes, yes, yes!' she cried as her tears turned to laughter and Ben stood, sweeping her up and swinging her around as he cried out a whoop of delight into the darkness.

Chapter 20

Two years later

Ben greeted his wife with a hug and lingering kiss as he came off stage, drawing catcalls and comments from the other band members. The tour had a tiring schedule but it was something they loved doing. Their shows were famous throughout the country music world for being so full of energy and life, and they knew it was a part of what helped them keep their fans. Despite the fact that it was exhausting, every member loved performing live, and for Ben this was the best tour yet because Ellie was with him.

'Five minutes,' a voice called from outside.

The band pulled themselves up from the comfy chairs they were sprawled on, kissed their partners and ran back out onto the stage to the screams and cheers of thousands of fans. The drummer launched into the beat of their latest single and the screams got even louder.

'Ladies and gentlemen, before we go any further, I'd like to introduce you all to the newest member of our band.' Lead singer, Marty, was picking up thrown offerings as he walked across the stage talking to the audience. Looking out into the crowd, he could see the fans nearest the stage peering at the other musicians, trying to see if the line-up had changed. He gave them a grin as he walked across to Ben.

Ben was only half listening as he adjusted the tuning of his guitar in his ear-piece, not looking up until Marty threw his arm around his shoulder.

'You want to do the introductions, buddy?'

But it appeared that no introductions were needed as the whole auditorium had already begun to chant 'Jake. Jake. Jake.' Ben smiled at his friend then glanced back towards the wings. Slipping his guitar over his head, he handed it to a roadie who had appeared from nowhere, Ben then went off stage for a moment, reappearing moments later with a baby boy cradled in his arms. The auditorium exploded with cheering as the bundle slept on, nestled in the crook of his father's arm. Marty leant in and admired him. 'Handsome little guy, huh?' Marty paused for effect. 'Obviously takes after his mama.' The audience cheered again. Ben grinned and turned to Ellie in the wings. 'Come get him?' he asked, his words filling the auditorium. A camera at the wings focused in as Ellie shook her head, beaming the image out onto the huge screens out in the theatre. Laughing, she beckoned at her husband to bring their son back, out of the limelight.

Ben turned back to the audience and confided in them. 'She's real shy.' He gently lifted one of his son's arms and gave the fans a wave as he smiled down at the child, winning back all the hearts he'd lost by marrying someone else. Walking back to the wings, his smile was broad as he delivered his baby back into the waiting arms of his mother. His wife. His Ellie.

Acknowledgements

First of all, thank you, as always, to James for his continual belief and support of both me and my writing. Without that, none of these novels would have been sent into the world, and far less would have been created in the first place. Thank you.

Thank you to my lovely editor, Clio, whose knowledge, kindness and support is so appreciated. Her guidance helps make these books so much better and for that, I'm truly thankful. Thanks also to Nia, and all the rest of the team at HQ.

As always, I'd like to send out a big hug to those fellow authors whose help and support can mean so very much. Chief among these is the fantastically talented, regularly hilarious and scarily intelligent Rachel Burton. PS, Eric says hi! Big hugs also go to Sarah Bennett and Lucy Knott for just being generally fabulous and lovely. I can't finish without saying a massive thank you to all the amazing book bloggers and readers who have helped spread the word about my books. I really do appreciate all the effort that goes into blog posts and reviews, and people just taking time out of their busy days to pass on a recommendation. It really does mean so much.

Read on for an extract from *Second Chance at the Ranch,* another gorgeous romance from Maxine Morrey...

Chapter 1

'Yes! Just like that! More! More!' Hero Scott turned her head this way and that, lifted her arms up, then down, the movements almost automatic now as the photographer prompted her unnecessarily. Her long dark hair swayed like a glossy curtain as she tilted her chin down further, maintaining the serious look the photographer had demanded for the shoot.

The studio was lit, almost over-lit, in accordance with the style wanted for the designer's advertising campaign. Loud music by the hottest current DJ blasted from speakers. Hero closed her eyes briefly from the glare, trying to halt the progression of a headache that had been rumbling in her skull for the last half an hour. Her throat was dry and she turned to one of the assistants hovering around the set and made a quick mime of drinking. The assistant grabbed a bottle of water, undid it and stuck a straw in the top. Just as she stepped towards Hero, the photographer roared.

'What are you doing?'

The assistant froze, colour immediately flooding her face as she stood, half on, half off the background roll.

'I ... erm ...'

'You've ruined the perfect shot! Ruined it! Where do we find these people, for God's sake?' he asked, turning on one of the others hovering around the shoot.

'I'm sorry. It won't happen again,' came the reply from a short but perfectly dressed woman, as a vicious glance was sent towards the assistant whose eyes were now brimming with tears.

'I cannot work with such—'

'It's my fault, Armand.' Hero's educated tones rose above the noise, interrupting the photographer's rant mid-flow.

Everyone turned to look at the supermodel. She casually tucked one hand behind her, the pose confident yet aloof. Behind her back, her other hand balled into a tight fist.

'I was thirsty and asked her to get me a drink. I'm sorry if it upset your process but I thought you were taking a break for a moment. So, the fault is completely mine, not hers.' Hero gave the briefest of smiles as she turned back to the young woman and took the bottle from her, placed the straw between glossy, deep-plum-coloured lips and took a brief sip. It wasn't enough, but Hero knew better than to test this particular photographer. He was well known for his diva-type tantrums and had the ability to end a budding career with just one vicious text. Hero had known him for over fifteen years now, both of their careers blooming at a similar time. Unfortunately, as Armand's career had blossomed so had his ego – something which hadn't been all that small to begin with.

No one spoke. No one moved. All were waiting for the explosion they knew was to come.

Instead, Armand let out a dramatic sigh and made a Gallic 'pfff' sort of noise. Hero met his eyes, the short nails on the hidden hand biting in to the soft skin of her palm.

'Fine. Let her keep her job. This time!' He held up his finger, highlighting the magnanimity of his decision. Hero nodded, and beside her the young assistant let out a strangled sob of relief.

'OK. Now! Can we get on?'

Hero dropped back into action as the shutter continued on

and on, the music still pounding, her throat still dry and the headache now full blown. Armand had returned to the shoot with even more drama than it had already been infused with. Hero had been there since 5 a.m., having make-up applied, touched up, and completely changed as fashion editors assigned assistants to curate outfits for the shoot. Hero stood patiently, being handed various clothes to try. Belts put on, belts taken off, her body moved this way and that as if she were no more than a shop mannequin. Which, in some ways, she supposed she was.

The incessant shutter finally ceased as Armand scrolled through a few of the last frames, his thin face becoming even more pinched as he frowned at the back of the camera. Hero took the opportunity to stretch her body, trying to ease the tension in her back and neck as she did so. Glancing across the studio, she smiled as she saw her best friend, Anya, a blonde, willowy Swede, talking to the assistant from earlier. Anya gave her a hug and bent to say something private to her. Whatever it was, Hero was glad of the smile it brought to the young woman. There were days she hated this world. But she knew she couldn't leave. Not yet.

Anya glanced up and over at Hero, her beautiful smile and funny double thumbs up making her friend grin and giggle.

'What are you doing?' Armand's attention, and ire, was now directed at Hero. She'd protected someone else, but Armand had to be seen to win. She knew the game.

'What is this?' he yelled, pulling a sarcastic version of the supermodel's wide smile. 'I do not want this! I want serious. Sultry! Mysterious! I do not want Coco the Clown! If I want to photograph clowns, I will go to the circus! Yet today I am wondering if the circus has not been brought to me!'

The photographer blustered on through his tirade. Hero knew Anya was trying to catch her eye again, but this time she refused to meet it. Instead, she blanked her expression, applying the metaphorical mask of disinterest she wore in these, and many other, situations now. They wouldn't get to her, she told herself. At least they wouldn't see, even if they had.

'Hey!' Anya hurried over to her friend once the photo shoot finally ended, and gave her a hug. 'You OK?'

Hero nodded. 'Yes, fine, thanks. You know what he's like.'

Anya rolled her eyes in agreement.

'Is that assistant all right?' Hero asked as Anya waited for her to change back into her own clothes.

'She's fine. I know her boss pretty well and had a gentle word.'

Hero flicked a glance up as she sat and tied the lace on her designer boots. 'Gentle?'

Anya shrugged, then grinned. 'The poor thing. Armand can be so awful sometimes. He thinks far too much of himself.'

Hero stood and pulled her hair into a low ponytail before pulling a baseball cap on. They had dinner reservations at a restaurant's opening night and, now that the photo shoot had run on far longer than it was supposed to, she didn't have time to go home and change. The make-up was much heavier than she would normally wear for something like this, but it would have to do now. The cap lent an air of casualness to her look and she knew, like so much in this world, if she acted like she was confident about it, no one would know the truth.

***

'How's your head?' Anya asked as they stepped out from the Tube carriage and into the mass of life that was a London Underground station at rush hour.

'It's going off, thanks.' Hero smiled.

The women exited the station within a swarm of others before managing to disentangle themselves from the crowd to walk the short distance to the restaurant. Anya tugged on her friend's sleeve to slow her.

'What's the matter?' Anya looked at her. 'You.'

Hero frowned.

'You still have a pounding headache, don't you?'

Anya was one of only three people who could read Hero. Everyone else was kept away from knowing what she really thought, or felt.

'No.'

Anya raised one fair and perfectly shaped brow.

'OK, fine.' Hero laughed. 'Yes, I still have it, but it is less now, I promise. Probably half of it is just dehydration.'

'Let's just go back home then,' Anya said, her voice soft and kind.

To Hero, that sounded like the perfect suggestion, but she knew Anya had been looking forward to this restaurant thing for ages now. Cooking and baking was sort of her thing. Not an ideal hobby when you were trying to keep your weight to a number decreed by the modelling agency. Hero had started running for longer since she and Anya had bought this flat together, and her friend demanded she be her guinea pig for each recipe she trialled in the gleaming steel and granite kitchen of their Kensington home. 'No, honestly.' Hero reached out for Anya's hand and gave it a brief squeeze. 'It really is going off now. I just need some water and some food and I'm sure that will take care of the rest of it. Come on.' She moved and linked Anya's arm through her own before tugging her along.

'OK. But if it gets worse again, just let me know and we can leave.'

Hero nodded in agreement. 'Promise.'

***

When Hero had begun modelling full-time, the world she had entered scared her and wore her down. She would sit at the castings, knowing that everyone there was analysing her, judging her, comparing her. She hated it. Finally, on a summer afternoon, she got up in the middle of one such go-see and walked out.

Hero sat on the wall of the ornate fountain in the gardens of the location and let out a huge sigh. It felt like a weight had been lifted off her shoulders. Another replaced it almost immediately. If she wasn't going to model, she had to find a job. The summer breeze blew the fountain into a mist and the fine spray was cool as it landed on her face. She closed her eyes to enjoy its soothing touch.

'Hello.'

Hero's eyes flew open and she found herself looking up into the face of a beautiful blonde. She was of a similar age to Hero, and looked vaguely familiar.

'Hello.'

'Are you coming back in?'

Hero looked warily at the door, then back at the blonde, then back at the door again.

She shook her head. 'I don't think so.'

The blonde took a seat next to Hero and held out her hand. 'I'm Anya.'

'Hero. It's nice to meet you.' Hero's etiquette switch engaged automatically.

'What a lovely name.'

'Thanks. My parents really liked Shakespeare.' She smiled awkwardly.

'It's very romantic.' The blonde smiled warmly again. There was an accent there, something Scandinavian, and she was the epitome of the stereotype with long, shiny, natural platinum hair, pale blue eyes and porcelain skin. Hero now remembered that she had seen her at other go-sees. That was why she looked familiar. Anya had a fantastic figure, a little curvier than Hero's. She wore no make-up, as per the preference for castings, allowing the clients to see bone structure and skin tone. Her long legs were clad in tight jeans and a white T-shirt clung to her upper curves.

Anya dug in the pocket of her jeans and pulled out a fresh pack of chewing gum. She unwrapped the outer packaging then offered the pack to Hero. 'Thanks,' Hero said and began to pull a stick out of the casing. Halfway through, she stopped. 'You bite your nails!' she blurted, before looking up at Anya, suddenly realising her comment had sounded like a criticism, which it hadn't been. 'I'm sorry, I didn't mean—'

Anya laughed. 'It's OK! I do! Terrible habit. They have to keep sticking on false ones if there's any chance my hands are going to show in a shot. Or I have to place them where they won't see them. It's a bad habit but I can't stop. I just tell myself there are worse habits to have!' She laughed but both of them knew that the statement was true. Drug habits were rife within their world so, as a vice, nail biting was pretty damn tame.

Hero quickly stuck out her hands in front of her, showing her own bitten nails – a connection of imperfection with her new friend in a world of false flawlessness. She laughed properly, easily, for what seemed like the first time in ages.

Anya persuaded Hero to return to the studio, which had resulted in bookings for both of them. The encounter marked the beginning of a strong bond of friendship between the two young women. They travelled to go-sees together and eventually shared a flat, both dismissing the financially available option of each girl purchasing one separately. Anya came from a close family in Sweden and missed the company. Hero had almost no family and also missed the company. Anya kept Hero's spirits from sinking and Hero returned the favour.

'Hello, gorgeous!' Rupert Thorne-Smith wrapped his arms around Hero from behind and gave her a big kiss on the cheek. The physical contact made a difference from all the air kisses she had received this evening. 'You look bored as hell,' he said, sliding into the empty seat opposite her.

Hero smiled. 'Of course I'm not.'

Rupert screwed up his nose and made a loud 'oink oink' noise, startling the group of older, clearly loaded, women sitting next to them.

'Stop it!' Hero laughed, batting her friend on the arm.

Rupert gave one more oink for good measure before lifting his champagne glass to his lips, a devilish grin on his face. 'That's what happens when you tell porkies to Uncle Rupert.'

Hero shook her head. 'Uncle Rupert' was seven years older than her and the only man she trusted.

'You on your own?' he asked.

'No, Anya's here ... somewhere,' she replied, looking around the now packed restaurant. 'I think she went off to try and talk to the chef. You know what she's like.'

'I also know what the chef is like. Real penchant for blondes. You should have brought a man. It's unlikely you'll see Anya again for some time yet.'

Hero shrugged.

'So?'

'So what?' She frowned.

'I wondered if there had been any change in the Ben Gale/ Hero Scott situation.'

Hero fixed him with a look. 'No. And there won't be.'

Rupert's face became more serious – the joker dispensed with for the moment. 'You two seemed really happy. Is it not worth trying again?'

'No. We were. Mostly. But between my career and his, it just wasn't working out.'

'But couldn't you—'

'No, Rupert. We couldn't. Besides, he's with someone else now, and so am I.'

'If you're referring to that sugar daddy, Jonathan Von Dries, then you already know my opinion of him, and your "relationship".'

'Don't be ridiculous. I don't need a sugar daddy!'

'And yet you have one.'

Hero blew out a sigh. 'I don't. And anyway, you're hardly one to talk. I'm not sure there's a lot of meeting of the minds in your current "relationship".' She made air quotes just as he had done, purposefully letting her gaze drift over to the peroxide blonde perched on the edge of a chair. His date was now on her fourth champagne and getting louder by the minute. Rupert followed his friend's eye line before looking back at her, unrepentant.

'That's completely different.'

'Of course it is. And how is that?'

'Because neither of us are wishing there was more to it than there is.'

'So, exactly the same then.'

Rupert looked at her and Hero did her best to hold his gaze. She couldn't.

'You deserve more than that, Hero.'

Her throat felt tight, and she looked away, out of the window at the passing foot traffic. Crowds of people hurried in all directions. A horn beeped and the wailing siren of an ambulance became louder as the blue lights flashed, competing with the huge neon signs for dominance. Sometimes she just wanted to get away. She didn't know where exactly but somewhere that was the direct opposite of all the noise, lights, crowds – all the constant demands on her senses. Sometimes she just wanted to sit and hear nothing but silence.

Rupert's hand caught hers across the table. 'You know it's just because I care about you.'

Hero nodded, her gaze still fixed on a point outside the window. 'I know.' And she did. Unlike most of the people she spent time with, she knew where she was with Rupert. He didn't take shit from anyone, including her, and she loved him for it.

Rupert Thorne-Smith's relationship with the model Hero Scott had always been cause for gossip. He was wealthy, good-looking, and successful with a reputation that was best described as gentleman playboy. Rupert adored Hero, but she was closer to being a younger sister to him than anything that the papers could dream up.

They had met at a party early on in Hero's career when he had found her sitting outside in the garden, away from the house and the noise and the beautiful people. She was extremely shy but something about her had made Rupert persevere – a new experience for Rupert and women – and it wasn't just her beauty. There was no doubt that the girl was stunning, but there was something else. She had looked lonely, and when he began to talk to her and ask her opinion on subjects, Rupert had never seen a person look so surprised at the interest. That night, a deep, enduring friendship was formed. Rupert took Hero to see a close friend of his, a financial whizz kid, who owned one of the top investment firms in London, and together they went over the best path for Hero to choose when it came to taking care of her earnings, which were rapidly becoming substantial. Thanks to Rupert, and Thorne-Smith Holdings, Hero's financial future was secure. She was already a very wealthy woman.

Rupert knew how the darker side of the glamorous career sometimes got to his friend. This was the side people didn't want the public to see. And to a certain extent, that wish was mutual. People didn't want to hear about the humiliation models sometimes felt, the lack of support from those who should have their backs. They didn't want to know about the drugs, the eating disorders, the ever-present knowledge that you could be the brightest star today and completely ignored tomorrow when a new star ascended. All that most people wanted to see were the highs. The glamour and glitz. The beautiful people living their beautiful lives, wearing the beautiful clothes. On days Rupert saw Hero or Anya looking exhausted, he urged them both to think about leaving modelling. Thankfully, Anya had already been thinking the same thing and was now making plans to return to Sweden and train as a chef. Having been lucky enough to sample some of her recipes, Rupert had absolutely no doubt of her success in her second career. It was Hero that held his concern.

He knew she was aware that, through savvy investments and careful control, she never had to work again. But whenever Rupert broached the subject, she would just smile and tell him not to worry. He knew that somewhere there was a reason she pushed on through, but neither he nor Anya had ever been able to find out what it was.

Hero stretched her long legs out in the hushed atmosphere of the first-class cabin. She'd come to enjoy long-haul flights, delighting in the fact that she was unobtainable for those hours. Her phone stayed switched off and in her bag – something Anya, who had completely embraced the whole Insta-life thing, teased her about relentlessly. It wasn't like Hero was stuck in the Dark Ages, although according to some of those within her circle, the fact that her phone wasn't glued to her hand and kept under her pillow meant she might as well have been. Hero smiled at their comments, but privately thought that neither of those actions seemed the healthiest and carried on doing her own thing.

And now, she had no one to answer to or anywhere else she needed to be except right here. Snuggling down under the duvet, she felt the stress leaving her body as she opened the new novel she'd bought at the airport and began reading.

When her sister, Juliet, had rung her a few weeks ago to say she had become engaged to a man she'd met on her holiday in Australia, Hero wasn't terribly surprised. Juliet had always been the most impulsive of the two sisters, and as Juliet had recounted the story of how she and her new fiancé, Pete, had met, Hero could hear the difference in her voice. Juliet was almost giddy with happiness as she told her about the sheep station that he owned and ran with the help of his younger brother, Nick, and the warmth of his mum and dad when they'd met her. A warm, welcoming family unit was something both Juliet and Hero knew very little about.

'He's a what?'

'A sheep farmer. His family own a sheep station outside Adelaide. They farm sheep. Merino sheep. Organically too,' she added, knowing how much of an animal lover her little sister was.

'Jules, I know models have a dumb reputation, but I think even I can work out what sheep farmers farm.' Hero's voice was teasing.

'I just thought you might appreciate knowing where your favourite sweater might have begun its life.'

'I'm pretty sure I knew it started off on a sheep, Jules, but thanks.'

Hero smiled under her lashes at her older sister. Despite the temptations having been scouted by a model agency when she was fifteen, Hero had continued her education, achieving good grades and fitting in modelling assignments around her academics until she was in a position to model full-time. Her looks, added to the fact that she was easy to work with, if a little distant, meant she hadn't stopped working since. 'Are you ready to be a bridesmaid for your big sister?'

'Ready and waiting.'

They had decided to marry in Australia as Pete had a large family and Juliet had almost none, only Hero. Her sister had been back in the UK finalising details on the sale of her flat, and was about to return back to Australia, and Pete. The wedding was in a month's time. Apparently, Pete's mum had been a godsend when it came to the arrangements, and Juliet was loving spending time with her and Jack, Pete's father. They in turn had loved her immediately.

'Are you really sure you'll be able to make it?' Juliet asked again.

Juliet was desperate for Hero to be with her on such a special day, but she also knew that her sister's job took her all over the world. As they said their goodbyes at Heathrow, she couldn't help checking one more time.

Hero waggled her phone. 'I have the date here and I'll book the time off with the agency first thing tomorrow. No problem. If someone wants me that bad during those weeks, they'll just have to wait. And if they don't want to wait, then that's their problem.'

Juliet looked concerned.

Hero laughed. 'Oh, stop worrying. I love you. You're more important than any shoot. I wouldn't miss this for anything! And I can't wait to meet Pete either. He sounds wonderful.'

'He is.'

'Jules?'

'Yes?'

'I'm going to miss you.'

Juliet pulled her little sister into her arms. 'I'm going to miss you too,' she said, holding Hero close, not wanting to let go.

'Call me when you get home.' Hero paused for a moment and looked at her sister. 'I love you.' 'Don't! I'll cry!'

'I know. You always do, you big blubberpuss.' Hero giggled and gave her sister a huge squeeze.

'I know. I'm a wimp! And I don't care.'

Hero grinned, her own eyes dry. 'I'll be there in a month.'

Hero nodded at the dedicated first-class security area in front of them. 'You'd better go. Don't want to keep him waiting.'

Juliet reached up to hug her baby sister again. At five foot eleven, Hero was three inches taller than her elder sibling and today she wore boots with heels that took her to over six feet. Juliet's feet were snug in trainers. Hero had upgraded her sister, despite Juliet's protests, but she still had a long flight ahead, and then another hop to Adelaide. Comfort was a priority.

'I hope you're not wearing those on the day?' Hero nodded down at her sister's footwear. Juliet followed her gaze, then laughed.

'No. Definitely not! With the groom and best man at six foot three and six foot four, I'm definitely wearing heels!'

'Good. Then if I wear flats, I won't tower over you.'

'You can be quite sweet when you want to, can't you?'

Hero pulled a face. 'Don't tell anyone!' she whispered, and then winked. 'Go on. Get on the plane, and I'll see you in a month.'

Four weeks later, Pete was back at the airport, waiting with his fiancée to meet her sister. Excited to see her, Juliet was incapable of standing still, constantly checking the screens and looking around.

Pete was intrigued. Juliet had told him all about Hero, her jet-set lifestyle, and her personality. From what he knew, it seemed that the sisters were a little like him and Nick, different in their make-up but close and reliant on each other. Even more so as a result of their parents' relative disinterest in them.

Hero stepped through the doors to Arrivals, a wheeled Louis Vuitton suitcase trailing behind her. Pete saw the difference immediately. He'd seen photos obviously, but it wasn't quite the same thing. The sisters might be similar in heart, but they didn't share such similarity in their looks as Nick and Pete did.

Pete watched as his sister-in-law-to-be glided through the crowds to meet them. Hero's brunette, waist-length hair fell in a shimmering sheet of rich brown as she crossed the space, her walk conveying absolute confidence. Her shoulders were strong and straight, with no hint of the roundness some tall people gain as they attempt to blend into the crowd. Hero certainly didn't blend. Couldn't blend. She was stunning. Completely, undeniably stunning.

Whereas Juliet's beauty was soft and crept over you, Hero's hit you straight away, right between the eyes. Pete watched the people around her and nudged Juliet as one poor guy, whose eyes were glued to Hero, got a whack from his girlfriend. Juliet pulled a sympathetic face.

'Oh dear! She can have that effect.'

Pete shrugged. 'She's very beautiful,' he said truthfully, 'but she's not you.' Juliet reached up and kissed him.

'You just remember that.'

'I hope that's Pete.' Hero appeared in front of them, a wide smile playing on perfectly painted lips. Juliet hugged her and introduced her fiancé.

'Pleased to meet you, Hero.' He leant down a placed a kiss on her cheek. It struck Hero that few men she met had to bend to do that. It felt rather nice.

Pete took control of the luggage and led the way back to the car. They loaded themselves into the offroader and started on the long drive back to the station. Juliet filled Hero in on the wedding arrangements and their plans for after the wedding.

Dear Reader,

Thank you so much for reading *No Place Like Home*. I really hope you enjoyed meeting Ellie and Ben, and following their story.

If you did, I'd be so grateful if you could leave me a review – a short one is absolutely fine! Reviews can make such a difference in helping spread the word about our books, so each one added really does help (especially on those leading sites for digital sales!). And of course, if you know anyone who enjoys a good romance, feel free to point them in the direction of my books!

For those of you who've enjoyed my previous romcoms, don't worry – I'm still writing those too. In fact, there's a new one due out very soon!

Thank you again for all your support. I always love to hear from my readers, so please feel free to contact me on any of my social media channels or by email. I look forward to hearing from you!

Happy reading!

Love Maxi xx